WORK | DONE

FOR | HIRE

WORK DONE
FOR HIRE

Joe Haldeman

ACE BOOKS, NEW YORK

THE BERKLEY PUBLISHING GROUP
Published by the Penguin Group
Penguin Group (USA) LLC
375 Hudson Street, New York, New York 10014

USA • Canada • UK • Ireland • Australia • New Zealand • India • South Africa • China

penguin.com

A Penguin Random House Company

This book is an original publication of The Berkley Publishing Group.

Ace Books are published by The Berkley Publishing Group.
ACE and the "A" design are trademarks of Penguin Group (USA) LLC.

Library of Congress Cataloging-in-Publication Data

Haldeman, Joe W.
Work done for hire / Joe Haldeman. — First Edition.
pages cm
ISBN 978-0-425-25688-6 (hardback)
1. Authorship—Fiction.   2. Snipers—Fiction.   I. Title.
PS3558.A353W67 2014
813'.54—dc23
2013034539

FIRST EDITION: January 2014

PRINTED IN THE UNITED STATES OF AMERICA

10 9 8 7 6 5 4 3 2 1

Cover photographs: rifle © Saulius L / Shutterstock; target © PILart/Shutterstock.
Cover design by Judith Lagerman.
Interior text design by Laura K. Corless.

For Gay, my not-so-secret agent

Sand in the Box

1.

A friend called me this morning and asked whether I could go shooting, and I said no, I couldn't. I made up something about work, but the fact is, I couldn't.

I was a sniper in the desert, in this war that it seems no one can really stop. I didn't volunteer for the job, not initially, but I wasn't smart enough to miss the targets in Basic Training. And "sniper" sounded cool, so I signed up for the school when they offered it.

I count back on all my fingers and it's been nine years. Sometimes it feels like yesterday, literally. I wake up in grainy grime and shit smell, the slimy cold of the damned plastic suit. Cold until the sun comes up and tries to kill you. That sounds too dramatic, but I'll leave it. The sun bakes you and broils you and disorients you, and it makes you a target. They have rifles, too. Not so many snipers.

In sixteen months I killed maybe twenty people, sixteen confirmed. What kind of a prick keeps track? Besides, as often as not, you can't tell.

The recoil usually knocks you off the sight picture, and with the scope at maximum power, it takes a second or two to get back. Your spotter will say, "Good shot," but what's he going to say? You're usually shooting at someone who's peeking out of a window or from behind the edge of a wall, and if an ounce and a half of lead buzzes by his ear at the speed of sound, he's not about to stand up and shout, "You missed!"

So I don't know whether I'm going to burn in Hell sixteen times or thirty or forty, or whether they even make you burn in Hell for not being smart enough to miss the god-damned target in Basic Training. I suspect I'll go wherever the people I killed went. But I don't expect to meet them.

I had a girlfriend all those sixteen months, and she e-mailed me every afternoon, morning her time, and I wrote back whenever I was near a hot point. We were going to get married.

But I know I'm not as nice in person as I am at the keyboard. That must happen all the time.

She put up with me for three or four months after I got out of the hospital. I think she still loved me for maybe half that time. But how long can you love someone who goes into bars just to beat people up? To get drunk enough to start fights. And then cry in movies. You can cry for Bambi or Meryl Streep, but crying in a zombie movie is a symptom that something is loose in your head.

That sounds so drama queen. I didn't really get that bad a deal, wounded once and out. The bullet that blew off my left pinkie also smashed a rib and bounced into my left lung, serious enough to get me six weeks in Bethesda and an early honorable discharge. Eighty percent disability pays for the rent and groceries and some of the beer.

For a few years the rest of the beer came out of the GI Bill, while I finished college and got an easy Master's. When that cow ran dry I did this and that, temp jobs like typing and answering phones. But I don't take orders well anymore, and tend to raise my voice. So I had lots of jobs, none of them for too long.

I've always written poetry, not a fast track to fame and fortune, and started writing stories when I was in the hospital. I actually sold one, for $150, before I was out of rehab. So the idea of doing it for a living was pretty natural. How far could it be from *Ellery Queen's Mystery Magazine* to the best-seller list?

I still don't know, but it's more than nine years.

I wrote a novel and it did about as well as most first novels, which is to say my mother bought ten copies and a few thousand other people must have thought I was a relative. It did get two or three good reviews, and a couple of poisonous ones, notably from the *Times*. It bothers me to know that I probably got into graduate school because I got reviewed in the *Times*. They hated the book but evidently thought it was important enough to warn potential readers away.

I guess every writer who's been a soldier has to write his war novel. I can't stand to read the damned thing anymore. Though I hate to think that maybe the *Times* was right.

Second novels are a hard sell, especially if you don't have cheerful blurbs from the first. "Puerile," shouts the *New York Times*. "A worthwhile journeyman effort," mumbles *Publishers Weekly*. My hometown newspaper called it a "good read," but I went to high school with the reviewer. So my second novel has been to some of the best addresses in New York, according to my agent, but it hasn't been invited to stay.

The agent, Barb Goldman, probably took me on because she's a vet, too. Twice my age, she was in the hundred-hour war that started the whole thing. Before 9/11 and Gehenna. When I go up to New York we get drunk together and remember the desert. Old sergeants whom we sincerely hope are dead by now.

Drinking with her, I've never felt the crazy urge to fight. Maybe because she's older than my mother and would die of embarrassment. Maybe because the bars we go to are a little nicer than the ones I frequent in Florida. Get into a fight in the Four Seasons and you might hurt somebody who could buy your book.

So she called and asked whether I'd like to make some easy money doing work for hire, and of course I said, "Who do you think I am?" She knew exactly who I was, and said I could make fifty thousand bucks, writing a sort of "novelization" of a movie by Ron Duquest. I said it sounded like a fun way to pay for the next two thousand cases of beer, and she said that's good, because she'd already accepted. She knew I liked fantasy and horror, and this was going to be a horror movie.

And that was not all, not by a long shot. Duquest had asked for me specifically. She showed me the note that had come with the request:

RONALD DUQUEST

HOLLYWOOD

If you got this you know my number

I really liked "High Kill," by your client Jack Daley. Good natural storytelling talent. Could he write a short book for me? We got an idea sounds right up his alley—a sci-fi monster and a returned vet. I can put a little up front: Ten grand to write the book, and he keeps all the book rights. We'll send another contract if we like the book for a movie: basically $50,000 for an 18-month option against $500,000 if the movie gets made. Make that "start of principal photography." Don't want to haggle but I have the check right here if you want it.

(signed) Duke D.

I wasn't sure quite how to take that. But I'd seen several features by Ron Duquest, and liked his light touch. I asked her what he meant by a "short book," and she said a novella, between a hundred and two hundred typed pages.

Sort of the opposite of what I normally thought of as a "novelization," which would be taking an existing movie script and cranking out a novel based on that. This might actually be easier, though. I could probably write a hundred pages of acceptable prose in a couple of weeks. For twice what I got for the last novel.

It would be a "work done for hire" in that Duquest would own the copyright. But since I'd keep the book rights, and also make a small fortune if a movie came out of it, what the hell.

She zapped me the two-page description. Pretty good story; the main character was my age and had gone to my war. He's a lawyer and a private eye but unsuccessful. I like that in a lawyer.

———

I spent the morning not writing. I'd never done anything like this, purely commercial stuff, but I had taken a screenwriting course in graduate school, and this was sort of the opposite. So I figured I'd do a diagram first, breaking down the supposed movie into acts and scenes, which I could reassemble into a book narrative.

While I was immersed in that, the phone rang and it was my current pelvic pal, Kit Majors, wondering whether I'd forgotten about lunch. I told her I was on my way out the door, and then I was.

I really should make myself notes. It was normally a ten-minute bike ride to the Irish restaurant, but I made it in five, sweating a little bit.

When I walked in, she signaled the bartender, and he started tapping me a Guinness. I was actually going to get us a nice bottle of wine, to celebrate, but that could come later. Kit liked to be in control, which was usually okay with me.

We kissed. "I got a job."

"Jesus, you're kidding. Someone put up a plaque."

"You peasants may laugh, but in fact it is a real job, real money. I'm gonna be a literary prostitute for fifty large. As much as a half million down the road."

"Wow. Room in that bed for another one?" Kit was a poet as well as a mathematician.

"You wouldn't want to do it. Novelization of a horror movie."

"Ew. People who go to those things read books?"

"Big words and all. This one's by Ron Duquest."

"I'm supposed to know who that is?"

"He did the Bradbury remake you liked, *Dandelion Wine*."

"That wasn't horror."

"Depends on what scares you." The bartender brought the beer and took our food order, a steak for her and a Cobb salad for me.

"You're gonna waste away."

"Not for a while." I've always been what they call "big-boned," but had never had to watch my diet, until the past year or so. I had to admit I was getting paunchy.

"Your mother called."

"What, she called you?"

She gave me a look. "No, she called the bartender. I couldn't help but overhear."

"All right. She always calls my cell. But I turn it off when I'm working."

"She said you promised to fix the porch, once it stopped raining."

"Oh, shit. Of course I'm gonna fix the god-damn porch. It's not like I had to write a book or something."

"I could come help."

"Nothing to it, really. Replace a step and stain it. But yeah, I could use the company. Talk to Mom, distract her."

"Tell her about our sex life?"

"No. She snores. You drive over?"

"What, you biked?"

"Two hundred calories. And the guy in the screenplay bikes. We could swing by Hawkeye's and pick up a plank and some stain. Then go surprise the old lady."

"You pay for lunch?"

"I'm a big Hollywood guy now. We always pay for lunch."

"Yeah, but you get blow jobs."

I rolled my eyes at her. "Everything has a price in this sorry world."

THE MONSTER

by

Christian Daley

CHAPTER ONE

He was so big that people couldn't help staring at him. If you guessed his weight, you might say four hundred pounds, but it was more like five. A relatively large head with small features pinched in the middle. Straggly long hair and no eyebrows. Ugly as hell. If he were on a television show he'd have a sweet disposition. In real life he was quite otherwise.

On police blotters in four states he was called Hunter. He was a monster, so far uncatchable, unobserved.

He hid his windowless van in a cul-de-sac and labored up a hill to a location he'd scouted out earlier. A jogging trail that had thick brush for cover, but by moving a couple of steps to the left and right, he could see a hundred yards or more in both directions.

He could hear for a mile. There was no one coming.

He tied a length of monofilament fishing line to a sapling and laid it across the path. It was almost invisible.

He hid in the bush and quickly applied military camouflage makeup to his face and hands, matching the green camouflage suit he'd made out of a tent. He snapped the wire up a couple of times, testing. It would do, catching the runner midway between ankle and knee.

The first jogger down the trail was a beautiful teenaged girl, blond hair streaming out behind her, breasts bouncing softly, her scarlet silken outfit clinging with sweat. He salivated at her beauty but let her pass. He was doing boy-girl-boy-girl and didn't want to confuse the police analysts. Not yet.

The next one was a boy, but he was too close behind, probably striving to catch up with the girl. If he made a noise, she might hear. If she saw the fat man at work, she would call 9-1-1. That would make things too complicated.

They both were well out of sight, though, when the next one came up, clearly exhausted, almost shuffling, a man of about forty. That was all right. He yanked on the monofilament and the man fell flat on his face.

He was up on his hands and knees by the time Hunter had lumbered out to the trail. He punched him once in the back of the head with a fist the size of a bowling ball, knocking him flat. He picked him up like a sleeping child and carried him back to the van.

The rear door was open. He laid the man out and wiped the blood away from his mouth, then slapped duct tape over it. Then he bound his hands and feet with tape, working quickly for one so fat, and handcuffed him to an eyebolt on the side, then quietly eased the door shut. The whole process took less than a minute.

He got a gallon jug of water out of the front seat and cleaned off the camo makeup. Then he took off the outfit; he had regular shorts and a tee underneath. Then he carried the water back up to the trail, made sure no one was coming, and rinsed away the spatter of blood the man's face had left. He thumbed open the large folding knife he always carried, severed the monofilament, and wrapped it around the jug as he walked back down to the van.

From the coffin-sized cooler in the back, he took out two quart bottles of Budweiser. Then he got in the driver's seat, the van dipping to the left in spite of its custom springs.

A lot of people drink beer while they're driving in Alabama. He decided not to take the chance. He drank both quarts sitting there, and finished off two bags of hot peanuts and a bag of bacon rinds. Life was good.

He put the empties and wrappers in a plastic bag and washed his hands and face. He ignored the faint sounds from the back and headed for the interstate.

2.

After I finished that little chapter, I checked the e-mail and lo, there was an $8,500 PayPal deposit from my agent, Duquest's down payment minus her fifteen percent. I actually clapped my hands together.

Duquest sent an e-mail, too, all lower case: "good so far." Hey, don't give me a swelled head.

Of course once the novella was in Duquest's hands, he could screw it up any way he wanted. But hell, he was paying for the privilege. I didn't much like surrendering control, even if it was a work done for hire. But I wrote HALF A MILLION BUCKS on a three-by-five card and taped it over the computer, in case I started to get depressed.

I decided to go buy a nice bike, like the private eye does in the story. Maybe I'll go buy a pistol, too; see how a 9-mm feels. But if somebody calls and tries to hire me to find a fat guy who kills joggers, I'm so outta here.

I printed out the first chapter and quit to clean house. Kit said her

parents wanted to meet me, and I had ignored the voice inside, screaming "Ah-ooga! Ah-ooga! Dive! Dive!" and invited them over for dinner.
So I had to weigh my options: good impression or self-defense food
poisoning. I opted for the former, but took the chicken out of the fridge
a tad early. Let the gods decide.

Maybe it's odd that I haven't met them, since they're only like ten
miles away and I've been seeing Kit for almost a year. The first couple
of months you wouldn't have wanted to take me home to Mother; some
asshole decked me with a Jack Daniels bottle, which broke my nose and
knocked out a tooth under a split lip. The VA fixed me up, but it took a
while.

That was a good bar, but I don't go there anymore. The bartender
turned out to be the owner. He bitched about the damage, and I sort of
picked up the broken bottle and offered him a colonoscopy. He went for
the phone and I decided to go bleed somewhere else.

Kit met me about a week later at a branch of the library, where I was
giving a reading from my second novel, which I think I will retitle *The
Fucking Albatross*. It had to be the worst reading in the history of literary
indecent exposure. I sounded exactly like a guy with a nose full of cotton,
and with the temporary cap on my front tooth, I whistled every time I
tried to pronounce "s" or "th." We had a beer afterwards and she took
me home for a mercy fuck that turned out to be a yearlong hobby,
maybe more.

So now to meet her parents. Shave, clean shirt, find some socks.
Hide the porn. I left my desk a random hellhole—I probably couldn't
find anything if I neatened it—but closed the office door.

Kit once asked me why male writers had offices and female ones
had studios or writing rooms. Maybe it's so we can pretend we're working.

I clicked "random classical" on the living room pod and made a salad and put it in the fridge. Dumped some coals in the grill and soaked them with starter fluid and waited. Normally, I'd make a drink at five, but that might not be a good idea. Wait and offer them one. I had a wild impulse to roll a joint; they'd be almost old enough to be hippies. No, that was the sixties and seventies. They were probably just born. Besides, Kit didn't smoke, so her parents probably didn't either. The family that smokes together croaks together.

They were exactly on time, and of course dressed down, for a picnic. Her father, Morrie, was wearing a T-shirt that half exposed a Marine Corps anchor tattoo on his beefy bicep. But it was a Princeton crew shirt, a little cognitive dissonance. Her mother, Trish, was delicate and quiet. Quietly observant.

Kit had brought the ingredients for sangria and took over the kitchen to make a pitcher. So I dumped a bag of potato chips in a bowl and escorted her parents out to the patio. That made things a little awkward, with no mediator. I braced myself for the usual "so you're a writer" excruciation.

It was worse. "Kitty says you were a sniper in the war," Morrie said. "In the army, was it?"

"Guard unit, actually."

"Same same." Not a good sign when a civilian uses military slang. "How long did they keep you over there?"

"Sixteen months."

"Not fair." He shook his head. "Ain't it a bitch, as we used to say." He glanced at his wife, and she gave him a tiny nod. "It would've been less if you'd gone RA."

"That was often a topic of discussion."

He smiled a kind of Princeton smile. "I can well imagine."

"Morrie was in the Marines," Trish said, somewhat unnecessarily.

"Just a grunt," he said. "We didn't get along with the snipers too well."

"We heard about that. They had a high opinion of themselves. Their school was a lot harder than ours, though."

"Yes. No question it was a difficult job. A lot of lying in wait."

"Like an alligator," I said.

"Alligator?"

"I used to spend a lot of time watching them, down in Florida. They lie still for hours, until all the other animals accept them as part of the landscape. One gets too close and they strike, fast, like a rattlesnake."

"Have you seen that?" Trish asked.

"Once. He got a big blue heron."

"I like alligators," she said. Why was I not surprised?

"Did you watch him for hours?" he said.

"Yes, I did. With a camera. But it happened too fast. All I got was a picture of his tail, sticking out of the water."

"Drowning the bird?"

"That's what they do."

"Are you guys talking about the war?" Kit brought out a tray with the pitcher of sangria. Three glasses with the wine punch and one of ice water. Her father took that one. "Two vets get together—"

"Not the war," I said. "Alligators."

She handed me a glass. "That's good. Some of my favorite people are cold-blooded animals."

"You even vote for one every now and then," her father said.

"Morrie . . ."

"Sorry. No politics."

"I'll get the coals going." I escaped to the lawn and squirted some fresh starter on the charcoal, then lit the pile in several places.

Nobody said anything until I came back. I picked up the drink and sipped it; extra brandy. "Thanks, sweetheart."

"Kitty says you write books, Jack," her mother said.

"I've written two and a half. Taking time off right now to do a purely commercial one, a kind of novelization."

To their blank look Kit said, "That's normally when they make a book out of a movie. In this case, Jack's writing the book first."

Her father tilted his head. "I would've thought that was the usual way."

"Kind of. Nobody seems eager to make a movie out of one of my books. But this isn't actually a movie yet; just a pitch."

Her mother shook her head slightly, with a blank look. "A pitch is a sales job," her father supplied.

"My literary agent actually came up with the deal," Jack said. "She was talking with a producer/director, Duke Duquest, and my name came up. He had a vague idea about doing a horror movie with its roots in present-day war. My war novel had just come out, with good reviews."

"It has a sort of horror angle," Kit said.

"Well, I'd call it fantasy. This one is real horror, though, a monster who hunts people."

"Like you," her mother said.

"What?"

"Isn't that what you did?" She looked honest and sincere and not judgmental. "Like a hunter after deer? With a rifle?"

"I suppose it is."

"If the deer had guns," her father said.

"It's good money," Kit said. "As much as a thousand dollars a page."

"My word. How many pages can you write a day?"

"Four or five, on a good day. Two or three's more common."

"Still damned good pay," her father said.

"I was lucky to get it." I decided not to mention that it would only be fifty pages. Kit said nothing to disillusion them, either, so the rest of the evening passed convivially, the Majors mistakenly thinking that their daughter was dating a budding millionaire rather than a starving artist. After they left, Kit rewarded me with a night of uncharacteristically inventive sex.

I didn't sleep well. Dreams about hunting.

CHAPTER TWO

Hunter crossed two state lines and wound up in backwoods Georgia. Then he drove an extra hour so he wouldn't be working too close to his own home. Following a smudged penciled map, he got off the interstate, then went a few miles down a pot-holed blacktop road, then turned onto a lime-rock road, and finally off that road, through crackling low brush for a few hundred yards, into a sunlit copse surrounded by thick forest. He backed and filled so that he would be able to drive straight out. He pulled on surgeon's gloves.

He opened the side door of the van and with a grunt lifted out the huge cooler. It held eight twenty-five-pound blocks of ice. He set it down so a rock tilted it up at a slight angle, and opened a petcock so that the excess water drained out. Then he set it squarely in front of a large tree.

He pulled the bound and gagged man out through the back door and dropped him next to the cooler. Then he returned to the van and brought back a large hook on a chain. He stood on the cooler and secured the hook to a stout limb. He pulled on it with all his weight, and it creaked but held.

The man was trying to scream, but with his mouth sealed by duct tape, he could only make a nasal whine. Hunter made sure the duct tape around his ankles was secure, and then easily lifted him up by his feet and hung him upside-down from the branch, the hook going between his ankles, holding him up by the tape.

He took the razor-sharp clasp knife from his pocket and sliced off the man's T-shirt and then his running shorts. He was wearing a jockstrap. He snapped it playfully and cut through the waistband and both leg straps, and tossed it away. The man had soiled himself, which was understandable and not unusual.

He put the knife away and delicately lifted the man's scrotum and testicles and looked underneath. The penis had retracted so far it was almost invisible in the nest of pubic hair. That was not unusual, either.

He walked back to the van and returned with a 12-gauge pump shotgun. He spoke for the first time, his voice curiously high-pitched and musical: "Don't be afraid. This is not for you." It was in case of interruption. He'd never had to use it.

He got a quart of beer from the cooler and twisted it open, and sat on the cooler with the shotgun in his lap. He sipped the beer slowly, studying the man.

When he'd finished the beer, he spoke again. "There's not a living soul within miles. If you scream, you will only annoy me." He reached down and carefully pulled an inch of tape away from his mouth. "What do you do for a living?"

"I'm a minister. But my father's a millionaire! He could—" Hunter pressed the tape back into place.

"A man of God. I respect that. I will be gentle." He opened the knife and with one sweep deeply cut the minister's throat, severing both carotid arteries. The man was probably dead before the gush of blood could blind him.

He didn't always do that. It wasn't necessary to bleed the corpse; the meat was going straight into the cooler. It was probably kinder to kill them quickly, but that wasn't much of an issue. Sometimes he played with them to see how they would react to his ministrations. Sometimes he even told them his life story, since they would never be able to pass it on, and their reaction to that was interesting, too.

A joke he played on the police was to dress out their bodies exactly as one does a deer, hence the name Hunter. But he had never killed a deer; he'd copied the instructions out of a library book, not wanting to leave a web trail, and practiced on roadkill until he was fairly expert, burying the remains to avoid suspicion.

He brought out his box of tools and supplies. He felt for the pubic bone and did a long ventral incision from there downward, using a sturdy plain hunting knife from Sears. He guided it with his fingers, careful not to nick the stomach or intestines. He cut through the pelvic bone with a Craftsman hacksaw, and cut away the diaphragm so he could remove the liver and heart, which he put in separate Ziploc bags and set in the cooler. Then he remembered the thymus gland and put it in a small bag to take home and add to the eleven he had in the freezer. Almost enough for a nice appetizer of sweetbreads.

He cut around the anus and severed the windpipe, and the offal slid out in a steaming pile at the base of the tree. He carefully stepped around it while he finished the job, skinning the man from ankles to chin. He left the head untouched, for his collection. He draped the skin artistically around the tree branches, tying it in places so an animal couldn't easily drag it away, then slipped a large yard bag over the blood-slick body and cut it down. Best to finish the job at home, where he had proper tools and plenty of time. He lay the body on the ice and dragged the cooler back to the van. Retrieved the hook and chain.

Tired. Lean people are harder to skin. He took a beer out of the cooler but put it back. Best to make a few miles first. There were already two turkey buzzards circling, and more would come. He stripped off the gloves and bloody clothes into a laundry bag and washed up, using the van's side mirror and a hand mirror to make sure there were no telltale speckles. He got a small erection but ignored it, then dressed in old clothes and quietly drove away.

3.

I woke up out of a terrible nightmare, reaching for Kit, who wasn't there; she left early to go to Chicago on family business. The nightmare wasn't about the cartoon monster in the script, but a related horror I saw in the war.

Artillery support had gotten the new "shock" rounds for the 175s, and the first one they fired fell way short, and it went off above a thing like a Muslim day care center or orphanage. Our camp was right on the edge of town, a place we called Honeypot, so they ordered most of us to run over and render aid.

It was all children except for four women, and all but one were dead or barely twitching. The shock round had blown off all their clothing and most of their skin. Most of them must have died instantly of cardiac arrest, but one was walking, a girl of ten or twelve who looked like a medical-school diagram, flayed from the waist up, just bloody muscles, and from the top of her butt trailed a bright flag of bloody skin like a gory wedding train. She fell over and died before the medics could do anything, but what would they have been able to do? Whole body skin graft; just grit your teeth, sweetheart.

It was two in the morning. I got up without dressing and turned on all the lights in the kitchen and sat drinking a beer very fast. Then I put some ice cubes in a glass and poured in a few inches of Kit's vodka. That got me tranquilized enough to go back to sleep and not dream, or at least not remember the dreams.

Woke up groggy and went for a walk. I took the next section of the script and a notebook, so I could at least pretend to be working. Went by a bike shop, but it wasn't open till ten, so dropped in the twenty-four-hour pool hall and had a healthy breakfast of Slim Jims and beer. I read the paper for a while and then went back to the bike shop.

The Steve in the story gets a really nice touring bike, but I didn't need anything that fancy or expensive. Just something to replace the old clunker I'd bought from a roommate in college.

The shop's pretty upscale, and most of the bikes are almost weightless and cost as much as a used car. But they did have a section with cheap kids' so-called mountain bikes—like there were mountains in Iowa—and adult "commuter" bikes. I can commute to work in ten seconds, barefoot, but I got one of those, a bright blue Cambridge. With an accessory package of lights and lock and saddle bags, it was just under $500. One percent of my eventual Monster money.

It was gloriously easy to ride, compared to my rust bucket. It had automatic shift and springs and nice wide handlebars, so you could sit upright and see the world go by. The old one had dropped handlebars, so you rode hunched over, and was so rigid your ass felt every pebble in the road.

Perfect weather for bicycling, sunny and slightly cool, so I pedaled around for an hour and a half, and wound up on the other side of town. There was a new Italian restaurant with outside tables, so I sat down there and took out the script and notebook. I got a half carafe of white wine and started to work.

CHAPTER THREE

Stephen Spenser thought he had the world by the tail when he left his father's New York law firm and joined a small one in Florida as junior partner. He liked the little town of Flagler Beach, and was usually inside only half the day, helping to prepare briefs and going over old files with the firm's gorgeous administrative assistant, Arlene. The rest of the time he was outside in the usually beautiful seaside weather, interviewing clients and respondents—and occasionally doing repossessions, a profitable sideline for the firm.

It was not just picking up and returning delinquent cars and boats, but sometimes children, who legally belonged to the other parent. Sometimes it got ugly, and although Steve was a big man and not easy to push around, the firm thought it prudent to get him a private investigator's license and a permit to carry a concealed weapon. Half the men in Florida own guns, his boss said, and more than half of the men who break the law.

Steve was no stranger to guns. Like most combat infantrymen, he had carried one everywhere; even eating and sleeping, it was never more than an arm's length away. It had been a comfort, even though he never fired it at anybody, and ultimately it didn't protect him from the enemy. On what turned out to be his last day in the army, an IED, improvised explosive device, filled both his legs with shrapnel in the form of dirty rusty nails and screws that had been mixed with human feces. He eventually recovered enough to finish pre-law and law school and join his father's firm—and then get tired of the other employees' attitudes and move to Florida.

He picked up a snub-nosed .38 Special, not very accurate or powerful, but small. He also got a 9-mm Beretta like the one he had carried in the army, but that size cannon is hard to conceal in light summer clothes. He'd never fired either one except at an indoor range in the local gun shop. The first of every month, he'd go there and run a couple of dozen rounds through each one.

After about a year, he proposed to Arlene and was overjoyed when she accepted. His mother sent a $250,000 "nest egg" check and his boss promoted him to full partner.

A couple of weeks later the boss sent him to the university law library in Gainesville to do a few days' research in tax law, and when he came back, the firm's office had a FOR LEASE sign on the door. He went home and found annulment papers on the kitchen table. His new wife had taken his new car and cleaned out their joint bank account. All their credit cards maxed for cash. The $2,000 rent was due, and he had less than a hundred bucks in his pocket.

The two disasters were not unrelated. She'd gone to Mexico with the boss and all the firm's liquid assets.

His parents' unlisted number was no longer in service. In the waiting mail, there was a note from his mother saying that Dad was furious about the unauthorized $250,000 gift, but he would get over it. Maybe not, Mom, under the circumstances.

The man who came to repossess the furniture, a fellow Steve had worked with a few times, was sympathetic and bought his old pickup truck. He also sold the expensive Beretta and his Lance Armstrong road bike, keeping the .38 Special and the rusty beach bike he kept for riding on the sand. With some reluctance, he sold his state-of-the art iLap, after downloading its files into a winkdrive. That gave him enough money to renew his PI license and rent a one-room office with a foldout couch. He had some cards printed up, whimsically calling himself "Spenser for Hire," and took out an ad in the weekly advertiser.

He'd been bicycling an hour or so a day, before work, both as therapy for his legs and to cut down on his smoking. He didn't desire tobacco while he was on the bike, so with no money for cigarettes and plenty of time on his hands, he started bicycling constantly. If he could give up a dangerous habit, one good thing would come out of this debacle.

Two good things, actually. For better or for worse, he was finally free of his father.

He got into a routine. He'd get out of bed at first light and take off on the bike for a long loop south of Daytona Beach and back, using his cell to check for calls back at the office every hour or so. There were never any really interesting calls, maybe one repo deal a week, but it did keep him from smoking. When he got home after sixty or seventy miles he would collapse into bed, where he also didn't smoke. He got to where he didn't even fold it back into a couch.

Some of the areas he biked through were not particularly safe, so he usually carried the .38—not in the shoulder holster, which would be a little conspicuous in a T-shirt, but in an innocuous zippered bag in his front basket. He had two big rear baskets for groceries, and he took to filling them up with aluminum cans, tossed from cars, worth about two cents apiece. It amused him to be beautifying the environment in exchange for lunch money.

After about a month of this, he was pedaling along with a few days' beard, old shabby clothes, on a squeaky rusty bike loaded down with trash, and a young cop stopped him and asked whether he could produce evidence that he shouldn't be arrested for vagrancy. In fact, he had left his wallet at home, so he didn't have any ID or money, but he did unfortunately have a gun, and the young fellow didn't want to listen to a lecture about unlawful search and seizure, least of all from a vagrant who claimed to be a lawyer.

Back at the police station, fingerprints and a retinal scan quickly verified he was Stephen Spenser, a lawyer with a PI ticket and a gun license. Why was he biking around looking like a penniless bum? A police reporter who was loitering around the station overheard some of that, and asked whether he would trade an interview for a steak dinner. Good human interest story, and it might drum up some business for Spenser for Hire.

The steak, at the local Denny's, wasn't too bad, but the story made him wince. It was in the Sunday edition of the Daytona Beach paper, leading off the People section. There was a big picture of him above the fold, scarfing up that cheap steak like a starving hobo. The story was sympathetic but condescending. He almost went out for a pack of Winstons.

But the story had his phone number, and that would change his life.

He read through the rest of the paper and was about to get on his bike when the phone rang. It was a man named Bayer Steinhart, who said he might have a job for a private investigator with a gun and a bicycle. Could they meet this morning? He gave an Ormond Beach address on A1A—Millionaire's Row—and Steve said he could be there at ten thirty.

He put on some decent clothes and pedaled south, going down the A1A sidewalk. He stopped and stared at the ocean just long enough to be five minutes late. It wouldn't do to appear too pathetically eager.

It was a mansion with architecture so idiosyncratic that Steve had stopped to look at it before. It was in the style of the twentieth-century Spanish architect Gaudí, the corners flowing as if melted. Fantastic gargoyle ornamentation. The lawn featured topiaries of unicorns and dragons, and there was a fountain where three beautiful nudes, life-sized and meticulously accurate, embraced laughing. The three Graces, having a better time than usual.

So the man had a surplus of money and a shortage of taste. Steve could live with both.

An attractive black maid a little older than Steve answered the door and escorted him through the house to a terrace that overlooked the ocean. Not too many people on the beach yet. Mr. Steinhart was scanning the horizon with a compact Questar telescope. Steve recognized it; his father owned one. They were built like a Swiss watch but cost considerably more.

He was wearing faded jeans and a light flannel shirt. Forty or fifty years old. As tall and muscular as Steve, he shook hands gently.

Without preamble: "One thing the article didn't say. When you were betrayed and lost everything, why didn't you just find a position with another firm? Law degree from Princeton?"

"I don't like lawyers. I've been around them all my life, and really wanted to do something else."

"What if I'm a lawyer?"

Steve paused. "I'll take your money."

He smiled. "Rest easy. I'm a mathematician, sort of. Self-taught. This all came from computer games."

"Of course. I thought the name sounded familiar."

The maid brought out a pitcher of lemonade and two glasses. She set it on a glass-covered wrought iron table.

"Thank you, Selma." To Steve: "If you biked here, you must be thirsty." They sat down and he poured two glasses.

"You've heard of Hunter."

"The assistant governor?" Slimeball.

"No. The serial killer."

"Oh, of course."

He rubbed his forehead and closed his eyes. "Five years ago . . . almost six now . . . my only son was his first victim."

"My god. I'm sorry."

"They found, the Georgia police"—his voice cracked—"they found his, his skin and insides. He'd been dressed out like a rabbit or a deer."

"I've read about that. I had no idea it had happened to you."

"We paid a lot to keep our identity secret. We thought it might have been a kidnapping, for ransom, that went awry. I had two younger daughters to protect."

"They're not here?" The place had a bachelor feel.

"No, they live with their mother up north. The marriage sort of fell apart. Understandable."

"The police weren't able to . . ."

"No, nothing. Of course it's federal now. Homeland Security and the FBI. They have no leads at all. And I just found out there was a new one, the twelfth, last week. A jogger in Alabama."

"I didn't know."

"Nobody does. The man had no family, so they kept it under wraps. If the murderer is after publicity, they think maybe not getting it might make him do something stupid."

"I read that he's pretty . . . not stupid."

"He's never left prints or DNA. He's left tire tracks, but no two are the same.

"I'll give you the FBI dossier, everything they gave me. I don't want to look at it anymore. Pictures."

"So . . . what do you want me to do? Find him when the FBI can't?"

"Basically, well, I want you to be a lure."

"Lure him to you?"

"To yourself. And then capture or kill him."

"Why would he want to come after me?"

"Everyone he's killed was alone, on a country road or path. All athletes, either jogging or running or, like my son, biking. All in Florida or Georgia or Alabama."

"I bike sixty miles a day in Florida. He hasn't come after me yet."

"My son and three others seem to have been on the same trail. It can't be a coincidence."

"What trail?"

"It's the Southern Tier Trail, three thousand miles of back roads and bike paths from St. Augustine to San Diego. Thousands of people bike it every year."

"You'd think the authorities would have it staked out. Parts of it."

"You'd think. But they call it 'weak circumstantial evidence.' None of them died near the trail, but they all were on or near it the day they died. My son's bike was found right off the trail outside Tallahassee, but he was taken to a remote part of Georgia to be killed."

"Well, I'm not a criminal lawyer. But I'd call it circumstantial evidence myself."

"Whatever, I'll pay you two thousand dollars a week to ride that trail by yourself, alone and apparently vulnerable, but armed. A hundred thousand if you capture the bastard. Two hundred if he's killed. It beats picking up cans off the road."

It was a crazy idea, but hell, the man could afford an expensive hobby. A quest. "Well, I'm not camping. I had enough of that in the army."

"I'll give you a credit card. Sleep in motels, eat in restaurants, best you can find out there in the sticks."

Steve rubbed his chin. "That piece of crap I'm riding wouldn't make it to Tallahassee. Need a new bike—and a new gun, more effective than the little peashooter I'm carrying now."

He reached into a beach bag and pulled out a fat wallet. "New bike." He counted out fifteen hundred-dollar bills. "New gun." Ten more. Then he put the wallet back and pulled out a thick manila folder that had "Dup. Hunter Case File" scrawled on it.

"Thank you, Mr. Steinhart." He stacked the bills together and folded them and put them in his pocket. "You've got a deal. Do you have a contract?"

He smiled. "I don't like lawyers, either. But if you draw something up, I'll sign it tomorrow." He stood up. "And then you'll be on the road."

Steve stood and shook his hand. "You've bought yourself the most expensive piece of bait in the state of Florida."

4.

Kit read the last page and set it on the small stack on the kitchen table in front of her. "Well, I like it so far, Jack. But the movie's script doesn't have all that stuff about the marriage and betrayal and all." She'd taken a copy of the script with her and read it on the plane.

"He wanted me to give the guy some depth, some history," I said. "In the movie, he's just a private dick with a bike."

She got up and tousled my hair on the way to the fridge. "Missed your private dick." She pulled some sandwich stuff out and put it on the counter. "Ham sandwich okay?"

"Sounds good." I watched her being methodical, four pieces of bread lined up along the edge of the cutting board. Mustard on one and three, mayo on two and four; ham slices folded over to precisely fit the bread. My head felt good where she'd rubbed it.

"Decide about the pseudonym?" The contract allowed me to make one up, or not.

"I don't think I'll do it. I'm not ashamed of having to work for a living."

"Are you sure?" She sliced the sandwiches in neat diagonals. " 'Jack, I mean Christian Daley . . . wasn't he the guy who wrote that awful monster book?' Not that it won't be a good book."

"You know, that's part of it? People will expect a piece of shit, and get a decent book. Besides, the movie might be a big hit. Sell millions of copies of the book."

She put the stuff back in the fridge. "So then what? You get lots of novelization offers?"

"Maybe a real book or two." Though in fact I wouldn't turn down another deal like this. A thousand bucks a day plus a quarter for every copy sold?

She set the sandwiches on plates and brought them over. "I've never been to Daytona Beach. Is there really a house like that?"

"No, I wouldn't risk using a real one. But there are plenty equally tasteful. Good sandwich."

"We ought to fly down when the snow gets deep. Call it research."

"Well, not much more of the story takes place there. I had an idea, though, actual research."

"You're gonna go kill a deer and cut it up."

"Hey, I didn't think of that! Seriously, I want to take a longish bike trip, get a feel for it."

"How long? You have snow tires for that thing?"

"Just a couple of weeks. Maybe over to Davenport and down the river a bit. Go through state parks as much as possible, no traffic. Maybe you could join me for a couple of days?"

She gave me an intense look. "Sure, pedal along through the deserted woods. Miles from nowhere. Why does that creep me out?" But she laughed.

"Just a thought. I mean, I could do it myself during the week."

"Actually, I could use the exercise." She stood up. "Glass of wine?"

"Half one. I'm going back to work."

"Like that's stopping me." She poured the glasses and brought them back. "I'll tell the boss that I had to have a drink because I just found out I'm in the middle of a Hitchcock movie where my boyfriend the writer is going to lure me out into the woods and dismember me."

"I'll be gentle and clean up afterwards. But that's a Stephen King movie, not Hitchcock."

"It's Stephen King if the script possesses him and makes him act it out. It's Hitchcock if he's just fucking crazy." We clinked glasses.

"Early Saturday, then? You could spend Friday night here."

"Oh, goodie. I've never slept with an axe murderer." She faked a three-syllable orgasm. "I'll put my bike in the car and bring it over after work. Movie and dinner?"

"Good. I'll see where the Trail comes closest. Maybe Ames. We can use my van."

"How do we handle that? I mean, it won't come when you whistle."

"Just pedal a half day or so and stop at a motel. Take the same route in reverse on Sunday, drive home."

"Okay. If it's the Bates Motel, though, I'm not going in."

"See? You do know horror movies."

"Just Hitchcock." She shuddered, or pretended to. "Could we talk about the weather, like normal people?"

"How 'bout them Hawkeyes?"

CHAPTER FOUR

There was no actual road or driveway to Hunter's lair. He had planted scrub pines across the original dirt road years before, and there was no trace of it anymore. You had to weave through trees to get there, and he meticulously alternated among a dozen different entrance points, so there was nothing like a path leading over the rise to the double-wide trailer that squatted hidden among a stand of ancient live oaks.

He maneuvered the van carefully through a mile of forest, mindful not to leave any broken saplings or flattened bushes. He parked the van under a lean-to of camouflage netting adjacent to the trailer, which was covered with the same stuff, made of immortal plastic.

He got out finishing the last of six Big Macs that came from the place in Macon where he usually bought lunch when he ate out. He carried three pizzas up the groaning stairs, for later. He always bought them at the same Pizza Hut, down the block from the McDonald's. He was known as a local character at fast-food joints more than fifty miles from where he actually lived and worked.

The double-wide had only two rooms, one of which was a large meat locker. The other room had a kitchen with a large professional range and oversized reinforced bed, chairs, shower, and toilet, with a long stainless steel worktable. A rolltop desk painted black sat at one end of the room, under a framed Star Trek poster and diagrams of male and female anatomy. All the other walls were solid with cheap metal bookcases crammed with science fiction paperbacks. All the books' spines were lined up exactly. All the metal surfaces glistened and the bed was made up with hospital precision. The tile floor was spotless and gleamed with wax.

He set the pizzas on the stove and emptied a tray of ice cubes into a large ceramic mug. He filled it partway with Coke from a plastic gallon container. Then he snapped the top off a half-gallon bottle of Old Crow bourbon and topped off the mug. He turned on a small TV mounted over the range and stirred the drink methodically.

Five minutes till six. He wouldn't be on the news yet, but he always checked. He sipped at the bourbon and Coke and ate half of one of the pizzas while he watched the inconsequential goings-on that consumed normal people's time—weather and war and human interest. He did have a special interest in humans.

After the news, he finished off the drink, washed the mug, and put it away. From under the sink he took a stack of newspapers and lay them down on the floor, overlapping, covering the area under and around the steel table. He lined a large trash can with a plastic bag and put it next to the table. He took cutlery out of a drawer and lined it up, just so.

He brought in the stiff body from the van and carefully unwrapped it. There wasn't too much blood, and he kept most of it in the bag, which he emptied into a waiting gallon jar. He labeled it with the date and set it by the freezer door.

First things first. He put a heavy cutting board under the man's neck and with one blow from a cleaver separated the head from the body. Holding a newspaper under it, he carried it to the meat locker, where it joined its eleven fellows on a shelf.

He wasn't squeamish, but it was easier to work without the head looking at you. Consulting a flowchart that he'd printed out and laminated, he started with the legs and worked his way up, carving the meat into generous but manageable steaks and chops, wrapping each with a Seal-a-Meal vacuum machine and dating it. Every now and then he carried the packages into the freezer and put each into its proper bin.

It took little more than an hour. He cracked the long bones with the cleaver, exposing the marrow, and put them in a slow oven to cook for brown sauce. Most of the rest went into a simmering stock pot. Then he cleaned all of his implements and the table.

He stacked up all the newspapers and set them aside to bury tomorrow; burning might attract attention. Besides, he liked to look at the pile every now and then.

He took a bracing shower and then finished off the pizza, watching MTV.

Time to make some money. Of course he couldn't have a regular job, but he could work at home. He opened the rolltop desk and turned on the computer and opened the Word file *Shandor Ascendent: Book Four of the Starfound Cycle.*

It wasn't great literature. But you do have to eat.

Cat in the Box

1.

I spent a couple of hours getting the damned bicycle carrier attached to the back of my old van. My own fault for buying it "as is"; it was missing a couple of bolts the previous owner probably hurled away in frustration.

Kit didn't mind the delay. She was going over last year's notes in Calculus III. I asked her whether that was in preparation for Calculus IV and she said "I wish," and told me the name of the course it was a prerequisite for. Three words, and the only one I understood was "analysis." Though I doubted it had anything to do with Freud.

We probably wouldn't need the carrier anyhow, this weekend. The plan was to bike up to Cedar Rapids, twenty-four miles on MapQuest, spend the night at a motel, and come back Sunday morning. Then I'd take a longer ride during the week, maybe to Des Moines and back, get a feel for it.

I've been riding a bike since I was a kid, a year-round thing in

Daytona, but haven't done a really long trip since my sophomore year, when a bunch of us spent the summer biking and staying in hostels in Holland and then England.

Since moving to Iowa I've grown a little flabby. Maybe more than a little. Doesn't take much energy to stare out the window at the snow and wish you were somewhere else. I tried skiing my first winter and fucked up both knees badly enough to need a wheelchair. Not anybody's vehicle of choice for ice and snow. A diet of beer and potato chips, seasoned with onion dip and self-pity, set me on the road to the 200-pound mark. Hit 203 before I got up on crutches.

Seem stuck at 190 now. Hoping to lose fifteen or twenty pounds biking, before winter sets in. Help get into the character, too.

Scrubbed the grease off my hands but decided against a shower. We'd want one when we got to the motel, anyhow.

Kit was hunched over her computer, which was on the low coffee table in the living room. Half a dozen books were spread around on the couch and table. She picked up a paper notebook and scribbled something down, not looking up when I came into the room.

"With you in a minute," she said.

"Want a beer?"

"Got tea."

I followed my nose into the kitchen. She'd put last night's soup on a back burner overnight, and the smell made me ravenous. It wasn't even eleven, though. Popped a beer and sat down at the kitchen table with a magazine and a 100-calorie bag of pretzels.

The bag had sixteen pretzels in it. A penny's worth of food and a dime's worth of plastic for half a dollar. But the principle was valid; if I had a regular box of pretzels I'd keep at them till I could see the bottom. Leave a few so I technically wouldn't have eaten the whole box.

Hunter would swallow the box whole. Cardboard, plastic, good roughage.

How often does he eat, anyhow? Big predators like lions kill a big animal, gorge themselves, and sleep. Maybe he should do something like that. But what do big ocean predators do? I think sharks have to keep moving. Do killer whales and porpoises sleep after they eat, floating in the waves? I'd look it up when Kit got off the machine.

My own computer was being random, files disappearing and re-appearing. So it was resting until the VA check came. The guy at the Apple Store said I'd need a rebuilt hard drive, which would suck up about a third of the check. But the uncertainty was driving me batfuck. So I was a madman writing about a lunatic on a mentally deficient machine. There's a recipe for a best seller.

So what's the appetite of a hugely fat person really like? Myrna the Mountain must've been well over three hundred pounds, fattest girl at GHS, but nobody ever saw her eat anything but salad. She said she had "fat genes," which generated obvious jokes.

Maybe when she wasn't eating lettuce she went after hikers on deserted trails.

Kit came in and opened the refrigerator. "How come you put the bike carrier on?"

"Had some time to kill." And it would save me 4.2 miles, biking from my place to here and back. It would make a difference, 48 miles instead of 52. Don't want to overdo it. "How often do you think a four-hundred-pound person would eat?"

She brought out a soda water and a pie pan with one wedge left. Key lime with whipped cream topping, graham cracker crust.

She laughed. "You should see your face—you, too, could be a four-hundred-pound guy! Split it with you?"

"I'll pass." Try not to drool.

"Maybe he'd eat all the time. If he ate like three huge meals a day, it would put stress on his digestive system. Didn't we used to be foragers?"

"Speak for yourself."

"You know what I mean, humans . . . roots and berries, nibble all the time?

"Yeah, but we're set up to be omnivores," I said. "If you kill a large animal, you can't just eat a nibble at a time. It would spoil."

"Wild animals don't mind a little rot. Remember that grizzly bear." We'd taken a helicopter ride over Yellowstone, and saw a bear that the pilot said had been eating on the same moose for weeks. He said that if we were on the ground, the smell would knock us over. She took a bite. "Yum . . . rotten moose pie. Maybe key lime."

"I guess this guy doesn't live on human flesh. He'd have to be killing people left and right."

"Well, I don't know," she said, stacking lunch meat and cheese. "He weighs four hundred pounds and looks like a creature from outer space. Maybe he doesn't just walk into a Hy-Vee and buy a side of beef. Maybe he *does* have to eat people."

"Or farm animals," I said. "That wouldn't draw as much attention."

"You ought to have him break into a zoo and eat a camel. Half a camel."

"Speaking of—"

"No. And I won't buy any more." Saturday night she'd come home with half a pack of Camels, and we shared it in an orgy of resolution-breaking. I could still feel the narcotic rush.

"You can't be virtuous all the time."

"So look up something really dirty in your Kama Sutra. Something

46

that doesn't cause cancer." She held up the mayonnaise jar. "And doesn't use condiments." We'd used mayonnaise once, and she complained it made her smell like a sandwich. So people will know where you hid the salami, I said, and she did have to laugh.

She didn't like to talk about sex, but was willing to do anything. Better than the opposite, I knew from experience. Lynette of recent memory. A modern kind of celibacy, I guess; talking dirty and being squeaky clean. All talk and no action, my father would have said.

I wondered where he and his girlfriend were now. It's not fair for old people to have so much fun. Or, be honest, it's creepy to think of your own dad fucking a girl not much older than you. Fucking anybody.

"Earth to Jack." She set the sandwich in front of me. "You're day-dreaming again. About your novel?"

"No, nothing." I drove the image from my mind. "The bike carrier, we might need it. Like if one of the bikes breaks down, one of us could pedal back to pick up the car, then come collect it."

"Oh, right. Good." She took one bite and got up to punch the little boom box by the fridge. "New Flash Point CD."

We shared a lot of musical likes and dislikes, but I didn't get her passion for Flash Point. Retro wannabes, what a combination. I nodded and concentrated on my sandwich.

"Maybe he'd like them rotten," she said. "The corpses. Like the French, they hang ducks and geese."

"What did they do?"

"Who do?"

"What did the ducks do, the French want to hang them?"

"You're kidding."

"No, I'm not. Who would hang a fucking duck?"

She laughed. "They like hang them in a shed. Let them rot to improve their flavor."

What an image. "Tell me you just made that up."

"I swear to God and *Gastronomique*. Go Google it."

"Oh, I believe you. What do they do with fish? Fuck them blind?"

"Not raw."

"'Course not. The bones." I put some more mustard on my sandwich. "Maybe he would, you know? He's got the big freezer, but maybe he'd stack them around for a while at room temperature first. The trailer'd smell like a dead moose, but he'd like it that way."

She nodded, munching. "That would make a good penultimate scene. Antepenultimate. The FBI men are closing in on Hunter's trailer, and they go, 'What's that godawful smell?'"

"He'd remember it from the war," I said, and had to stop and swallow twice.

"You all right?"

I coughed and swallowed again. "Yeah. Nothing."

"*You* remember it. Don't you?"

"Sure. But it's not like a big thing." The first time, it wasn't. They'd been dead so long they'd dried out, and we didn't smell it till we were right on them. But the next was a woman and two babies, bloated up and burst, and as soon as we smelled them we heard the flies, and followed the sound, and if it hadn't been for the X-rays, the demo squad, we might have snagged a trip wire in the sand and gotten claymored all over the fucking desert.

"Jack, you're pale." She touched the back of my hand and I jerked it away in reflex.

I rubbed my face with both hands. "Fucking shit."

"Tell me."

"No, really. I'm all right." I took a bite and tried to smile and chew at the same time.

"If you don't talk to me about it, who are you going to talk to?" I shrugged, or cringed. "You stopped going to the VA shrink."

"She just gave me pills."

"And you didn't like the pills, I understand. I didn't like what they did to you. But you do have to talk to someone."

"Okay. I will."

"Promise?"

"Yeah. I'll open up. Let it all out."

Into the book.

Twenty-six miles turned out to be more in practice than it had seemed in theory. The idea of Iowa being flat was also a theoretical premise not borne out by fact. At the nineteen-mile mark there was a forlorn-looking motel, the Tidy Inn, and we turned into it after a two-word discussion.

The owner was a fat woman with sparse yellow hair, in a faded floral print dress at least a size too small. I had to pay her in cash, and if we'd wanted a phone, that would've been another $50 cash deposit. I wondered when she'd last had a customer who didn't bring his own.

The room was too large for its small bed and desk and chair. It had a stale smell and was dark as night. Kit kept me from turning on the lights when we unlocked the door. She'd unclamped the strong headlight from her handlebars. She crept over to the bed and pulled the covers over as she snapped it on. No bugs went scurrying for shelter. That should have comforted me, but instead I worried that she might not have been fast enough. Armies of bedbugs waiting to carry us off into the night.

One welcome surprise was an old-fashioned bathtub sitting on claw feet. It was big enough for two, a little crowded. She filled it up with steaming water, only a little rust-colored, while I did a quick maintenance routine on the bikes and brought them inside.

She was already undressed, standing in the water, and lowered herself down with an expression of bliss. "Oh, my aching butt."

I peeled off my Lycra bicycle togs and slipped in facing her, interlacing legs. The hot water was a relief, technically for the perineum rather than the butt proper, but she knew that. "Oh, my pulsating perineum" might be misconstrued.

I tickled her with my toe. "What do you want to do tonight?"

"Something besides that. Maybe trim your toenails." I jerked back. "Kidding." She put my foot back in place, gently, and then leaned forward while she reached behind her back to run some more hot water into the tub.

"Besides the obvious, we might try to find something to eat." We'd packed an emergency dinner of beans and franks, but there might be a roadside café or, more likely, a fast-food joint.

"Should've asked Dragon Lady," I said. "Wonder how close we are to the Amanas." The Amana Colonies were a cluster of pseudo-Amish towns that featured home-cooking restaurants.

"Ask her when we're cleaned up." She took the little bar of soap and started to work on me. After a couple of minutes we dried off hastily and moved to the squeaky bed.

Afterwards, she fell asleep with her head on my shoulder, her breath tickling my neck. Her body still glowing from the tub and sex.

As often happens, I was miles from sleep, no matter how tired I was from the neck down. Should think about the book. Hard to put myself into the head of an inhuman flesh-eating monster with this cute flesh doll cuddled up alongside me. My deflated dick shrank even more at the thought.

I looked down at her body and had a terrible instant of transport. In front of a mosque, a civilian body carelessly ground under tank treads, bare legs unaffected, relaxed. Don't go there. Don't go back there.

CHAPTER FIVE

Stephen Spenser wasn't impressed by money, having grown up surrounded by rich people he didn't like. But there was a comfortable talismanic feel to the tight roll of C-notes, held with a fat rubber band, that rode in his left front pocket. Faded torn jeans, to go with his faded flannel shirt and well-worn tennis shoes.

The bicycle was a marvel of camouflage, or misdirection; a sturdy ancient Schwinn with a flaking paint job and a touch of rust. But the running gear and brakes were brand-new Campy and Shimano, the tires were Gators, and the seat cost more than the frame. It was comfortable and stopped on a dime and got forty miles to the gallon of Heineken.

It had two big reed baskets, one of which held his travel bag, carefully chosen after a couple of hours' browsing in pawn shops and thrift stores. It was beat-up khaki nylon, scuffed but strong, with lots of compartments and a lock. The middle part held a week's worth of clothes and dehydrated meals, and side pockets held wallet and change and a notebook, along with hardware like a bottle opener and flashlight and Swiss Army knife. What had really sold him on this one was a side pocket under a Velcro flap, large enough for a Glock 9-mm and two spare clips.

Under his shirt he carried a snub-nosed Smith & Wesson Chief's Special .38 Airweight—the kind of gun a private eye always had in the movies. But Steve knew too much about guns to rely on it alone. And Hunter was doubtless a big man. In Alabama he'd left three footprints in mud while he was carrying a two-hundred-pound victim. A police lab report said that it would take at least five hundred pounds to drive his size fourteens that deep. To kill him with a .38, you'd have to hit him in the eye or right down the ear, and Steve didn't want to get that close while the beast was still alive.

He recited the LAPD mantra: "Two in the chest, one in the head." The first would get his attention, the second would kill him, and the third would kill him again. If he were human.

At Mr. Steinhart's insistence, he had a radio beacon Superglued to the underside of the seat. It used two hearing-aid batteries and would run for more than a year. If he were killed and the bike tossed somewhere, the cops could track it from fifty miles away. They might even find his body nearby.

If he were actually following the Southern Tier Trail, he'd start in the middle of St. Augustine. But Hunter wasn't going to nab anyone off a city street, so he studied the bus route and had the Greyhound drop him and his bike off at Molasses Junction.

It was like a scene out of *The Grapes of Wrath*. Bare dirt from horizon to horizon, a steady north wind, cold in the bleak sunshine, blowing needle-sharp sand into his face. He'd be headed west, so only his right ear would fill up with dirt.

The only building at the Molasses Junction crossroads was a general store. He locked his bike up, feeling foolishly urban, and carried his bag inside the dark dusty place. Mostly bare shelves. With the dust storm rattling the windows, it all felt like a set from a Woody Guthrie movie. With himself a fugitive from a Humphrey Bogart *noir* flick, armed to the teeth with no target in sight.

A tired old woman came out of a back room, wiping her hands on a bloody rag. Actually tomato guts. Behind her he could see a canning setup boiling, and a case of empty catsup bottles.

"What you want, somethin'?" She wasn't really that old. Her face was creased with fatigue, the lines stark in deep sunburn, maybe kitchen heat. Her body was not old, curves and muscle straining tight jeans and tank top. She turned halfway to adjust a Slim Jims display and not incidentally reveal that she was wearing a snub-nosed pistol in a butt holster. Probably smart in an isolated place like this. But the opposite of sexy.

He considered buying a box of .38 Special rounds to establish fellow-feeling, but decided against it. "Just a Coke, um, and a Slim Jim."

"In the machine there."

It was the kind of cooler he hadn't seen since he was a little boy, a big red icebox with a sliding top; inside, bottles of drinks racked in ice-cold water. He pulled out a twelve-ounce Coke in a heavy returnable bottle, also a time trip. There was a bottle opener at the cash register, which clanged and made satisfying greased-metal sounds. He got a quarter change for his dollar, and a finger-touch of warm flesh. "You need somethin', just holler." He watched the .38 swivel back to the stockroom.

A good place to begin an adventure. Sex and guns and Mother Nature outside playing the noir witch. Forget Arlene and the evaporating check and weepy Mom and dear old Dad.

Just you and me, monster. I'm coming to get you.

2.

I was able to finish most of a chapter while she slept. She envied me for being able to get along on five or six hours' sleep; I envied her for being able to stay down for ten. She was always more rested than me, but then I theoretically had more time to work. An extra forty-hour week every ten days. If only I could get paid for reading trash fiction and watching TV, I'd be a wealthy man.

But this particular morning, I did write, and was pretty happy with it.

So was Kit. She read through it while we had motel-room instant in paper cups.

"Would they really have to shoot him in the eye, or the ear? I mean in the real world."

"They say people who kill people for a living don't like .38s. The army stopped using them in the Spanish-American War, the Philippine part. The enraged Moro natives would absorb several shots and just keep coming."

"Pretty tough customers."

"Well, they tied leather thongs around their balls before they went into combat. The leather got wet and constricted, and the pain drove them mad."

"That's got to be bullshit," she said. "Racist bullshit. They couldn't walk."

"Hey. I read it in a book. That's why the army changed from the .38 to the .45. The .45 bullet was big enough to knock them down."

"But they don't use the .45 anymore. You said you had a 9-mm in the desert. That's got to be smaller." She rubbed her chin. "Forty-five hundredths of an inch is like twelve millimeters. Way smaller."

"Yeah, I guess. But it knocks them down better."

"Goodness. Smaller is better. Where will it all end?"

"A tiny little bullet, obviously, that moves at the speed of light. A photon."

"Have to be a heavy photon."

"I'm sure they're working on it." I should've paid attention in physics. How could a photon weigh anything, if it always moved at the speed of light? If it didn't move at the speed of light, it wouldn't be a photon.

"So is the monster really from another planet?"

"He thinks he is."

"Yeah, but *you* know. Don't you?"

"Right now he's Schrödinger's Cat. And I haven't opened the box."

"Ah." She took a sip of coffee. "So you don't know yet."

I wagged a pedantic finger at her. "That's not what I said."

She squinted at me while wheels turned—she was the one who first told me about the paradox: Mr. S's cat is in a box, presumably soundproof, with a gun pointed at its helpless little head. The gun will go off if the trigger is struck by an alpha particle from an alpha-particle generator that the cat's sadistic owner purchased at the local quantum hardware store. Schrödinger's point was that because of the quantum nature of elementary particles, there was only a probability, not a certainty, that the alpha particle had done its job. You couldn't tell whether the cat was alive or dead without opening the box—which takes the problem out of the quantum universe and into the real world.

Of course in the real world, there would or would not be a smoking hole in the box and cat brains all over the place. But that's not what scientists mean by "real."

"That's cute, Jack. You mean it literally?"

I shrugged.

"So right now—in your mind—the monster is both a human and an alien."

I almost didn't say anything. I trickled a little bit of rum into my coffee. "Until I open the box," I said.

I had a WeatherCard but hadn't charged it, and of course didn't bring the adaptor, but the morning sky was seamless blue and the weekend forecast had been good when we left home. So we filled our water bottles and pedaled off into deepest darkest Iowa, which is to say sunny rolling hills with wildflowers anthropomorphically nodding approval as we cruised by on our modest quest. Then the smallest grey cloud peeked over the western horizon, and then it loomed, and then all hell broke loose, lightning and thunder and a screaming gale pelting us with fast fat drops.

Lightning blasted a copse of trees not a hundred yards in front of us, while I was looking at it and trying to decide whether to stop there for shelter. Then Kit's bike slipped on gravel and she went down hard. Gloves protected her hands, but her left knee was torn and the shoulder hurt.

The bike was all right but she couldn't ride it, left leg stiffening. She couldn't even push it, really.

Neither of our cell phones got a signal. "Let's just lock it and leave it here," I shouted over the wind. "If somebody steals it, they steal it."

She nodded, her face screwed tight. "You go on for help. Or back to the motel?"

"No! I'm not leaving you."

We compromised by hiding the bike behind a sign and piling all her stuff on the back of mine, which I then trundled back toward the Tidy Inn while she limped alongside.

I wasn't much of a companion, pushing the double load through pelting rain and grit. I sort of wasn't there, going into a kind of zen state familiar from the desert: you can get through anything, one minute at a time. When the minute's up, do another minute. Go blank, stay blank.

So she startled me when she cried out "There! There it is!" A dim red VACANCY sign flickering in the gathering gloom. Only two hours and twenty minutes of trudge.

The cruddy place did look a thousand percent more comfortable than it had the evening before. The old crone got all maternal and taped up Kit's leg. She let us have the same room for ten dollars off, since it hadn't been made up yet. I could've collapsed into a pile of dirty laundry and slept for a week.

Kit filled the tub while I worked over the bike a little with paper towels and WD-40. Slipping into the water was pure heaven. Almost literally, like dying quietly and drifting off to a somnolent reward. We both fell asleep and woke up in cooling soup. While the tub drained we scrubbed each other with the hand shower attachment, more giggles than hygiene.

We carried lightweight emergency meals, dehydrated ramen or rice with mystery meat—just add hot water and pray—but decided to have regular food whenever it was available. So when we checked in we'd made a call to one of the Amana Colony restaurants, the Wheel, that did home dinner deliveries. I got dressed enough to open the door at eight, and a teenaged boy brought in armloads of Styrofoam boxes—the minimum order, a family dinner for four. Famished, we tore into the mountain of roast pork and sausage, mashed potatoes, green beans, beets, yams, and all. We didn't open the container of pickled ham, the place's specialty, saving it for tomorrow, wrapped up along with a loaf of fresh bread and some butter.

The motel TV only had network, so we lay in bed and watched mind-rot for a while. I fell asleep in the middle of the first sitcom, and when I woke up the room was dark except for the luminous clock, 4:44, a lucky-looking number. Kit snored quietly while I set up the laptop on the desk, angled so the light wouldn't bother her. I made some instant with hot water from the tap and sweetened it with rum, and let the screen take me into Hunter's world.

CHAPTER SIX

Hunter kept his police-band radio going all night while he sat on the steps of the dark trailer and peered out into the night with infrared goggles. He saw a fight between an owl and a weasel, but no human activity. If anybody was missing Lane Jared, PhD, they hadn't told the police.

You should know as much as possible about the things you eat. From his flat sharkskin wallet, Hunter could tell that Dr. Jared was thirty-two, single, and perhaps did not drive; he had a "non-driver's license," a state ID, issued in Atlanta, and his leg muscles were so tough and stringy that if he owned a car he had probably only pushed it around for exercise.

He had a membership card for a vegetarian co-op, which no doubt was why he tasted so bland. Not enough poisons. He was either gay or complex; a hidden pocket in the wallet held a much handled photo of a plain-looking young man wearing only a smile and an erection. It also hid three tightly folded hundred-dollar bills; otherwise, Jared had only a single, a fiver, and a ten. No credit cards. An eight-year-old university ID showed him with a Rasputin-style black beard; the head freezing in Hunter's cooler was clean-shaven and going grey.

Most of the wallets Hunter collected from his meals were full of documents like membership cards and business cards and receipts. Dr. Jared was parsimonious in that regard. He wished now that he'd talked with the man awhile. He'd said he was a minister; was that a lie? Probably not. Maybe he was a Christian who believed in transubstantiation, and eating him would be a kind of perverse sacrament. It would have been fun to discuss that with him.

He would probably just scream, though, or get all weepy, like the last female. How could this happen to me? She asked that over and over. Perhaps you were a bad girl. Though you didn't taste bad. Lots of good fat.

When the sun came up, Hunter lumbered around the perimeter of his camp checking the alarm devices. Monofilament stretched at toe height. When he first set it up, touching the lines would ring little chimes. Now the system was more sophisticated; lights on a computer map inside would show where the intruder was.

If it was just one, he could shoot him from the dark. If it was a group, he would arm the trailer's timer and drive off in the van. The trailer would blow up after five minutes. The van would unroll two mats of nails on the gravel road to slow down pursuers, and where it intersected the state road, he'd buried a hundred-pound crate of dynamite topped with buckets of rusty nails.

Still, he might be caught. He hadn't decided whether to be taken alive. An autopsy would immediately reveal that he wasn't human, which would displease his masters. If he were captured, he would have a good chance of escaping before they found out the truth. But in the process of escaping, he might reveal his superhuman strength.

Exercise time. Hunter squatted over a truck axle, red with rust except for the two places where he gripped it, and smoothly he lifted it over his head. He pressed and curled it silently fifty times and let it drop.

Breathing a little hard, he crossed the clearing to where an ancient live oak had grown a stout limb about eight feet off the ground. He grabbed it and did twelve pull-ups, the tree groaning in protest, and then reversed the position of his grip and did twelve more. Then he did three with his right arm alone, grunting.

He could not run like a human, not in this gravity and atmosphere, but he staggered around his property three times in a well-worn figure eight path.

It made him hungry. He had a few cuts that had gone straight into the refrigerator's meat compartment. He took out two arm steaks and smeared them with chopped garlic in olive oil, then sliced an onion and fried it up in butter. Seared the steaks on both sides and lowered the heat to braise them in red wine with some rosemary. He took the jug of Gallo burgundy and sat on the steps, drinking from it while attacking a large can of Sam's Club potato chips.

Once each minute, he would stop chewing and listen. He could hear birds and animals going about their business and the quiet simmer of the steaks under the heavy cast-iron skillet top. The smell of rosemary and garlic and sweet flesh was intoxicating.

A large car or small pickup whispered by on the state road, more than a mile away. A human would not have heard it, he was sure; nor could a human smell the cooking so far away. Hikers were his only worry.

It smelled so good, we had to come and check.

You must join me, then.

3.

I finished the short chapter and quietly got dressed. Peeked through the blinds and it was full daylight outside.

"Time to?" Kit muttered, half asleep.

"Sleep," I said. "I'm gonna go back and get the van."

"I could come with," she said, half sitting up.

"No way. Get some rest." She grunted and fell back with a thump, and mumbled thanks into the pillow.

I pedaled off into the bright cool morning. This was going to be the pattern of my life, I realized, a lark married to a dove, and I liked it. Almost all my writing, I did while she slept through the morning. True, I wasn't much of a party animal at night, but neither was she. Our nights often ended with me snugged next to her while she read a book or watched TV or a movie on her pad, but I think she liked that. Part of her independence from the conventional world. Her parents' world.

The morning sun had dried everything off and it was perfect

bicycling weather. A slight breeze at my back, a hard smooth bike lane. I pushed it up to twenty and kept it there, enough to break a nice sweat.

I stopped once to carry a turtle across the road, feeling kind of stupid. He'd probably just turn himself around and get squashed on the way back. Turtles bothered me more than most roadkills, though. The pathos factor. They thought they had everything covered, and then these mammals evolved to where they had eighteen wheels and hurtled along at ninety miles per hour. Your shell might just as well be tissue paper. Be patient; we'll evolve up over the road and leave you alone again.

The turtle was once my "totem animal." In high school, a friend had read about the idea, or come up with it on his own—that we should all adopt some species of animal that stood for what we wanted to be. Among all the ferocious and fast and clever menagerie my friends allied themselves with, I was the lone turtle. Slow, careful, observing everything. Safe within my shell.

I wasn't much different now. Faster, at least to the outside observer. A slow brain, that tried not to miss anything.

That had been my big beef with the army, at least in training. Everything fast, by the numbers, hup-toop-threep. Until I found my niche.

A sniper doesn't do anything fast. Watch and wait, wait and watch, don't move. Total zen, except for the bit at the end. You squeeze the trigger and someone a half a mile or more away falls over dead.

I read a library book by a woman who had interviewed all kinds of combat veterans. Before my war, but she had guys from the Gulf and Vietnam and even WWII, and she came up with an unsurprising generalization: the farther away you were from the person you killed, the less fucked up you were by the killing. Seems pretty obvious. You choke some poor bastard to death with your bare hands, it's going to bother you more than squeezing a trigger a half mile away from him.

I don't remember whether she talked to the guys who pushed the button on Hiroshima and Nagasaki. Pretty remote, but times a hundred thousand? Maybe they had bad dreams. Worse than mine.

I didn't usually see the results of my "sniper craft," as they called it. They'd drag them away, or there'd be a pile, your victim one among many. Twice I was sure, though. One guy looked like TV, lying back with his eyes closed, a dark wet spot on his chest. The other had the top of his head popped off, like if he'd worn a helmet he might have been okay. My big moment of fame in the platoon—confirmed-kill head shot, a raghead sniper.

I never told anybody I hadn't aimed for the head. It was a long shot, about five hundred meters, and the bastard was prone, aiming at some of our guys off to the left. I had a solid braced position, and aimed about four feet over his chest. Maybe a breath of wind caught the bullet. "Head shot," my spotter said. "You da man." I made E-5 the next week, for one week. Then got busted back for boozing.

Then got the stripe back and lost it again, I'm still not sure how. I supposedly got into a fight and knocked out some E-8 asshole. But I didn't get into fights, not then, and I don't know how I was supposed to've knocked out a bruiser a head taller than me without even hurting my knuckles. But it was his drunken word against mine. So we both got busted, but I had to clean out latrines for a week. Officer latrines, so of course it didn't smell bad at all.

My supposed head shot, though. The bullet hit his head about two inches above the ear, and it was like a sledgehammer. Blood and brains everywhere, bone chips. But if the wind had gone the other way I would have hit him in the butt, or not at all.

What did all this have to do with Hunter, I wondered as I pedaled along. I was a hunter then, in the broadest sense of the word. Civilians who do it for fun sneak around with a high-powered rifle like mine, looking for woodsy "targets of opportunity," though theirs don't shoot back. Less sporting, if you ask me.

I didn't like the actual sniper-ing much, but was surprised to find that I loved the shooting itself, burning up ammo on the rifle range, trying for smaller and smaller groups. In sniper school I often got the day's best MOA—number of hits within a minute of arc—which was good for a half-day pass on the weekend. Take a cab to a scummy bar off base and try to pick up some girl who didn't have a financial motive.

I never did pay for it, neither stateside nor in the desert. Maybe I pretended it was virtue. But I was a virgin when I got drafted, and had a grim anti-fantasy about doing something stupid, and the whore laughing at me.

Which of my regrets about the army was strongest—killing people? Following orders from idiots? Wasting three of my most productive years?

Maybe it was not getting laid. Being too shy or scared, when really I was in a horny guy's heaven. Some of those hookers in Columbus were stunning, but the ones who peopled my fantasies were ordinary cute girls who looked like the coeds I'd spent so much undergraduate time and energy not fucking.

After combat, it was easy. Just ask the damned girl! What's she going to do, chuck a grenade at you? And combat veterans my age and education were pretty rare still, that early in the war. I learned to play that mystique pretty well, the year between army "separation" and the night Kit ignored my bashed-in mouth and rescued me from my wicked ways.

It was not yet noon when I pulled into the English & Philosophy Building parking lot. I called Kit and discussed possibilities, then drove out to the Coralville Strip and got a two-foot-long loaded submarine to split.

Funny how driving a route you've just biked seems to take about the same length of time. The bike ride had been almost three hours and the trip back was not even thirty minutes. But I enjoy biking along in a meditative state; driving, I had to put it on cruise control to keep from speeding out of boredom. Plus a little submarine hunger, even though I'd shortened my half by a couple of bites.

She or a maid had made up the bed, and she was sitting in the lone chair, reading. She had showered and changed her bandage, a less dramatic single wrap of gauze. We went outdoors to a picnic table to attack the sub.

She rode the length of the motel parking lot and decided that discretion was the better part of valor, though I think being a mathematician, she might express that differently. "$D \gg V$"?

We drove back to my place because I had tools and a workstand, and we drank wine while I cleaned and adjusted her bike. I even tuned the spokes on her rear wheel, ping-ping-ping, a process she'd never seen, which delighted her.

She picked up a family portrait that was sitting on top of my nailed-together bookcase. "Hear from your dad recently?"

"Still boning what's-her-name in Chicago, I guess. I did get an e-mail day before yesterday that went to a couple hundred of his closest friends. He's opening in Chicago next week. Probably go up." Dad was a sometime actor, though most of his money came from teaching drama in adult ed, a sure road to big bucks.

"That would be a good gesture," she said carefully. "It wouldn't bother you if what's-her-name was there?"

"No, no. She's all right. I guess collecting fossils is a legitimate hobby."

She studied the picture. "I don't know. I'd say he looks pretty good. He looks like you."

"Not anymore. He has a bushy white beard now, and horn-rim glasses. Not as much hair. Closer to Lear than Hamlet."

"Hamlet's overrated. Who wants a worrywart?

"Careful, there. I played Hamlet in high school."

"No, really? I've known you all this time and I didn't know that?"

"Wasn't a big deal. I'd already decided not to follow in Dad's footsteps."

"Trotting in front of the footlights. Was he disappointed?"

"Funny, no; not at all. He was all for me getting a doctorate and teaching. It was Mom who wanted me to act."

She laughed. "While your dad was cheating on her with actresses?"

"Funny business." I shrugged. "She might've known back then; maybe not. It didn't all come out until the divorce." Five years ago.

"Did your dad ever say . . . did you know?"

"Oh, hell, yes. Not in so many words, just a wink or a raised eyebrow now and then. And when he was happy he really showed it. By the time I was sixteen I could tell that his being happy didn't have much to do with what was going on at home. Then Mother caught them together, I think by accident."

" 'There are no accidents.' Who said that?"

"Schiller? Maybe the captain of the *Titanic*."

"Was it what's-her-name?"

"No, not even an actress. She was a tech person, a lighting engineer. Not even pretty—that annoyed the hell out of Mother."

She traced her finger over the glass of the picture. "Your mother's more than pretty. Glamorous."

"Yeah, I guess. Little life lesson there."

"I'm glad you're not attracted to beautiful women."

Nothing safe to say to that. I touched her nose, then kissed her gently. She giggled while we were kissing. "Sorry! I can be so awful!"

"Naw. You just need an editor sometimes."

She stood up and pulled her T-shirt off in one cross-arm jerk, and then stepped out of her shorts. "So come edit me. If you're done with the bicycle."

I wasn't, quite. But it could wait.

CHAPTER SEVEN

Relaxing after a big meal, Hunter sometimes let his mind wander back to other times and places.

His home planet, Vantor, was beautiful but not pleasant, a hard place to grow up—if you lived long enough to grow. Of his twelve littermates, all male, only one other lived to become adult.

There had been four, but on the eve of their tenth birthday they went into the pit together, and only two were allowed to come out. He could still taste his brothers' blood, and feel it splashing on his face.

He would not dishonor that memory by eating humans raw. Their taste was insipid anyhow, and needed cooking with spices and herbs. Especially the taste of their sexual parts, pallid and tame. They fought fiercely over that part, the last birthday, thinking it gave strength and courage.

After the tenth, they didn't count birthdays. You lived until you died, and that would be a long time.

He was not sure how he had gotten to Earth, or what his purpose was here. He was content to wait, and hunt, and eat.

He sat there unmoving through the night, neither asleep nor awake. At first light, he took a shovel with a sharp square blade and cut out a rectangle of turf. He carefully squared out the hole, depositing the dirt on a canvas drop cloth. When the hole was handle-deep, he went into the trailer and brought out the inedible remnants of the luckless jogger. Before covering it with dirt he undressed, straddled the hole, and evacuated generously into it. Then he filled the grave, stamping the soil down tightly, and carefully replaced the turf. He saturated the area with his alien urine, which he knew contained butyric acid. No bloodhound would come near it.

He went back into his trailer and turned the heat up to a comfortable hundred degrees. Then he carefully eased himself onto the oversized recliner and opened up his paperback book: *The Pawns of Null-A*, by A. E. Van Vogt.

He had read it before, but that was all right. He didn't read for information.

4.

Kit stared at the last page and set it down carefully. "So he eats this guy's balls and then shits on his bones and pisses on his grave. Couldn't you be a little less tasteful?"

"Well, actually, it's his brother's balls."

"Oh, okay. That's all right." She laughed. "Keep it in the family."

I had to laugh, too. "Hey, if you can't appreciate good literature, you don't have to expose yourself to it."

"It's not me who's exposing myself. Are you going to let your mother read this? Your *shrink*?"

"I wouldn't show it to the shrink. Mother would say, 'Can't you sex it up a little? Have him jerk off into the grave?'"

"No wonder you're such a delicate soul."

"Everything I am today, I owe to dear old Mom."

I loaded up on carbs with a double stack of pancakes—or used the bike as an excuse to stuff myself, take your pick—and then Kit drove me back to where the weather and road had stopped us the night before. The plan was for her to keep the van while I completed the loop to Des Moines and back; if I ran into trouble she would come rescue me.

I wasn't going to rough it; I had a map with all the motels on the route and their phone numbers, so when I decided to quit for the day I could call ahead. (That seemed prudent because there weren't all that many places to stay.)

When she dropped me off and drove away, I felt a guilty glow of freedom. Four or five days of being a carefree bachelor, the wind at my back and nothing in front of me but the road.

The carefree feeling ended with a bang after an hour and ten minutes. I had somehow managed to run over a nail more than two inches long. It wasn't even the same color as the road, cruddy with rust. But sharp enough to blow me out.

I was carrying two spare tubes, but repaired the flat one out of prudence and pessimism, remembering one day I managed to have three flats in three hours. All of them less dramatic than this one, relatively slow leaks, which can take longer to fix—not obvious where the hole is. Or it turns out to be the valve, unfixable.

I let the glue on the repaired tube rest and pumped up a new one and was on my way—twenty minutes to fix the tube, change the tire, and be back on the road. Short of my best by five or six minutes, but I wasn't in a hurry.

I should have been. Of course the weather couldn't last. I slogged through a driving rain until I fetched up on the shores of the Angel Bless Motel. A flashing neon cross would normally repel me like a vampire, but the rain had weakened my resistance.

I was suddenly on the set of a Hitchcock movie that never got made.

I staggered dripping into a small Victorian room, a half-dozen cut-glass lamps giving a warm glow to the complicated floral wallpaper. Smiling older hostess wearing a full skirt and an apron. She didn't say the only room left was #13, which might have sent me back out into the rain. But she did insist on showing me around the six glass cases along the walls, her late husband's life work. Lots of miniature trains and airplanes and hundreds of butterflies pinned to velvet. She had been a widow for nine years, four months, and seven days.

The room she led me to had only one butterfly, a big purple one pinned under glass, hanging over the bed like an invertebrate crucifix. There's a sad irony to a moth-eaten butterfly.

I set the coffeemaker to just heat some water, and took as hot a shower as the motel's plumbing and budget would allow. A quick ramen dinner, and then I made weak tea with just a pinch of sugar. I didn't want to stay awake.

The TV's depth axis was shot, so rather than watch crap in two and a half dimensions, I flipped through the various books on my notebook and settled on *Down the River*, a collection of short stories by recent Iowa graduates. I had a paper copy at home, a contributor's freebie, but the only story I'd read in it was my own, checking for typos. Mildly curious about the competition, I got halfway through the second story before I turned off the notebook and the light.

———————

It was still raining when I woke up. Not cold or windy, so I guess if I were a serious cyclist I'd just man up and pedal out into it.

Instead, I made a double-strong, double-sugar cup of coffee with

ReelCreme™ and took the motel's chair out under the eaves and sat looking at and listening to the rain, not thinking about the novel or anything in particular. Then I went back inside, made another cup, and unrolled the notebook and its keyboard.

What would Hunter do in the rain? Not a scene from the movie, but what the hell.

CHAPTER EIGHT

Hunter liked the sound of rain drumming on his metal roof. The fact of the rain, though, was a little annoying. He had eaten one frozen meal and wanted a fresh one, but there wouldn't be many joggers out.

Not many potential witnesses, either.

No diversions left. He was tired of reading, and television was earnest documentaries and Saturday morning cartoons, which offered sufficient violence but no appetizing consequences.

With no particular destination in mind, he got in the van and headed north, playing a Jacksonville radio station on the radio but not hearing the music, listening for weather updates. He got gas in Georgia, filling up at a place that was too ramshackle and open to have surveillance cameras. He did have to go inside to pay, and considered the risk/benefit ratio of killing the dimwitted clerk and emptying the register.

The boy was skinny and sallow and smelled bad, which may have saved his life. And there could have been a hidden camera amidst the chaotic jumble of merchandise behind him. Hunter bought eight Super Red Hot sausages and, unseen back in the van, ate them like a sword-swallower, one after the another, while he studied the map.

The rain had let up when he stopped, but now it continued with redoubled force. He took a left turn and then angled down a county road that pointed into Alabama.

He came upon his prize only fifteen minutes down the road. A large woman on the gravel margin hunched against the force of the rain, working on an upside-down bicycle. He slowed down and waved at her, blinking his lights. She waved back and he pulled off the road in front of her, and backed up.

He rolled down the window as she came up, wiping the water from her long hair. She was big, not quite half his size, and he salivated at the thought of all that delicious fat.

"Golly, thanks, mister—" He flung the door open with such force that she sprawled almost to the middle of the road. But she was standing, staggering, by the time he heaved himself out of the van. He took two ponderous steps and dropped her with a punch to the solar plexus.

Faster, now. He grabbed her wrist and roughly dragged her to the back of the van. Locked. Stupid of him.

The driver's-side door was still open. He lumbered back to it and stretched to reach the keys in the ignition.

Sudden sharp pain in his back. He turned and she was standing there with a narrow-blade knife, a switchblade stiletto, staring at the color of his blood.

The wound was not serious. He backhanded her so hard her neck snapped.

She was limp but still alive as he tied her up and manacled her in the back. She managed some incoherent growls and moans, too soft to annoy him or attract attention, so he didn't bother with the duct tape.

"Be happy," he called back. "You're out of the rain."

Decisions. Maybe leave Georgia for this one, so as not to have the same group of state police studying his spoor. Drive on into Alabama, or maybe all the way through to Mississippi.

No. The need was growing in him. Alabama would do.

He was across the border in thirty minutes, and stopped at a McDonald's for a bag of small burgers and ten orders of fries. He gulped it all down, driving one-handed but with intense care, before he left the interstate. He had memorized the map and the Googlemaps screen that showed the nameless dead-end dirt road that was his tentative destination.

At the first small road he pulled over to the shoulder to check on his quarry. He was too big to crawl through the van, so he chanced opening the rear doors. Her eyes were closed, but when he forced her mouth open and poured in some water, she coughed and gagged.

"That's good. It won't be long now."

"Please," she croaked. "Do . . . do whatever you want. . . ."

"Don't worry. I will." He eased the doors shut and went back toward the front of the van, but she started to scream. Annoying.

He went back to the rear doors, swung them open, and hit her head twice on the metal floor, just hard enough to stun her.

"Please. You only cause trouble for yourself." He tore off a piece of duct tape and smoothed it over her mouth. Then he tore off a small piece and closed one nostril. "Wouldn't that be an awful way to die?"

Before getting back into the van, he stepped into the forest, studying the loam. The van would leave tracks when he went off the road.

If it rained harder, they would be obliterated, but the forecast called for the rain to taper off and stop in a couple of hours.

He studied his memory of the Googlemaps images. The topographical map showed a ridge to the east, and a gravel road in a few miles that ran up it. He would drive up there and check the soil and underbrush.

In the small cooler between the seats he'd stashed alternating quarts of beer and Coke. Took a Coke to be on the safe side. Wouldn't do to be stopped in the middle of nowhere and forced to kill a state trooper. Two, probably.

He almost missed the unmarked gravel road and reversed back up to it. He drove up the rise and pulled over, out of sight from the paved road, and stopped to listen for a couple of minutes. No traffic; no sound but the ticking of his engine and the patter of raindrops.

He drove on slowly for about a mile and a half. The road ended at the grey ruin of a clapboard shack with a collapsed roof. Saplings grew out of the interior. The front door was missing and there was no glass in the windows.

Still, some indigent might have sought shelter there. He quietly shucked a shell into the 12-gauge and eased heavily out of the van, alert.

His eyes adjusted to the gloom inside the cabin. Sound of a rat or squirrel scurrying away. No other signs of life except spiders and millipedes. Woodsy smell with a touch of mildew.

The exposed beams under the part of the roof that was intact were strong enough to support his weight. He went back to the van and brought out the chains and hook and large cooler.

When he returned for the woman, her eyes were open, unblinking.

She didn't resist when he handcuffed her wrists together, and then her ankles.

Should he rape her? He had done that to the first two women, and one man, but there was no special joy in it, and it proved nothing; he already had total control over them, so sticking a protuberance into an opening was a trivial exercise. Besides, if he were interrupted and had to leave body parts behind, the fluid they found in her vagina would not be human in chemistry or biology.

He hung her up by the heels and stooped to remove the duct tape. "Don't scream. There's no one around to hear you, and you'll just annoy me."

She winced when he jerked the tape off, then worked her jaw and said, "This is the weirdest dream I've ever had."

"It's not a dream, Cooper." He'd looked in her wallet. "It's not even a nightmare."

"I refuse to believe that. You'll kill me, and then I'll wake up."

He almost smiled. "That's a new way of coping. None of the others have said that." He unrolled her Lycra shorts and left them bunched around her knees. "Most girls your age shave around the pubic region. The bathing suit part, at least."

"I'm sure you're an expert." Her voice was conversational but quaking. "You can say 'cunt.' Under the circumstances."

"Heavens, no. I don't know you well enough." He sliced her T-shirt from neck to waist and then cut both sleeves to remove it. She was wearing a red sports bra. He snapped the elastic but left it alone.

"How many . . . how many others?"

"Twelve; you'll be lucky thirteen. The newspapers call me Hunter. You haven't heard of me?"

"I—I never read the paper. Or watch the news."

"Oh. Is it too depressing?" He made small nicks over each kneecap and watched the blood trickle down. "If you read the newspapers, you might have thought twice before bicycling alone out in the woods."

"My boyfriend and parents know where—"

"I'm sure they do. We'll be in another state before they get around to calling the police. You'll be in quite another state." He wiped one stream of blood with his forefinger and tasted it. "Type O, I believe?"

"Look. If this is a gag—"

"There may be gagging." He stuck out his tongue and licked the trickle of blood from the other leg in one slow sweep. Then he wiped his mouth with the back of his hand. "You are delicious."

He went outside and came back with a large plastic bucket with a lid. He pried off the lid and put the bucket on the floor underneath her head. Then he sat down cross-legged, facing her eye to eye.

"Carolyn Cooper. You must bike a lot."

"No. Yes." Tears were running down her forehead.

"Your thighs and calves are very muscular. But not *too* lean. Do you go to school?"

She shook her head no.

"Church? Do you go to church?"

"You . . . United Southern Baptist."

"Southern Baptist. So you'll be in heaven soon."

She cried harder and tried to wipe her nose on her shoulder. He held up a Kleenex and said, "Blow." She wouldn't.

"I bet you're still a virgin. Are you?"

She nodded slowly. "And yet you say 'cunt.' How people have changed since I was a boy." He reached up and she cringed away, and so started to swing and bob, a complex pendulum.

He waited until she stopped. "What if I promised to let you go if you let me make love to you? Have sex. Here on the floor?"

She glared at him and shook her head, just an inch, back and forth.

"If you don't, I'll kill you."

"You will anyhow. You godless bastard."

He stared into her eyes, brow furrowed in thought. "It's a complicated moral dilemma—for you, not for me—though you may be too upset to appreciate it right now."

He held up one finger. "You refuse to have sex with me and I kill you. You go to heaven. If you were headed there anyhow."

Two fingers. "You let me make love to you and I keep my word, and let you go. Technically, you sinned the sin of fucking—but is your God so petty he would send you to Hell over that? If so, I would posit that you don't have a snowball's chance of getting through life without doing something that will send you there."

Three fingers. "You let me make love to you and I kill you anyhow. As you have suggested. I would concede that that could be bad. Go directly to Hell, do not collect two hundred dollars." He laughed. "You're looking at me as if I were crazy. Haven't you ever heard of Monopoly?"

He shook his head at her crying. "There is a fourth, necrophilia. I could kill you first and then have sex with your remains. But that would be sick. I've never done that, not really. They were always alive when I started."

He stood, set the blade on her abdomen, and pressed slightly. "The last time, I cut his throat and then opened him like *this*." With his finger, not the blade, he swept down from pubic bone to sternum. She screamed.

He sat back down. It took all his strength to hold her head still while he replaced the duct tape.

"Please try not to pee. That doesn't help anything." Instead of cutting her throat, he just opened a carotid artery, which resulted in a mess. He must have saved only half the blood, the rest of it spurting all around as she struggled. By the time there was a regular flow into the bucket, the floor of the musty room looked like a macabre Jackson Pollock painting.

He wouldn't do it that way again. It was nice to have the blood, but the out-of-control disorder was vulgar.

When he made the long ventral incision, she was so close to being dead that she hardly reacted, just flinching. Before he cut her down, he severed the intestines at ileum and rectum, and laid them out in a neat circle around the locus where she was hanging, which remedied some of the randomness. He separated the edible parts from the steaming pile of offal and sealed them in plastic bags, which he set on the block of ice in the cooler.

She was a little too large to fit into the cooler until he took out the ice block and jointed her. Then he split the ice into eight chunks and arranged them in various hollows, and propped the bucket upright inside her circled arms.

Before moving the ice chest, he took the shotgun and went out the cabin's back door, and silently reconnoitered. The rain had stopped and the forest was utterly quiet.

He found the remains of a rabbit that had been torn apart, probably by a hawk, and smiled in empathy. He thought of what was inside the cooler and his stomach growled.

5.

The rain stopped abruptly just after 10:00. I finished the chapter I'd been working on, rolled up my gear, and punched the phone for automatic checkout. Figured I could cover half the distance to Des Moines before lunch if I poured on the coal.

Perfect weather and road. Cool fresh-washed air and pebbly asphalt that hadn't gone through too many Iowa winters.

Sometimes the bicycle is a perfect place to think. Maybe the rhythm and slight exertion. But especially like this, with no distractions from weather or traffic—the mind roams and grazes. Not a mind-set for doing the taxes or solving scholarly problems, but good for free association and inspiration.

So what would Hunter be if I were writing the story free of constraints from the script? Like this last chapter. That went easily and was pretty interesting. Pretty good writing.

How close did the book really have to be to the movie?

Well, the movie didn't actually exist yet, as a movie. They were supposed to start shooting July first, two weeks before the book was due. They were going to wrap the movie six weeks later, 15 August. That date was set in stone; another company would be moving into the studio the next day.

My contract required me to rewrite the novelization if there were "fundamental" changes between the script and the movie. I hadn't minded agreeing to that clause—hell, if I had to write the whole novel over, it was still a fortune compared to real fiction.

But wait. Consider the obverse—what if *I* made fundamental changes to the story myself? And delivered before shooting started? If they liked it better, they might use that version, or some part of it.

They wouldn't pay me any more—talk about fantasy!—but it could enhance my reputation. And if they *didn't* like it, how much work would it be to return it to Duquest's original inspired version?

Barb Goldman said I'd be lucky if the Great Man even saw the first page of the book. Most likely it would go to the "script girl" (of whatever gender) or some similar minion, who would write up a page or two about it, to be filed and forgotten.

But what if the report said, "Hey, this is really good! Somebody should send it up to Duquest before he starts to shoot!"

Doesn't hurt to dream. With a free hand, what about the script would I change?

The action really wouldn't have to be that different. Maybe a little more believable. I was already taking some liberties with the characters, who were pretty cardboard in the script, and I had the studio's blessing for that. When I talked to Duquest's agent on the phone, what he said he wanted, in so many words, was "really good writing, just not too literary." Sort of like really good soup, but without any seasoning.

What does a Hollywood guy mean by "literary"? Big words? No problem. Complex characterization? Keep it subtle. Layers of meaning? They won't worry about the cake if the icing looks pretty.

As I'd told Kit, but of course hadn't mentioned to the movie people, that was the most interesting aspect of the job; the most challenging: writing two books simultaneously, a literary one and a commercial one. The hat trick was that both novels were made up of the same sequence of words.

Maybe that was kind of quantum-mechanical? Like a particle being in two places at the same time. Though I could never get my literal-minded brain around that one, quite.

With writing it's simple to do two things at once. The Marquis de Sade's "novels" are masturbation adjuncts but also exquisitely detailed maps of a deranged mind examining itself. *Ulysses* is a microscopic deconstruction of one day in Dublin, but the same sequence of words adds up to a daring experiment in the limits of the novel form.

So my job was simple wordsmithing in comparison: write a good novel that follows someone else's story line—like *Ulysses*, both Homer's and Joyce's, to go from the ridiculous to the sublime.

In theory, I could write two different versions, literary and commercial. But that way lies legal madness. The book will be a "work done for hire," and is the sole property of Ronald Duquest. Once I cash the check, I'm out of the picture. If I tried to copyright a book with the same story and title, but better words, the people who owned the commercial version would not be amused. It's probably a good life rule not to piss off people who keep lawyers on the payroll.

The new bike was very pleasant for the first fifteen miles or so, but somewhere between twenty and thirty I started to wonder about the wisdom of my choice. The "commuter" bike was exactly that, and its cushiony ride would be perfect for going back and forth to and from work. The softness of the ride ultimately came from your own muscles, though, pushing against springs. A road bike's ride might be harder on your butt, but all the energy you expended went to getting you from point A to point B.

Maybe I could put that in the book. Our hero gets an oversprung commuter bike with the guy's money, but goes back the next day for one that's more practical for the long haul. Not in the script, but a nice bit of verisimilitude for bike-savvy readers.

The author of the book, unlike the character, doesn't have an employer with a fat wallet. Well, they *do* have billions, but not for the peons who humbly till the literary soil for them. Not for the comfort of their butts.

It was worth a few miles of daydreaming. I'd only spent $500 on this bike, leaving $49,500 for other stuff like rent. Minus Barb's 15 percent. A decent road bike would run about $1,500, and they'd probably give me $400 trade-in. Call it a thousand-dollar investment, finally, out of the fifty I was getting for the book.

I almost had myself convinced, but a reality check came creeping in. How often, in real life, would I do even ten miles in a day, let alone fifty or a hundred? Going to the 7-Eleven for a six-pack, I'd rather have this comfy blue Cambridge than a sexy hard-riding racer. And it would be really stupid to buy both—where would I put them? I wouldn't even leave my Salvation Army junker locked up overnight outside my apartment. Even if nobody was desperate enough to steal it, kids liked to demonstrate their budding manliness by stomping on spokes—and frames, if they were big kids.

Even the one bike dominated my so-called living room. Two would make it look like a bike shop.

I did have a get-thee-behind-me-Satan moment as I pedaled wearily into the suburbs of Des Moines. Two Guys Bike Shoppe had a signboard out front saying THIS WEEKEND ONLY ALL CAMPYS 25% OFF LIST!!! A Campagnolo would be just the right level of wretched excess— a Caddy, but not a Rolls.

I went past it a couple of blocks to a motel that was conveniently just behind a liquor store. A six-pack and a miniature of dark rum would take the kinks out fine. A burger and a couple of cookies for dinner, from the 7-Eleven beside it. It wasn't dinner on the French Riviera with Duquest and his bevy of bimbos. But that might come in time.

CHAPTER NINE

He roasted a whole leg slowly, sawed in two to accommodate the oven, sealed up in heavy foil with herbs and spices and wine. After a few hours, timing by smell and touch, he used a long filleting knife to extract the bones for stock. He chunked the meat and browned it carefully under the broiler.

He wolfed a quarter of it down and then rested for a day. He checked his garbage-disposal map and dug a new hole for the cooked-out bones and burned her clothing on top of them, then relieved himself there before replacing the dirt and mat of humus and undergrowth. Three drops of butyric acid to keep away curious dogs and other digging animals.

Prudence dictated that he ought to change his location soon. This little patch of Alabama was perfect, but that perfection was a danger. People looking for him would eventually close in and be on his doorstep, by a process of elimination.

Where next? The challenge of living in a city had a perverse appeal. The probability of detection would be high, though; almost certain. He was prepared to face, and escape from, a squad car or two of country-bumpkin state troopers, but a city SWAT team would be formidable, and if he bested them there would be a small army after him, federal as well as state. He couldn't afford to be tightly surrounded and observed in action. If they realized he wasn't human, they would want to capture him alive and find out what he was. His masters would not like that.

He opened a third quart of Pabst Blue Ribbon and thought. Moving the trailer would be conspicuous and difficult. Burning it in place would be simple, but would draw investigators. If they found all the buried bones there would be trouble. He was too physically conspicuous to hide among humans, but he could find another place like this.

Maybe he *should* consider moving the trailer. It would be conspicuous on the road, but more conspicuous as a burned-out ruin. Fire inspectors might wonder why a hermit needed a big meat locker. If they checked it for DNA they would find out.

He considered burning on a monumental scale, a forest fire that incidentally consumed the trailer. That might not call attention to him if he planned it properly.

It would be unthinkable to abandon this place before he had a destination. Not very difficult to find, with time and resources. The past two homes, he'd arranged through the same Atlanta firm, a rural acreage broker who only worked online. Hunter's Atlanta bank account was administered by computer and fueled by nighttime cash deposits.

Cooper's purse had yielded an unexpected treasure: a roll of fifty hundred-dollar bills sewn into the lining. He had handled them only while wearing gloves. There was no pattern to the serial numbers; they were an assortment of five bills that looked and smelled brand new, with forty-five that had been in circulation. He crumpled them all up and soaked them in water with a little dirt, and dried them between sheets of newspaper.

It was interesting. Perhaps he should have talked to her longer. There was no way that money came from a regular paycheck, and details mattered. The more he knew about humans, the better his chance of eluding capture.

How long had he been doing this? He remembered recent events in microscopic detail, but only back to his first Alabama victim, six years ago. He had evidently not been programmed to "remember" anything before that. In a plastic envelope he had a birth certificate and a high-school diploma, along with drivers' licenses from four states, with the same picture but different names.

He didn't remember acquiring those documents, though he knew how he might buy replacements. They must have been with him when his masters brought him to Earth, probably just before his detailed memories began.

That had been in a run-down log cabin in a scrub pine swamp in Georgia. He had this old van and a cooler full of meat and a collection of fading memories, along with carefully sealed boxes of books and magazines.

He knew the meat was human but wasn't sure how he had come by it. A memory of a lot of blood, and screams that stopped abruptly. From his aches he could tell he had been driving a long time. That was all.

He knew he wasn't human; every human he'd seen was small and weak. He could deduce something of his heritage from the books and magazines, full of encoded references to his origin. The nature of his destiny unclear, ambiguous. He probably would have to die to fulfill it.

But he was not to die alone.

6.

You got a new bike?" She was trying to smile, but her expression had an element of wide-eyed incredulity. Two new bikes the same month?

"Isn't it a beauty?" I had rolled it up to her door, which she opened as I reached for the doorbell.

"But where's the old one? I mean the old new one?"

"At a bike shop in Des Moines. I sort of traded it in—"

"*Sort* of? What, it was two weeks old?"

"This is sort of like a long test ride. I can take it back."

"A hundred miles?"

I checked the cyclometer. "A hundred seven point two."

"It is pretty," she admitted. Sleek and classic, deep red lacquer. "How much?"

"A thousand dollars. Minus a penny."

"Well, that was generous. How much you get for the old one? The old new one."

"Three-fifty." She pursed her lips and nodded. She probably thought that meant the total transaction had been $650; I didn't elaborate. It was a thousand after the trade-in. A grand for a $1,350 bike was okay, even though a mathematical literalist, like Kit, might say it was actually $1,500, plus two weeks' use of an increasingly clunky commuter bike. The Campy was like gliding on glass. I was still totally in love. But I hadn't even had it long enough to add air to the tires.

"Can I try it?"

"Sure, go ahead." She took it by the handlebars and looked down at the pedals and front chain ring, then the rear gear cluster.

"There's no computer," I said.

"Yeah, I see." She frowned. "I had one like this when I was a kid, no computer."

"Don't worry about shifting. No hills around here." I lowered the seat about an inch.

"Don't you need magnetic shoes?"

"Works without 'em." She mounted the bike not too ungracefully and wobbled off. By the end of the block she seemed to be in control.

She turned around the corner and was gone just long enough for me to start worrying. Then she came flying back around the same corner and stopped right in front of me with a little chirp of rubber, smiling.

"When you make your first million, buy me one?"

"Half million," I said. "You approve?"

"It's hardly like a bike at all. But why no computer shift?"

"Well, it adds weight, I guess a pound or so. One more thing to go wrong. It doesn't take long to master the gears."

"Lots of levers," she said doubtfully. Only five, really, and you didn't use the "overdrive" one until you were going twenty-five or thirty miles per hour.

"I'll run you through them later. Tomorrow? I could use some air-conditioning."

"Your place or here?"

"Airco's off at mine, but . . ." I took out my phone and punched the home utility number and turned it on. "It'll be cool in half an hour. Get some lunch at the Mill?"

"Sure. You put the bike on the car and I'll get my stuff. Spend the night?"

"Twist my arm."

"That would be different." She went halfway down the walk and turned. "I'm, um, a little indisposed?"

Probably the yeast thing again. "That's okay. I love you for your mind."

"Sure, you do. Head, anyway."

———

Actually, her mind was working well. After lunch we went back to my place and she read the most recent chapter.

"So is he really an alien? From where?"

"I'm glad you can't tell yet."

"But, like, do *you* know?"

I shook my head. "What do you think?"

She topped off her tumbler of wine. "Well, I have an unfair advantage. I do know the author."

"I hear you've slept with him."

"Not that well. He snores." She riffled through the pages, mumbling, "Alien, human, alien, human . . ."

She set the manuscript down and tapped it three times. "I'm gonna take a chance and say 'none of the above.' Most of the rest of it, I've read several times, and this new part doesn't change anything basic. He's neither fish nor fowl. You can't tell whether he's a nut job who thinks he's an alien or an alien who acts like a nut job. True?"

I leaned back and smiled at her.

"So are you a Cheshire cat or a Schrödinger one?"

I tried not to react to the good guess, but think my eyebrows shot up.

"It's not that mysterious. I remember the conversation. But I wonder what you're going to do with it. In real life, sooner or later you open the box, and the cat is either dead or alive."

"But a story isn't real life," I said. "I could leave the box closed."

"And the reader never finds out whether Hunter is an alien or not? I don't think your average reader is going to like that."

I shrugged. "Why should the reader know more about the story than I do?"

Gun in the Box

1.

Kit never needed an alarm to get up early. I came half awake when she quietly got out of bed and dressed in the dark. I mumbled something and she gave me a sleepy kiss and slipped out the front door. Her car door didn't slam; I remembered she was letting me use the car for the day tomorrow.

It could have been a minute later or an hour when the doorbell rang. Funny, I thought; she should have had a key.

I put on some pants and was grabbing a T-shirt when a car door did slam. The car squealed away from the parking lot and then squealed again as it tore out onto Second.

Not Kit. I opened the front door a crack and peered out, the car long gone.

A brown cardboard box more than a yard long lay on the doormat. I picked it up—heavy—and turned it over. No address or postage. I took it inside and put it on the dining room table and turned on the overhead. Low light for romance; I clapped it up twice.

The box was secured with a single piece of broad strapping tape. Too strong for my thumbnail, so I got a knife from the kitchen rack.

Inside, packed in crumpled paper and inflated plastic bags, was a gleaming new M2010AW-9, exactly the same rifle I'd used in the desert, though I'd never seen a new one.

I reached to pull it out but then stopped. What the hell was going on?

Under the sink there was a box of throwaway plastic gloves some previous tenant had left. I stripped off a pair and put them on clumsily, feeling melodramatic. This thing was going straight to the police, and if there were fingerprints on it, they wouldn't be mine.

It had a good smell, gunmetal and walnut wood. I liked the wood stock, even though it was heavier than the more modern one, and some guys said it had harder recoil, without the spring. But it felt like a rifle.

I took it out and set it on the table. There was also a box of twenty-five rounds of match-quality .300 Magnum ammunition, with a round battery taped to the top. That would be for the scope, night use. A threaded chrome cylinder that must be a silencer; at least that's what they looked like in movies. A plastic bag with a dozen paper targets.

It had a shorter magazine than we had used in combat. I thumbed the release and found that it held six rounds and a folded-up note. Plain bond paper, printed out in what appeared to be 20-point Courier:

> `I will pay you $100,000 to do what you`
> `once did for privates pay. Youre target`

```
will be a bad man. You will agree that
the World is a better place without him.


Down payment in the butt stock.


I will be in touch.
```

Deficient in grammar, but intriguing. I got a small screwdriver and removed the butt plate. On top of the cleaning supplies, ten of the new $1,000 bills, neatly folded into thirds.

That was military. Bedding, uniforms, ponchos, all folded in thirds. The friendly sergeant we'd had in sniper school said by the time we got out of the army *we'd* be folded in thirds.

For a person with pretty bad spelling and grammar, he certainly had lots of money. I creased the bills so they would lie flat, and brought the desk lamp and magnifier over to study them.

Ten dead Kennedys. I'd never seen one before, except for pictures when they started circulating them a couple of years ago.

They didn't show any wear, but then not many people would crumple one up and stuff it in a pocket. Rumor had it that they were manufactured with nanocircuitry that broadcast the location of each bill. The government denied that with just the right degree of "Who, us?"

If they were counterfeit, an amateur like me probably couldn't tell. I took the magnifying glass and examined Kennedy's right eye on each one, and they all looked the same. The paper had authentic-looking threads, but I'd seen how counterfeiters could bleach out a one-dollar bill and photoprint any denomination onto it.

The e-mail hoax. A few months after I got back, I got a bunch of e-mails that tried to hire me to kill the president. But that was a kid, Timmy something. He'd never confessed, but went to juvenile court and got a suspended sentence.

Could they be related? I ought to find out what became of young Timmy. Maybe he came into money.

I picked up the phone. Don't use 9-1-1 unless it's an emergency. I clicked on the directory. Call the Iowa City cops or the state troopers? Or Coralville or the Kampus Kops, for that matter. Or go straight to the FBI or Homeland Security?

Well, I didn't especially like any of those organizations. Which one would cause me the least trouble?

I wished I still smoked. This would be the time to stoke up a pipe and emulate Sherlock Holmes. But I didn't even have any tobacco, just a little marijuana and some rolling papers stashed away. That would be a real good idea.

Would I be breaking a law by inaction? I assumed so, but what would the law be?

Technically, I was in possession of an unregistered military weapon, but the selector switch only said SAFE and SEMI. If it didn't shoot full auto, I assumed it was legal.

I could put the ten grand in the bank while I decided what to do. But no. At 3.5 percent it would earn less than a dollar a day. And it probably wouldn't be in there a day, before the cops came knocking.

Was I accessory to a crime? A conspiracy to kill some unidentified bad guy. That might be a crime once the bad guy was identified, but right now you could argue that I just had a legal gun and a hypothetical use for it.

Plus ten dead Kennedys.

It couldn't be real. Somebody was setting me up. But for what, a joke? A blackmail deal? It would be an expensive joke, not very funny, and if they blackmailed me they could get a three-figure check and a comic-book collection, which I'd have to collect from Mother's attic.

I went to the computer and found that a new rifle like this, with a standard high-power scope, would run $2,600 out of the box. I ought to just take it down to Gun 'n' Porn. But they probably wouldn't take a weapon that didn't have papers.

Or I could wait and see who they wanted dead. There were a couple of people I'd gladly kill for free; maybe I'd be lucky.

It occurred to me that that was a thing any guy might say casually. But it does mean something different if you once assassinated people for $1,300 a month and all the army chow you could eat.

Presumably most of the people I'd killed as a sniper were guys like me, ordinary people snared by chance or circumstance and turned into killers by their own government. I told myself that I could feel sorry that they were dead, without feeling guilty for being an instrument in the chain of events that led to our unfortunate meeting. I was drafted, and most of them were forced into uniform by poverty and politics.

This was completely different, except for the tool engaged. The target would probably not know he was a target, and presumably wouldn't be shooting back.

And the person shooting him would not be a just-following-orders soldier. He'd be a hired assassin.

I should take the whole thing, money and all, down to the police station, and wash my hands of it. Any normal person would.

Instead, I stared at it and thought.

If I did have an immortal soul, it was already forfeit. So ponder the ponderable: first, could I do it and not get caught?

With no wind deflection and a clear shot, working from a stable platform, I could put a bullet into "the head zone," head or neck, from two thousand meters, call it a mile and some change. One or two follow-up rounds into the thorax. A little less accurate with a silencer, I assumed; I'd never used one.

My first thought was that if it was a city situation, like Kennedy, King, or Semple, then no way. Of course those assassins hadn't used silencers. Still, there would probably be witnesses and then a short chase.

With a silencer, though? From a mile away? It could be done. But could it be done by me?

I supposed it would depend on the target. If it was somebody I would kill for free, then sure, I'd do it for money. If it was some random stranger, then not. Maybe not.

The phone rang.

2.

It wasn't Kit; she always called the cell. And not before dawn. I let it ring four times and picked it up. "Well?" I said.

A woman's voice. "If it was the right person, would you do it?"

I should have said, "I don't know what you're talking about," and hung up. Instead, I said, "I don't know enough. Who are you?"

"I can't tell you that. I can tell you that we are not the government or enemies of the government; it's not a political assassination."

"Why should that be a plus? Being a gun for hire, with no principles involved, isn't appealing."

"You didn't agree with the principles behind the war for which you killed sixteen people."

"Apples and oranges. I didn't have a choice."

"You did, though. As you have said and written. If you had gone to jail for refusing the draft, it would have been less time out of your life. Less moral complication."

"Yeah, happy hindsight." Any way I could trace this call? I took the cell phone out of my shirt pocket.

"Put the cell down," she said. "If you call anyone I'll hang up."

The blinds were closed. "You have a bug in this room?"

"There are other ways we can tell what you are doing. I need an answer."

"Why me? I need *that* answered."

"Expert marksman, unmarried, apolitical and agnostic, low-income disabled veteran against the war."

"Okay, that must narrow it down to a thousand. Why me?"

"Because we can trust you to do the right thing. You wouldn't want Kit to come down with a rare blood disease and die slowly. Would you?"

"What? *Blood* disease?"

"Timothy Unger. Google him. We're serious." The line went dead.

That was Timmy's name, the e-mail ammunition boy. I looked him up and found that he was born in Iowa City twenty years ago and died last year of a heart attack.

Too young. There was an autopsy, the obit said, but no follow-up story except for funeral arrangements. But then I tried "rare blood disease" + "Iowa City" + "fatality" and his name came up, dead last year. It was supposedly myelofibrosis rapidly transformed into secondary acute myelogenous leukemia leading to massive cardiac failure. The doctors were "mystified" by the sudden onset of the disease.

Maybe there was some mysterious poison that mimicked myelofibrosis, whatever that was. Or maybe they just put a nickel in the Google machine and asked it for the name of someone local who had died of a rare disease last year.

No. That wouldn't explain the e-mailings.

Anyhow, this was way beyond the possibility of a hoax, for any reason. Too complicated and expensive and incriminating.

I sat down by the rifle and rubbed its smooth stock. They're giving me time to think this over, before they identify the victim. I have to kill X or they kill Kit. For what values of X would I refuse?

How had they found me; why had they chosen me? My slight prominence as a writer? Well, I did write about war and about being a sniper. I should've chosen Gothic romance.

The phone rang. I picked it up and got a recorded message—same female voice—that was repeated once: "Take the rifle and targets and ammunition *right now* and drive to the east end of the Coralville dump, where people go for shooting. When there's enough light, sight in the rifle. Collect all your brass and your targets and leave. You will be watched."

It was just starting to get light in the east. I zapped a big mug of water and stirred in enough instant coffee and cocoa to wake up the dead, and took it out to the car, and came back for the weapon and targets and ammunition. It felt odd, carrying a rifle without a sling, just walking out to the car like any garden-variety nutcase out to shoot a president or a classroom full of innocents. I knew the bad guys were watching me, but who else? Was one of my nutty neighbors calling the cops, and would they listen? *He always acts funny and keeps to himself, says he's some kinda writer. I always knew there was somethin' wrong with him.*

So if I zero in the rifle, am I complicit? Yes and no; I could still decide not to shoot or to miss the target.

No car was following me as I drove out to the Coralville dump. If they really would be watching me, as they said, they were already there. Or in orbit, for all I knew.

Tried to hatch a plan as I drove through the hazy dawn. There was one aspect I could control: I didn't have to sight the rifle accurately. I could misalign the finderscope and send the bullet anywhere.

Sighting in a rifle-and-scope combination is simple if the equipment is good. This was all solid and new, the same combination I used in the desert, a red-dot Insight MRD on the M2010 sniper rifle. To sight it in you put a "dot" target—a spot on a piece of paper—a measured distance away, and fire carefully from a stable platform. Once you're comfortable with the rifle, you try to get three-shot groups within about a one-inch circle—smaller circle for a real pro. Then you click the rifle sight for windage (left and right) and drop (up and down) until that group consistently appears where the scope's crosshairs intersect, on the printed spot.

Hunters often sight for seventy-five yards; in the desert we usually went out to four hundred. So I was to do half that.

There were no obvious witnesses at the Coralville dump. A lot of crows and a slightly pungent atmosphere. A hand-lettered sign saying SHOOTERS led me to the left.

The setup was simple. Two weathered picnic tables set up with sandbags, next to a plank platform for sighting in from a prone position. I would sit.

There were thick wooden supports about a yard square, spray-painted 100, 200, and 400. I went out to the 400-yard one and thumbtacked four targets there, and returned to the picnic tables.

I filled the magazine and slid it into place, seated the first round, and clicked off the safety. It was going to be loud. What would I say if a cop showed up? "Don't bother me; I'm getting ready to shoot a bad person." I put earplugs in deep, lined up the rifle, and peered through the scope.

It was so dim. Well, it was barely dawn. A long way from desert glare.

There was nobody around, but I said, "Ready on the firing line" in a loud voice. What did civilians say?

The first shot was pretty loud, even with the earplugs. Missed the target completely. They obviously had the wrong guy for this job.

I took a couple of deep breaths and did the zen thing, floating up there watching myself calm down. I quietly touched the hair-trigger and willed the bullet downrange. It did hit the target, about 11:00.

It had occurred to me that someday I might wind up being the target of this rifle, rather than the shooter. One way to protect myself would be to zero it off-center.

Upper left-hand quadrant, about 10:30, halfway from the crosshairs to the edge. So if anybody else used the rifle on you, the bullet would whish by harmlessly over your right shoulder.

And I didn't plan to kill anybody with it anyway.

3.

Zeroing took less than an hour. No witnesses until I was packing up to leave. He nodded hello, unsmiling, and went to set up his equipment on the other picnic table. Checking on me? Not obviously. Old guy in an old car, local plates. I wrote down the plate number just in case, feeling a little foolish.

So I had taken the first step leading to a rewarding career in civilian assassination. Or the second step; I should have called the cops when I opened the box. Called the feds.

First I had to protect Kit. Get her way out of town before I went to the cops. The woman on the phone had been scarily specific.

I was going to meet Kit for lunch. She'd probably be safe at work. Better not call. Just pick her up and go to some random place.

Money. I could get $500 from the ATM. But the bank would be

open in an hour. Empty out my accounts. Then have Kit do the same, and run like hell?

Maybe I was thinking too much like a storyteller. I should do the rational thing and go to the authorities.

Did I have enough evidence? A note that could be printed anywhere, a phone call I didn't record, a rifle you could buy at Sears. And a story that sounds like something a storyteller would make up. A storyteller who wanted publicity, they would assume.

I should at least wait until I knew who the target was supposed to be. A recording of the next time they call wouldn't hurt, either.

Did Kit still have a recorder in the glove compartment? I pulled over and found it, but it was the big high-fidelity one we'd used to interview Grand-dude. I'd want one I could carry in a pocket—surely the cops or spooks could extract the other side of a telephone conversation recorded from a couple of feet away.

If I went straight to the Radio Shack at the mall, it would be open in an hour. The rearview mirror showed a half mile of open road behind me; no one on my tail.

Do it. Get the small recorder . . . but also go to the savings bank and empty that account, then go to the checking bank and max out cash on AmEx and Visa. Then have Kit do the same?

Maybe I shouldn't go home at all. They were watching. It wouldn't be smart to rush in and start packing suitcases. But what *would* be smart?

My heart was hammering and my breath was short. Try to stop shaking. Try to think. Make a list.

1. Go to the police.

But then *they* would control whatever "2." was going to be, and every number thereafter. My own main concern was protecting Kit, and then covering my own ass—or maybe it was the other way around, to be honest. Whatever came third was a distant third, though.

Would the police actually be protecting us? The mystery woman watching me would know when they showed up. How long would they stay interested if nothing else happened? Whoever was behind the rifle must have an agenda, but I didn't even know whether they were left, right or orthogonal. Or how patient they might be.

If not the police, our only protection would be flight. No way we could hide in Iowa City.

I could pursue my writing career online; my agent could make credit transfers to a bank anywhere. I knew from research for my first book how to build a new identity, a bogus paper trail, without spending a fortune or breaking any serious laws.

I'd be asking Kit to throw away her past and future. But if we were going to stay together, we didn't have much choice.

Well, we did have one, Plan A. Go to the police. This is not a TV show. Just go to the fucking cops.

My reverie was broken by the crunch of gravel behind me, and I looked in the rearview mirror . . . and saw that I didn't have to go to the cops. They had come to me. State trooper.

A short muscular guy with a Smokey-the-Bear hat stepped out of the car. Sunglasses. I rolled down the window while he was writing my license number into his notebook.

"Good morning, sir," he said, exhaling tobacco and Clorets. "Is there a problem?"

"No, sir, nothing."

He looked into the backseat. "Nice rifle."

"Yes, sir. I was just down at the dump—"

"We know. We got a call."

My mouth went dry. But why should it? "I haven't . . . have I broken some law?"

"No, not really. The dump isn't open to the public till nine, but it's not posted. Some sport stole the sign." He studied the gun. "You had pulled over, and we thought you might need assistance."

"No, um . . . I was going to make a call. I don't like to use the cell while I'm driving."

"That's smart; that's good." He was still looking at the rifle. "New gun?"

Better not say *I think so.* "Yes, sir."

He nodded slowly. "You have papers on it?"

"Papers?" Oh, shit. "Do I need a permit for a rifle?"

"No. Not unless it's full automatic. You got a bill of sale?"

"It was a gift."

"Mind if I take a look?"

"Of course not." Not a good time to rant about "search and seizure." I started to open the door.

"Stay in the car. Sir." He opened the back door and lifted the weapon out. He looked it over carefully and sniffed at the receiver.

"I just fired it," I said helpfully.

"Hm . . . excuse me." He carried it back to the squad car. He and the other cop sat there for a few minutes. I could hear the radio crackling but couldn't understand what it was saying.

He came back without the rifle and asked for my driver's license and registration. I gave him the license. "I don't know where the registration is. It's not my car."

"No. You're not Catherine Majors," he said, deadpan. He walked back to the squad car and returned with the rifle. He put it in the back and closed the door with a quiet click.

"Thank you for your cooperation." He gave the license back. "Please drive carefully."

———————

I looked at the batteries and recorder on the seat next to me and had a melancholy recollection: the last time I saw my grandfather before he died, just before I shipped for the desert. He and my dad and I had all had too much to drink. It was his eightieth birthday, and we had a recorder like this one going, while he talked about the past.

Grand-dude and I shared the bond of both having been drafted (Dad's generation was spared), and we traded Basic Training memories. Then he started to talk about combat, which he never had done before.

He started to cry—not weeping, just his eyes leaking a little, dabbing, and he delivered a slurred soliloquy about how useless it all had been— how much *less* freedom we had after his war, Vietnam, than before; how the government used war to increase its control over its citizens, what a fucking waste it had all been. Dad got upset with him, me headed overseas in a couple of days.

But I said it wasn't that different from what I heard in the barracks every night. Grand-dude said yeah, same-same. Soldiers aren't fools.

But we go anyhow.

4.

Kit's office was in the main administration building, a short walk from the cluster of student-oriented shops and restaurants downtown. It cost half as much as lunch to park anywhere nearby, so I found a place down in the student ghetto and walked the half mile through quiet streets, checking out every car that passed. This is where the bad guys would appear out of nowhere and tackle me and put a bag over my head and stuff me into the trunk of a car, and no one would notice.

In fact, every car seemed to be a student looking for a parking place. Perfect disguise.

I called Kit and suggested Hamburger Haven, not a ritzy place, but small enough so that no one could come in unobserved. I called her from the door, so I could just step inside to watch and wait.

There must have been something in my voice. She asked me what was wrong.

"Nothing. I just got pulled over by a cop," I half lied. "No ticket, no problem."

I sat down at the counter and ordered a cup of coffee, but then realized I was too fucking jumpy already, and changed it to a beer. "Breakfast of champions," the waitress said, although it was after eleven. I guess I looked like someone who had just gotten up. And found an early Christmas present on the doormat.

I smiled at her and realized for the first time that I smelled like smokeless powder. Would anybody notice? With my current luck, I expected an off-duty cop to sit down next to me and say, "Been shootin'?"

Yeah, think I'll go assassinate some stranger so the bad guys don't give my girlfriend myelofibrosis. You ever have a day like that?

I finished the beer pretty fast, and the waitress was delivering my second as Kit walked through the door. She smiled. "Starting early?"

"You have no idea." I picked up the beer. "Let's sit in the back."

The waitress trailed us with menus; we waved them off and ordered burgers. Kit sat down with a pleasant expectant smile. "How's the bike?"

"Um, it's good, good. We have a real problem."

"We?"

"Not like you and me. I mean . . ." Where to start? "I'm in deep shit. And I'm afraid you are, too."

"What'd you do? We?"

"Nothing! It's just . . . right after you left this morning, the doorbell rang."

"Before *dawn*?"

"Yeah." I took a deep breath and told her about the rifle, the phone call, the rifle range, and the state trooper, talking low and fast. She listened silently, eyes widening.

"And you haven't gone to the police?"

"They wouldn't believe me! It's too fantastic."

"But you have proof. You have the rifle. The state trooper's report will verify that you took it straight out to the dump and . . . well, yeah. That's a problem."

"Like why didn't I tell any of this to the Smokey? I guess it was the timing. Like he was part of it, following me." Our burgers came and I took a bite and struggled to swallow it. Drank some beer. "I should've called the cops first thing, right after I found the rifle and the woman called. Hell, I shouldn't have picked up the phone when it rang."

"Let me smell your hand." She took my right hand in hers and sniffed it. "You still smell like gunpowder. If we went to the police right now, that would strengthen your case."

I wasn't sure. "It'd mean I've fired a gun recently. But that's already on record."

She frowned. "Guess so."

"Am I just being paranoid? Maybe I *should* go straight to the cops. But the woman on the phone expressly told me not to, or they'd come after you. Like Timmy what's-his-name."

"Jesus." She sat back and looked around. "'Damned if you do and damned if you don't,' my father would say."

I bit my lip but then said it: "I've thought about your father."

"What about him?"

"People who might have a reason to do this."

She frowned and shook her head slightly. "No way. He *likes* you."

"So he says, but he's not sanguine about my earning potential. And he's a hunter; he does know all about guns."

"And a fellow veteran. He wouldn't do this—not to you, not to me."

"Yeah, I know. Grasping at straws."

"Grasp at a different one." She touched both my hands. "Who else would do this?"

"No one, or anyone. You write a book and you sort of become a target."

"Some of the characters in your first book were based on real people, weren't they? Maybe somebody didn't like what you said."

I shrugged. "Not saying it couldn't happen. But an e-mail would get the message across better . . . besides, it's too oblique for that, and too expensive. You could scare me as much with a postcard, if you said the right thing."

" 'I'm going to trash your book in the *New York Times*.' "

"That might work. But I sort of favor 'I will get you when you least expect it.' "

"You've given it some thought."

"Well, yeah. Trying to put myself in the head of someone who would do this."

She chewed thoughtfully. "Maybe it's not personal."

"*You're* the one they're threatening to murder. That's not personal?"

"What I mean is, think of it as a business proposition. They want you to do something illegal and probably dangerous. So they offer incentives, positive and negative. If the money isn't enough, then maybe saving my life would be."

I felt a tight squeezing in my chest. If it were just me being threatened, I'd have wiggle room; it would be hypothetical, and I could bargain with them—kill me and you won't have anything. But I wouldn't gamble with Kit's life, and they knew that.

Kit took a paper notebook out of her purse and scribbled on a page. Tore it out and showed it to me: *Assume we're being watched and listened to. Pay the bill and follow me and don't say anything about it.*

"Yeah, sure." I left a twenty on the table, nice tip, and followed her out the door. When we got to my car, she tugged on my sleeve and we kept walking. Her car was at the end of the block. I slid in on the passenger side. She got in and wrote another note: *Could your clothes be bugged?*

I shrugged and wrote *possible*.

She drove wordlessly to the Kmart on the outskirts of town. Parked in the fire lane and wrote, *Get clothes and cash, change clothes. I'll be back.*

I'd already emptied out my cash card's account, and maxed out advances on AmEx and Visa. Good thing Kmart takes cash.

I got some prewashed jeans and a plain shirt. On impulse I went back to the sporting goods section. They had plenty of firearms there, but I'd read about the new two-day waiting period.

So I couldn't get a real gun, but there was a CO_2-powered pellet gun that looked just like a service Glock, except for a bright orange nose, which I could spray-paint black.

I didn't think these people would bluff too easily. But it was better than nothing.

There was no way I could just change clothes in the Kmart dressing room and walk out. So I paid for the jeans and shirt and took them to the adjoining McDonald's. Broke a lifelong vow and bought a Coke there, and went into the men's room. Changed into the new clothes and stuffed my old ones into the trash, must happen all the time. I got back to the Kmart entrance just as Kit pulled up. There was a big pink suitcase in the backseat, a red sock sticking out like a limp tongue.

She looked at me and smiled. "Okay. So let's do a disappearing act."

"What about your job?"

"I e-mailed him, death in the family, don't know how long I'll be gone."

"Get some money?"

"Yes. I emptied out both accounts, about four grand."

"Wow. I just had a little over a thousand."

Her mouth made a small O and we stared at each other for a second, then it clicked. "Remember?" I said. "I don't have the Hollywood money yet."

"Shit, of course. I knew that and spaced it." She faced forward and put the car in gear. "Left or right?"

"I-80, I guess. Put some miles between us and them."

She hesitated. "Maybe back roads would be better."

"Just a second. Let's think." She put it back into Park and looked at me with a forced expression of patience, or resignation.

"We leave my car in Iowa City, gun in the trunk, and head off to parts unknown. What happens to the car?"

"I think after two tickets they tow it away. Then wait for you to come bail it out. Auction it if you don't show up."

"But I don't think so. Not in my case. They'll run the license plate and find I was stopped by Smokies this morning. They'll read about the gun and pop the trunk, and voilà, I'm a fleeing criminal."

"But you aren't a criminal."

"Thanks for the vote of confidence."

"I mean really. They can't search your car without a warrant. You didn't break any law this morning—but even if you had, could they just pop your trunk and rummage around looking for nothing in particular? Don't they have to have 'probable cause'?"

"Hell, I don't know. If a car's impounded that means a law was broken. There's probably another law that allows them to break into it and sell everything on eBay. I mean, who makes the laws?"

We sat for a few seconds, breathing hard, maybe thinking hard.

"Wonder how far we could go," she said, "on five thousand dollars. I don't have a passport."

"Maybe we shouldn't even leave Iowa. Cross a state line and we've got the feds on our tail." I said that last like a movie tough guy, but she didn't smile.

"When do you expect the check?"

"Probably not till the end of the month. Let's not even think about it. We've got five grand of our own money and ten of the bad guys'."

"With fifteen thousand dollars," she said carefully, "we could do like that guy in your book. Manufacture new identities. Or is that all fantasy?"

"No, you really could do it. But it takes some time and planning. And a lot more than fifteen grand; call it a hundred. Each."

She laughed without any humor. "That much. Buying off officials?"

"No, just side-stepping computers. Like, his first step was taking the identity of someone in another state who was born the same time as him, but died an infant. That won't work anymore. You're in the federal system from womb to tomb, no matter how little time you spend in between."

"That's comforting."

"Yeah, 'Big Brother Is Watching You.' We'll be okay if we're careful. Don't use any credit cards or IDs, and don't go anyplace where they scan faces, like the courthouse."

"Don't leave any fingerprints on corpses." She had read my first book, all right.

"I'll wear gloves if we kill anybody. So you're the driver. Where to?"

"I asked you first." She rubbed her face. "Damn. I was thinking get lost in a big city, Chicago. But as you say, face scanners. Liquor stores have them, banks. I guess convenience stores in high-crime areas."

"So we go to a small town?"

"I'd say so. Stay in Iowa," she said.

"The Amana Colonies? We'd eat well."

"Not a tourist place, not too close to Iowa City. Sioux City? Is Davenport too big?"

"Davenport. We could hop on a riverboat and escape to New Orleans. Except I think they're all permanently anchored."

"It's an idea, though," she said. "It's one place in Iowa where you could get a G-note changed without drawing a lot of attention."

"The casino, that's good. Find some mom-and-pop place out in the country, dash into the casino to change the bills, then move on."

"No, wait. I'm sure they scan faces on the way into the casino. If anywhere. But they may not be looking for you."

"Yeah. It's not as if there was a warrant out for me." It still felt shaky. "Are there casinos on the Illinois side of the river?"

"Don't know." She took the iPak out of her purse, shook it, and asked it, "Search. Riverboat. Casino. Illinois." It came back with "Harrah's" and an address.

"Worth the extra couple of miles. That was a state trooper, and I don't imagine Iowa and Illinois share data down to that level. Not even a parking ticket," I said optimistically. Just a murder weapon on the backseat.

We picked up bad coffee and a couple of McDeathburgers, compromising culinary standards for speed, and headed straight for I-80. Unlike mine, her two-year-old car had Supercruise, so once we got on the superhighway, she went all the way to the left, shifted it to Traction, and asked it for a Davenport warning. "Finish my coffee if you want," she said, and cranked her seat back and closed her eyes.

I'd never had Supercruise, and it still made me a little nervous. But it really was safer than driving manually, especially at high speed, so I just watched the pastures and cows blur by and tried to think of something that wouldn't make me nervous. I closed my eyes and recalled about ten of Shakespeare's sonnets. I'd memorized all of them when I was sixteen, with a little help from Merck's Forget-me-not™, but that mostly evaporated after a few months. I could still bore people with the famous ones, and my favorite obscurity, "Oh truant muse / what shall be thy amends . . ." My muse was kind of truant, running for its life.

When the car chimed her awake, she stretched and took over, drifting slowly through three lanes of sub-cruise traffic to cross the Mississippi bridge in the slow lane and take the first Illinois exit. There was a big blinking billboard directing you to Harrah's Showboat West. "You want to go straight there?" she asked.

"Sure, let's do it. Run the money through and get back on the road. Be in Indiana by nightfall. Kentucky." Panic and caffeine overdose, a real recipe for casino success. Take a couple of deep breaths.

The parking lot was huge, serving both the casino and a miniature Disneyworld that didn't have any Disney characters. We parked at Tombstone A-5 and discussed strategy.

Kit had been to Vegas with her parents, and knew how to play blackjack conservatively. I could do the same with side bets on the craps table, though it took more concentration, and the ambience at craps was loud and testosterone-soaked. So we'd stick to blackjack and not play at the same tables.

We'd move around, playing for a couple of hours, cashing the G-notes at different tables. There were $100-minimum games where the big bills wouldn't be uncommon. I was hoping that if we cashed them at the tables rather than at the cashier, the serial numbers wouldn't be scanned immediately.

This was the overall plan: lose steadily but not spectacularly. Quit when we still had 80 or 90 percent of our stake, converted into somewhat used C-notes and fifties.

We quizzed each other on betting strategy for half an hour, using the iPak to deal out of a four-deck shoe, which is what Google said they used here. Then we got on the slidewalk a few minutes apart, agreeing to meet at the main entrance at 5:00.

The entrance foyer was ice-cold and not too loud, a good distance from the muted clang of slot machines and susurrus of crowd noise. As I approached it, it was like walking toward crashing surf.

Trying to look casual, half expecting some cop to appear out of nowhere, I strolled into the slots area and sacrificed a few tens and twenties, keeping track. I put in $210 and got back two hundred. A little slow, and the machine wouldn't take anything bigger than a fifty. It paid back in metal-and-plastic medallions, of course, and dollar coins. They weighed down my left pocket as I walked toward the table games.

Kit had a small stack of gold and silver chips in front of her. We waved, as prearranged—there were cameras all over the place, and they probably had our names and Social Security numbers locked in before we bought a chip. The probability that the casino's computer knew we had come in the same car was high enough that ignoring each other might be suspicious. We didn't want to play at the same table, though, two people who knew each other flashing G-notes together.

I went on to a smoking table, since it had a couple of empty chairs and I could stand the smoke for a little while. It would also be a good cover if I wanted to leave early, coughing.

"Hundreds," I said, and set down two bills. The dealer didn't blink and slid over two short stacks of silver chips. The G-notes went straight into a slot without being scanned, good.

We had agreed that the best strategy would be the least conspicuous, simply "by the book." I knew that a lot of high-rollers played with dramatic sloppiness, either not knowing better or demonstrating how little money meant to them, or for some peculiar thrill, but most of them knew the basic algorithm and won or lost more slowly. Hit sixteen unless the dealer shows less than seven; stand on seventeen or more, always. Split any pair under nines, and nines if the dealer has between three and eight. Double down on eleven, or on ten if the dealer has shit.

There were about a dozen exceptions to those rules, but we weren't playing to win. We wanted to appear mildly interested for a short while and then leave with a handful of high-denomination chips.

The casino was quite happy with people who played this way, bleeding customers by transfusion rather than amputation. Some places even handed out business cards with the strategy printed on the back, which is how I learned it as a kid, a souvenir that Dad brought back from Mississippi.

Even careful players presented less of a gamble for the house than putting money in a savings account. A bank can fail, but hope is constantly reborn—not to mention greed.

I was down three hundred when the dealer played out the shoe and shuffled. Feigning impatience, I tossed out three more notes. "Gold, please," I said, and he gave me twelve chips. They did have platinum thousand-dollar chips, but I didn't want to hemorrhage all over the table.

With the fresh shoe I had a disconcerting run of luck betting the gold chips, but then bet heavily and lost three times in a row. Just a little behind, I said I wanted to take a walk, and went to the cashier window and cashed in all my chips. So I'd gotten rid of five of the G-notes, and still had $4,900 in a thick roll in my pocket, mostly hundreds. Headed for Kit, I took a detour through the slot area and turned ten of the C-notes into twenties, a separate roll in the other pocket.

I panicked a moment when Kit wasn't at her place at the table, but then she came up behind me: "Hey, sailor! New in town?"

I turned and asked her sotto voce how she was doing.

"I could leave," she said with a broad grin. "Have you cashed in?"

"A hundred behind."

"My hero." She took my arm. "Let's not go straight out to the car." She steered me into a bar area, and ordered two Heinekens. We sat at the bar.

"You're drinking beer?"

"Oh, yeah." She touched the back of my hand with her little finger and opened her palm for a second. On it she'd written with eyeliner: WATCHED PICK U UP EXACT 5:17. "What time you have?"

I checked. "Quarter to five."

"Good." She launched into a long anecdote about her Aunt Betty going to Vegas, which I'd just heard. I made appropriate responses, ignoring my watch until she said she had to go to the "little girls' room," a phrase she never used.

I finished my beer and left a good tip and carried her bottle out with me. Sat and played poker machines until 5:11. Wandered toward the entrance, stopped to take a leak, and stepped out into the wall of dry heat at exactly 5:17. She pulled up and I got into the car and we rolled away.

I exhaled heavily. "So you were being watched?"

"Who knows. Probably just a casino cop; maybe they check you out when you flash a thousand-dollar bill. Maybe he was a gigolo, about to make a move. Or I might just be paranoid."

"Paranoid is good."

"I changed tables twice and he followed me like a shadow, not even trying to be subtle. Smiled at me all the time."

"Maybe he was just interested in rich beautiful women."

"Oh, stop it. If he wasn't trying to scare me, he would have made some small talk. Not just stalking."

"Think you got rid of him?"

"Went in the ladies' room and straight out the other door, then out the exit and walked halfway around the building. He didn't follow me out through the parking lot, for whatever that's worth." She checked her mirrors.

"Yeah, he could—"

"Hold on!" She crossed three lanes without signaling, gunned through a left-turn light as it turned red, and spun the car in a fast U-turn and accelerated through another yellow light, then braked sharply and pulled into a side road and parked.

I was still clinging to the seat. "That . . . that should do it."

She mopped her face with a balled-up tissue. "Whatever 'it' is." She turned on the radio and tapped the search bar until she got some classical music, and turned it up to maximum volume.

She leaned against my shoulder and whispered in my ear: "What now?"

I turned on the car's dash map and tapped it till it showed all of Illinois and part of Indiana. I touched the border town Oak Grove and raised eyebrows at her. She nodded and put it into gear.

I took a page out of her paper notebook and printed big capital letters as she drove along.

WORST CASE: THERE'S A NANODEVICE IN OUR CLOTHES OR ON OUR SKIN OR HAIR. MY CLOTHES ARE NEW AND RANDOM. ARE YOURS? She shook her head.

Another page. ASSUME THE CAR IS BUGGED. WE'LL LEAVE IT AT A MOTEL W/A NOTE TO THE OWNER & SOME CASH.

Another page. WALK TO THE BUS STATION & GET A TICKET

TO NOWHERE. Another page. LIE LOW FOR A YEAR & WATCH THE NEWS.

Meanwhile, we talked about music, art, and science. She liked Mozart, Monet, and math. I was more like Van Halen, Vermeer, and voodoo. But we already knew all that about each other.

For some reason—perhaps not to avoid the obvious—she asked me about the desert, about being a sniper. "You said it bothered you less when you were actually doing it."

"Well, yeah," I said. "Partly it's tit for tat; they're shooting at you, so you shoot back.

"But it wasn't like an even exchange. I was only seriously shot at twice before the one that got me. I mean, they sometimes mortared us at night and all, but that's just weather. Most of the first six months I was there, the death rate was higher for troops stateside, like drunk driving. I was a mile away from the people I was shooting at, and they usually had Marines fucking with them a lot closer.

"It was like that woman said in the book about killing. Without the scope, you could hardly see the targets at all. You squeeze the trigger, bang, the guy falls over three seconds later. If you get your sight picture back you might see him go down."

"You had a spotter watching with a more powerful telescope?"

"Usually. Sometimes we just did targets of opportunity, fuck with them long-distance. Even if you miss, it's not by much. 'Course they do it back. That's how I got hit, I think."

"You told me they never got the guy."

"No, shit, he was in some dunes in the middle of nowhere. We'd used up all the drones, the rubber-band guys, and he had ten minutes to get lost before we had air support."

"And before you were medivaced."

"More like fifteen. But our medic was cool. Some superglue spray kept the lung from deflating, pneumothorax. But the hand, that was bad."

"Yeah." She knew that one; they'd bound my hand up tight to stop the bleeding, and hadn't seen that the little finger was only hanging on with a little skin. By the time they got around to it, it might as well have been blown off and lost. Rather lose a finger than a lung, though.

"It was brave of you to relearn the guitar, the new fingerings."

"Not much else to do in rehab." Actually, after a year, I was playing better than I ever had with all my fingers. A thousand hours of compulsive repetition.

Losing that finger didn't affect my writing because I could never type worth a shit anyhow.

"You'd sit and think," she said.

"Yeah, too much of that." That was when the PTSD first crawled into bed with me, and I started to get the high-octane drugs. I try to remember what that felt like and I can't, quite. Just a fog and a memory of a memory of nightmares. While the guitar sort of learned how to play itself.

I dozed for a while. "Over the state line," she said, waking me. "How does the Oak Grove Motel sound?"

"Sounds like Indiana. Or is it Kentucky?"

It was Indiana; Hoosiers not horses. The eponymous grove only had one tree, but it was an oak—a pin oak, the only leaf I remembered from freshman botany. It has a pin on the end. Like a grenade.

While Kit was showering (definitely a one-person stall) I went down the road for a six-pack and a bag of ice, and on impulse snagged a homemade bag of red-hot pork rinds. She ate a bite of one and made a face. I scarfed down most of a bag, leaving a little room for dinner. Can't get them in Iowa.

We went back across the state line to a pizza place that had a 2-for-1 special and a rear parking lot, where the car couldn't be spotted from the road. The second pizza we'd keep for breakfast.

It wasn't exactly a relaxing place, all bright primary colors and loud music. But the benches were comfortable and the guy turned the music down to a whisper when I asked him to. He also politely wiped the crumbs off the table, onto the floor.

I asked for wine and got a half carafe of ice-cold Chianti. Kit unfolded a large-scale roadmap and studied it.

"We want to go south," she said.

"Down to the Gulf? And over to Florida."

"I don't know. We're not exactly on vacation."

"Nothing wrong with Florida."

"Except that it's an obvious destination. If the bad guys know we're headed south."

"Maybe so," I said. "But if they go looking for us in Florida, they have to find us in the middle of a million tourists. If we're in Pigsty, Arkansas, we'll stand out."

"That's 'Piggott.' Didn't Hemingway write there?"

"Another reason to go somewhere else. I'd start doing short declarative sentences."

She smiled and lowered her voice. "My instinct is to look for run-down small places that might not be on the Net. Once the car's registered somewhere, we're vulnerable."

"Well, we don't really need a motel. We could just pull over on a back road and catch some Zs, then move on."

"No way." She laughed. "I read that book. Some homicidal alien'll cut us up and eat the pieces."

"I bet he made that up." A cockroach came out of a crack in the wall and skipped toward the pizza. I slapped at it and it scuttled back. "Yuck. Kind of glad I missed." More than an inch long.

"They're bigger in Florida," she said.

"Maybe slower, too. Pity I left the gun behind."

She was staring at the crack. "Maybe we should get one."

"What?"

"Just a thought. Stupid, I guess."

It had crossed my mind, too, of course. "Not stupid. But not a rifle. I can't imagine any scenario where that would work. Maybe a conceal-able pistol, like a Derringer, if we get cornered."

"But you can't just buy one in a store, can you? Without showing ID? The guy in your book, Steve, he had a permit and everything."

"Yeah, he needed a concealed-weapon permit, which was true down in Florida . . . but when I went down there as a kid, my uncle kept a handgun in his tackle box, and it wasn't a big deal that he didn't have a permit; he joked about it with my dad. But I remember he hadn't bought the gun; it was an old thing he got from his own father."

"So the trick is to choose your grandparents wisely?"

"Always. There used to be a used-gun section in the want ads. I remember when they stopped doing that, ran a sanctimonious notice for weeks."

"So it will have to be a back-alley deal," she said.

"Yeah, and Oak Grove doesn't even have any *front* alleys." I snagged her a glass from the counter and we finished the last of the wine.

It had gotten dark, crickets chirping. Maybe one car a minute went by outside. A quarter moon shone down.

"Glad to be off the road," she said. "Quiet here."

She looked good, girlish, just-washed hair back in a ponytail. The neon sign in the window made her skin look warm.

"We could go make some noise."

It took her a second to react. If she blushed, I couldn't tell. "Sure. I'd like that."

We got back to the motel in about two minutes, breaking two states' speed limits. We parked in the back, where we'd been before, and rushed around to the door, my arm around her waist.

While she was wiggling the key in the lock, I started to get a bad feeling.

The key had worked fine earlier.

Had we left a light on?

She pushed the door open and suddenly gasped. "Oh, shit."

In the center of the bed, the long cardboard box with my name and address on it. Beside it, a fresh box of ammunition.

The phone rang.

Jack in the Box

1.

I picked up the phone and didn't say anything. "Are you done wasting gasoline?" the female voice said. I turned on the recorder in my shirt pocket.

"Who *are* you?"

"You asked that before. I can't tell you."

"Then I can't do anything for you."

"Not to wax philosophical, but for whom were you working when you killed all those people in the desert?"

"I'm not going to go there."

"You were killing people in order to stabilize the price of a barrel of oil. To use your own words."

"I was drafted."

"Yes, and as you've said, you could have gone to jail instead. You don't have that option now."

"Why don't you just do the job yourself? You threaten me and Kit with murder. Why not just kill this poor schlub yourself?"

"That may be clear later."

Kit had written a note: PLAY ALONG SEE WHAT THEY WANT.

I nodded, but could feel a slippery slope under my feet. "Maybe if you told me something about who the target is."

"That's progress. But not yet."

"So at least tell me why you're using *me*. There must be a thousand guys who would do it for pocket change."

"You already know part of the reason. The rest will become clear."

"Maybe if I knew who you were . . ."

"You will never know that."

I took a deep breath. "So okay. Tell me what to do." Kit's eyes widened but she nodded, lips pursed.

"The first thing is to take that recorder out of your pocket and leave it on the end table. Second, put the rifle in the trunk of Ms. Majors's car. Third, get a good night's sleep. Finally, in the morning, keep driving south, toward the Gulf of Mexico." She hung up.

"What is it?"

"Keep going south, she said. First get a good night's sleep."

"Sure. Lots of luck on that."

I put the recorder on the end table. "And leave this, she said. I guess we should assume they can hear everything we say."

She nodded. "I hope you all eat shit and die," I said to the recorder. "I mean that sincerely. I want to watch."

"I don't know if we should provoke them," she said quietly. "These people are crazy."

"And I'm fucking getting there."

We hadn't slept two hours when the sun started to show through the blinds. I set up the coffeemaker and we squeezed into the shower together, unsexily. One small bar of soap and no shampoo.

Over a breakfast of acid coffee and stale chocolate-chip cookies, she said it before I could: WE CAN'T HANDLE THIS BY OURSELVES, she wrote down. COPS OR FBI OR WHAT?

I nodded and wrote, HOMELAND SECURITY? ASSASSINA-TION? She thumbed a query on her iPak and showed me the screen: a map of Springfield, Illinois, with an arrow pointing to the Homeland Security office.

We didn't say anything about it; just got in the car and headed east. It might have been an excess of caution, but we didn't even use the car's route guide; she'd drawn out a map on a piece of paper.

About two hours of secondary roads through farmland and small towns, then a half hour on high-speed cruise, and we parked below an oblong grey building with extrusions like upside-down ells, which managed to look both heavy and arachnid.

"Imposing," she said.

"Haunted by the ghost of J. Edgar Hoover. I don't suppose we want to take the gun in with us."

The reception area was arctic cold and government-grey. The room listing by the elevator didn't have a Department of Mysterious Weapons Left in Cars, so we opted for Domestic Terrorism.

A matronly clerk listened to our story and settled us in a waiting room with a curious selection of magazines, a mixture of well-thumbed hunting and fishing journals with three pristine copies of *Harvard Law Review*, not the swimsuit edition. After more than an hour, she asked for my driver's license and escorted us into the office of agent James "Pepper" Blackstone.

Blackstone was a slightly plump pale white man with aquiline features. He seriously studied us as we came in and sat down, and then glanced at the screen inlaid on his desktop. There was nothing else on the desk, and nothing on the walls but a standard picture of the president and a calendar.

"This rifle," he said with no preamble, "we knew it was in your trunk, of course, before you got out of the car. If you'd tried to take it out of the trunk, you would have been stopped."

"Good to know you guys are on the ball," I said, and he didn't react. "Of course the rifle is why we're here."

He looked at his screen.

"You found it in your car . . . twice?"

"Once outside my door," I said. "I left it in Iowa City, in the trunk of a parked car, but someone evidently retrieved it and put it in our motel, while we went out for dinner last night. They also broke into my apartment and took the mailing carton it had been in."

"Why would they do that?"

"*I* don't know! To scare me."

He considered that for a long moment. "A preliminary investigation shows three sets of fingerprints."

"You took it out of my car?" Kit said.

"It's a weapon associated with a crime, Ms. Majors. We're allowed to." He didn't look at her. "Your fingerprints, Mr. Daley, and those of the two Iowa state troopers. There are no other fingerprints at all, which is interesting. What is more interesting is that the surface of the rifle is completely sterile, outside of those points of contact. There's not one nanogram of organic substance. It's as if the weapon had been autoclaved and then put in the car's trunk by someone wearing sterile gloves."

"Not just wiped clean?" I said.

"No; that might obliterate the fingerprints, but there would still be traces of organic material, or perhaps of a solvent used to remove it. This was a very careful job."

"Well, I'm glad it's not just a bunch of amateurs."

"I wouldn't rule that out. Amateurs can be compulsive." He took off his glasses and leaned back in his chair, which squeaked, and began a long soliloquy. "Being a writer, Mr. Daley, perhaps you can appreciate this: the tropes of terrorism and the mechanical aspects of spy business are so deeply imbedded in our culture that private citizens have used them to harass other private citizens; make them think they're being followed by someone—us or the FBI, the CIA, the KGB . . . or some mysterious organization whose three initials are known only to a few. Ask yourself this: If you had the desire to do to someone else exactly what is being done to you . . . would it be impossible? Would it even be difficult? If you did have the desire and the money to spare."

I thought for a second. "The rifle is common enough, though I'm not sure how I could buy one without leaving a paper trail. Hire somebody to do it; a mule, I guess. The phone calls could be made with throwaway cells. But these people know exactly what I'm doing, all the time, as if they were in the same room! How could I do that?"

There was a single knock at the door and a bland young man in a coat and tie strode in, put a manila folder on the desk, and left.

Blackstone spent a few seconds looking at each of three sheets of paper. "On June eleventh of last year, someone who looks like you and had your driver's license bought that rifle at a sporting goods store in Des Moines." He slid over one sheet, a grainy photograph apparently from a store's security camera. A person who looked something like me was buying an M2010-AW9.

"That's not me," I said. "I mean, I know it's not me because I wasn't there; I've never been in that store. But it doesn't really look like me, anyhow."

He took the picture back and examined it. Shook his head and got a jeweler's loupe from a drawer and looked again. "Maybe, maybe not. Can you explain the driver's license?"

"Well, no. Not if they had the neutron-counting thing." I'd been sent a new license a couple of years ago with the ID dot: traces of two radioactive elements, the proportions different for each person's license, impossible to forge. Some small stores didn't have the neutron counters, but probably all gun retailers did.

He handed me my license. "This checks out. It is the one that was used to buy the gun." He looked at Kit. "Ms. Majors, you are a mathematician. You know Occam's razor."

I knew that one; the simplest explanation is probably the right one. But she knew the whole thing: "Entities must not be multiplied beyond necessity."

"Exactly. So for your story to be true, Mr. Daley, these are the entities: a miscreant had to steal your driver's license before June eleventh, use it to buy a weapon, and return it undetected to your wallet before today. That is not impossible. But a simpler explanation is that the picture *is* you. And you had some arcane reason for setting this up."

I looked at Kit. "That's what I said you people would say. That it was just a publicity stunt."

"Can you prove you were somewhere else on June eleventh?"

"June tenth is my birthday," Kit said. "He took me out to dinner in Iowa City—did you use a credit card?"

"Probably."

"That's less than compelling. You could still be in Des Moines the next day." He slid the picture an inch toward me. "I think the burden of proof is on you."

"We slept together," she said, her voice strained. "I was with him the next day, and he didn't buy any *gun*."

"Were you with him all day? Do you remember?"

"No, I wasn't. That was a Wednesday and I taught at 10:00."

He tapped the picture. "And you? Do you know where you were on that Wednesday?" He leaned forward and read the date stamp. "At 12:30 in the afternoon?"

"Hell, I probably slept in." I took the picture and studied it. The guy was wearing clothes that could have come out of my closet, which proved nothing: jean jacket and blue jeans, white shirt.

"I don't have boots like that," I said, not expecting him to be impressed. "Wait, though . . . I looked it up, and a gun like this costs $2,600 new. I don't have that kind of money to spend on anything. You can check my bank and credit card records."

"We have, of course." He slid over another sheet, with a scanned copy of a receipt. "You paid cash. There's no record of your having withdrawn that amount, but . . ." He shrugged.

"Absence of proof is not proof of absence," I supplied. "But if this *were* a publicity stunt, why didn't I try to get some publicity?"

"I never used that word," he said. "Many of the people who come through this office have done things for reasons I don't understand— reasons *they* don't understand."

"So now I'm crazy."

"That's a layman's term, Mr. Daley. Not very useful to us."

"Who is 'us'? Are you a shrink as well as an agent?"

He almost smiled. "In fact, I am an 'analyst,' but not a psychoanalyst. And all I meant was that perfectly reasonable people do things that are not reasonable—literally not for reason.

"In the absence of further evidence . . ." He took a business card out of a tray and handed it to me. "I'm afraid Mr. Occam has raised his razor. Do contact us if you have evidence of a law being broken."

"It's a sniper weapon, for Christ's sake! You're not concerned about a sniper weapon appearing and disappearing?"

"It's a hunting rifle, a very popular model." He leaned forward and put the card in my shirt pocket. "It has been returned to your trunk."

"Along with a bug of some kind, I trust?"

"That's not my department, Mr. Daley, but I sincerely doubt it. We have a lot of work to do without making more." He peered into the desk screen. "Do let us know if you have a change of address or phone number. Good day?"

"You think this is some kind of a gag I set up?"

"Your words, Mr. Daley. Do you need help finding your way out?"

"You can't . . ." A big black guy in a tight dark suit was walking toward us. "No. We're outta here."

"One thing, please," Kit said in a strained voice. "How can you say for sure that this photo isn't a fake? Please?"

He picked it up and scowled at it. "Any electronic image could be manufactured from the ground up, Ms. Majors, pixel by pixel." He tapped the date stamp in the corner, with its bar code. "This part would be almost impossible, though. You would have to know the security protocols of the company that made the camera, just to start."

"*You* could do it."

"Homeland Security? No, we don't have any facilities for that—or none that I know of. I suppose some other agency might—but the cost, to make a counterfeit security image that we couldn't detect? Unless you're a closet millionaire, or indeed some kind of super spy, no." The black guy loomed next to him. "Thank you for your concern. You have been good citizens, bringing this to our attention. We'll keep our eyes open." His own eyes looked back down into the screen. The black guy's eyes gestured toward the elevator.

The shimmering oven of the parking lot was momentarily a relief, after that huge tax-funded refrigerator. The asphalt was so hot it felt spongy.

"Do you think that's it?" Kit said.

"I hope not. I mean, the guys who're after us must know we've been here. That might up the ante."

"Or they might decide to give up," she said. "Rather than risk the wrath of James 'Pepper' Blackstone."

"Whatever. I guess we want to drive slowly and leave a trail of bread crumbs."

We paused in the shade of a tree, incongruously planted in the middle of the lot, and stood on its grass. "Suppose we're wrong," I said, "in assuming that your car is bugged."

"What do you mean?"

"Well, how could they have bugged it in Iowa City? They might have followed me to the Hamburger Haven. But there's no way they could've known you'd stop there and drive off with me a few minutes later. Mess with your car in broad daylight. So it's me they're following, my body."

"Or they were at the time," she said. "They've had plenty of time to work on the car since."

"Yeah. They probably buy bugs by the six-pack." I suddenly felt nauseated. "What if it is my body? Like they put it in my food and it attached itself to my stomach."

"Could they do that?"

"I don't know. They can make them really small."

"I mean, it would pass on through. Really. If something attached itself to your stomach or intestines, it would make you sick, wouldn't it?"

I was dangerously close to demonstrating it. "The idea does. But hold it." An idea was crystallizing. "You wouldn't do that. You'd hide it in a muscle mass."

"How could they do that without your knowledge?"

"In the hospital. Not here, but in fucking Germany!" She shook her head slightly, not following me. "When I was in the army—when I was *wounded*!"

"But that was years ago."

"See, that's the mistake I've been making. This shit didn't start a couple of weeks ago—it was set up while I was still in the army. They just didn't activate it until they needed me."

"'They'? You think the army's behind all this?"

I actually went cold in all the rippling heat. Some ductless gland that had evolved in order to deal with agencies that had three initials. "No. Huh-uh." I pointed toward the car.

While we walked I asked about her aunt, who was dying of cancer. She made up a sob story that would melt the ice-cold heart of whoever was listening to parking-lot conversations.

As we approached the car I asked her to pop the trunk. "I want to take a look at the rifle," I whispered.

"They'll be watching."

"Probably." The trunk sprang open and I reached past the rifle box to a tackle box that I knew was full of tools. I selected a pair of pliers and slipped them into my front pocket while I was lifting the clumsy rifle box and struggling to open it.

I set the rifle on top of the box, still hidden to outside eyes. While running my left hand over the stock, I used my right to gently press the magazine release button. I slipped the top round off and then slid the magazine partway back, and returned the rifle to the box. But one round was in my shirt pocket now, and the magazine was loose, not pushed in. Kit looked mystified; she knew I had done something fishy but hadn't followed it.

I scribbled a note, GUN WON'T WORK, though I was still a step away from that.

When we were up to speed on the highway I took out the cartridge and used the pliers to wiggle the bullet and separate it from the brass casing. While Kit chattered about music I emptied the powder out of the cartridge and rolled the window down and let the breeze blow the grey powder away. Then I reassembled the bullet, tapping it home firmly with the pliers, and put it back in my pocket.

It was an old saboteur's trick. With the cartridge back in place, the emptied top round in the magazine, the rifle was a passive booby trap. If someone pulled the trigger, the hammer would fall on the empty cartridge's primer, which would make a small explosion—just enough force to drive the bullet partway up the barrel and be stuck. When the next bullet was fired, full power, it would strike the first one, and the gun would blow up in the shooter's face.

I could fire the weapon safely, because I knew to eject the first round before pulling the trigger. For anyone else it would be a nasty and perhaps fatal surprise.

I scrolled the map down and left and enlarged it. She looked over and held her finger over a small town, Carlinville, not tapping it. I nodded and we studied it for a second, and then turned off the map, and resumed talking about Steven Spielberg.

Interstate 55 had the cruise lane, so we took less than half an hour to get down to the Carlinville exit. Meanwhile I fiddled with her iPak and found out that Carlinville once had more houses ordered from the Sears catalog than anyplace else in the country, and was once the home of the woman H. G. Wells called "the most intelligent woman in America." I passed that morsel on to Kit, and she said, "We just have to stop there and pay our respects."

We passed by a small park in the middle of town; she looked at me and I nodded. Parked a block away and walked back, picking up a couple of ice cream cones on the way. We could watch the car from the park, in case somebody tried to put a dead body or an H-bomb in the trunk.

There was a bench in the shade of a tree next to a playground area. The kids were raising all kinds of hell. I spoke quietly.

"None of this makes any difference if they have a microphone up my ass."

"I would have felt it." She smiled. "Here's my logic: I think they do have a device in or on your body, which they can track for location. But not listening."

"Which 'they' are we talking about?"

"Does it make any difference now? Them versus us. But I don't think it's a listening device or a video bug, if we're talking about Agent Blackstone and his gang. If they'd been listening to us, they'd know you're innocent."

I nodded. "Unless they think *we* think we're being listened to all the time. Saying things to avert suspicion."

"Yeah, but how far down that rabbit hole do you want to go? Blackstone being manipulated to feed us lines?"

I took his card out of my shirt pocket. Nothing fancy: plain picture, not a holo; James "Pepper" Blackstone, Analyst, Domestic Terrorism, Department of Homeland Security.

I held it up to my mouth. "Hello? Jimmy boy?"

"He probably likes to be called 'Pepper.'"

I studied the card. "You know, you're right. This has to stop somewhere. Blackstone didn't know where the gun had come from. They didn't have time to set up some damned phony scene in a gun shop in Des Moines."

"Okay."

"So that means someone *who wasn't working for them* set me up. Nobody who buys a weapon in a gun shop doesn't know he's on *Candid Camera*. They got somebody who looks kind of like me."

"What about the driver's license?"

"That is a problem. The feds can't get past that because they lack one crucial piece of evidence that I have: I do know I wasn't there. Nobody did some voodoo crap and made me drive to Des Moines and buy a fucking gun!

"It's simple. Someone hacked the god-damned system. If someone can program it, someone else can program around it. The ID dot on your license really boils down to a string of ones and zeros. Somebody got ahold of my string and put it in the system."

"How?"

I had to laugh. "*I* don't know! I'm not a fucking criminal!"

She put a finger on my arm. A woman on the other side of the play area was staring at me with a cross expression. No doubt a prissy G-man in drag.

I lowered my voice again. "Let's just assume as a starting point that Blackstone is what he says he is. Tonight when we stop, we'll write him a long e-mail with chapter and verse, everything that's happened. 'Here it is, take it or leave it.' Even if they think I'm lying, at least it'll go into my dossier. In case."

"In case you die, you mean."

"Well, yeah." I started to frame something sarcastic to say but it evaporated on my lips. In that dappled noisy playground she was trembling, and looked like she was about to burst into tears.

"Sometimes I forget," she said. "People trying to kill you is not a new thing."

"Yeah. Me, too. I forget."

But not really. Not ever.

2.

James "Pepper" Blackstone, M.S.
Analyst
Domestic Terrorism Working Group
Department of Homeland Security
800 East Monroe Street
Springfield, IL 62701-1099

Dear Agent Blackstone:

This is just to put down on paper some of the things we said, and perhaps forgot to say, when we spoke with you at your office May 18th, this afternoon.

For the record, I, Christian "Jack" Daley, have no active connection with the U.S. (or any other) government, except for monthly disability checks from the Veterans Administration, and

*occasional medical examinations there. I have never been
employed by the government in any way other than the
straightforward, if unwilling, relationship I had with the Selective
Service Commission and the U.S. Army: I was drafted and then
chose to "volunteer for the draft," as the official language has it:
I was told that I could get a better assignment that way, and still
serve only two years, after training.*

*Whether my eventual assignment as a sniper was actually
"better" than whatever would have happened to me, if it had been
left up to chance, is not relevant anymore. I served out my time as
a sniper in Operation Desert Freeze, and was wounded and given
the usual handful of medals, and came home.*

*I was subsequently diagnosed with Posttraumatic Stress
Disorder, and have gone to the Iowa City VA Hospital off and on
for medication and talk therapy.*

*(I don't dispute the diagnosis, but would like to repeat my
opinion here, that anyone who has had the experience of being a
soldier, killing people, and being wounded, and does not suffer a
"stress disorder" from the experience, would have to be ipso facto
mentally ill.)*

*I think the record will confirm that PTSD has not greatly
affected my behavior since I separated from the Army.*

*You surely have access to my military records, but I would be
surprised if you found anything there of interest beyond the simple
fact of my sniper training. I was moderately skilled as a marksman
but had no enthusiasm for killing strangers.*

*It's a mystery to me why anyone would select me for this
cryptic and surely criminal enterprise. I was not that great a
sniper—I did get the sniper cluster on my rifleman's badge, but*

*that really means that I managed to hit some of the enemy and
didn't shoot anyone on our own side. My politics lean toward the
left, but I'm far from being anyone's candidate for an instrument
of violence against the government. I mainly want to be left alone.*

*Of course, politics didn't really come up with whoever gave me
that rifle. They threatened my lover's life, and my own, if I didn't
kill a "bad man" for good pay. They haven't yet said why he was
so bad.*

*You were confident that Homeland Security, with the help of
the FBI and police, can put a quick end to this matter. I would like
to share your confidence, but Kit and I are both very scared, and
have to act with exaggerated caution.*

*If you have any message for me and Kit, please leave it on my
home phone recorder. We will be travelling.*

C. Jack Daley

I printed out a copy on the library's printer and Kit proofread it.
"Looks okay."

"Good." I folded the paper up and put it in my back pocket. "Go get
the car. When I see you pull up in front, I'll click on SEND and come
get in the car, and we're off for the highway."

She breathed out heavily. "Whatever you say, boss." She wasn't 100
percent with me on this, but couldn't come up with a better plan. I
wanted Homeland Security to feel we were cooperating, but we couldn't
know whether the bad guys might intercept a message, or might even
be hiding there, safe in some corner of the bureaucratic web.

Even if they, the menacing "they," were hooked up with the government, they didn't necessarily know that we'd gone to see Blackstone. But

it would be prudent to assume that they did know, as soon as the agent filed a report. They might have known as soon as his secretary typed in my name—or maybe even as soon as we rolled into the parking lot. Where some scanner evidently noted that we had a gun in the trunk. That might ring a few alarm bells even if I were just a forgetful hunter.

Her bronze car rolled up and I pushed SEND. Anybody who really wanted to know could find out that I was in the public library in Litchfield, Illinois, at 12:39 on May eighteenth. Just passing through, though. Leaving behind some cybernetic spoor.

She had the radio playing loud. Taped on the dash over it, where we both could see it, our complex route to Baton Rouge, which we'd researched and printed out in the library. It was "blue highways" all the way, a slow crawl but one that ought to avoid stoplight cameras and toll booths. Getting off the grid by burrowing under it.

We were plainly in no hurry. No real destination. Baton Rouge was big enough to hide in, and dodgy enough that we wouldn't have any trouble finding odd jobs that wouldn't require ID.

But we weren't really going there. It was a feint.

Without saying a word about it, we drove straight into St. Louis and left the car in a low-rent long-term parking lot outside the airport. Took the airport shuttle to the East Terminal and transferred to one of the hotel shuttles headed into downtown St. Louis. Ninety minutes after we ditched the car, we were in the Greyhound station with tickets south, bought from a machine with cash, no IDs.

We had about $9,000 in cash, split evenly. We were taking different busses—hers direct to New Orleans and mine via Joplin. We would meet in two days in the line waiting for breakfast at Brennan's—and then go someplace more reasonable for a meal and planning session.

If they managed to follow us through that maze, it was hopeless. Maybe learn Chinese and go join their space program. No way Homeland Security, or the nameless "they," could follow us to the moon.

Of course they might already be there, hiding behind some fucking crater.

I hoped the clue we left in the Litchfield library was subtle enough not to look planted. I'd noticed that the connection between the computer and printer was wireless, so any cloak-and-dagger types who'd followed us there could pick it up from the parking lot. We talked about going to California while Kit typed up unrelated directions to Baton Rouge.

Of course they would eventually find the car in the long-term parking lot outside of the airport, the gun still in the trunk. Whether they were the government or some more sinister "they," we knew the car was bugged. We would probably be caught on camera outside the airport if they were the government, but even so, we might lose them between the airport and the bus station. When did a self-respecting spy or terrorist ever go Greyhound?

Before her bus left, she downloaded her e-mail and mine. Blackstone had sent a pro forma "thank you for cooperating with Homeland Security" message, and there was a note from my father asking why I wasn't picking up the phone.

And Hollywood raised its ugly head. A note from Ronald Duquest's office reminded me that the next chapter was due yesterday. Golly, slipped my mind.

I would normally e-mail the manuscript to myself, as I always do at the end of the writing day. Kit was taking the iPak with her, of course. I could write the next chapter out by hand and type it in later, but there was a Woolworth's down the street. So I went in and bought a kids' laptop for $99, bright red with big rubbery keys. An economy-sized twelve-pack of batteries, enough to get me to New Orleans.

The first thing I wrote on it was an e-mail to Dad, copied to Mother, explaining that I'd been accepted to a special writers' retreat at a Trappist monastery. Total silence for a month, no street mail or e-mail, complete isolation from the modern world. By the time I'd written out a description of it, I wanted to sign up. Just write for a month, no guns or spies. Not sure about "plain food cooked by nuns." Kit was confident I could find the one nun who was a gourmet cook, and maybe a closet nympho-maniac, besides.

Anybody who was really interested would be able to figure out that the message came from St. Louis, but in a couple of minutes I'd be headed south in anonymity. I clicked on SEND and kissed Kit and got on the bus. Waved to her as it pulled out, and then opened up the file with Duquest's story line and my minim opus.

CHAPTER TEN

Hunter slept for ten hours, woke up famished, and microwaved the heart and kidneys. They were not tender but juicy and tangy. He drank a pint of whiskey and a gallon of water and slept again.

When he awoke, he hacked the remaining leg into two pieces, and put the foot half into a big pan with onions and a handful of wild rosemary. He stabbed it a dozen times and pushed garlic cloves deep into the muscle. He opened a can of camper's bacon and draped it all over the leg and put it in a slow oven.

He sat on the trailer stairs for exactly one hour, listening intently. Two cars and a motorcycle went by, and as he was rising to go back in, he heard the whir and labored breathing of a bicyclist slowly climbing the slight grade.

It would not be smart to hunt so close to home. But just for practice he slipped quietly through the underbrush and crouched down behind a dense thicket of bramble. He nibbled on some berries and watched.

He would be a beautiful catch, young and plump. He must be local, since he couldn't have pedaled very far on the old Schwinn, fat patched tires and faded blue paint held together with skeins of rust.

Hunter's stomach made a noise and the boy heard it. He stopped and looked around wildly, and Hunter tensed to attack. But then he turned the bike around and fled downhill.

Some ancient instinct urged him to bound after the quarry and bring it down, and something like saliva squirted into his mouth in anticipation. His long muscles tensed to spring, but the brain interfered and he relaxed.

There would be another day.

He would be cautious, as usual. He sat unmoving long after the sound of the bike receded into nothing. The clock in his brain ticked off an hour, and then another hour.

No villagers with torches and pitchforks. No steady-eyed deputy adjusting his Stetson and saying, "Maybe the boy did hear somethin', Sheriff." No rumble of tanks and scream of jets converging on the invader from another world.

But he was not an invader, he thought; he belonged here as surely as a shark belongs in the sea.

A rabbit advanced slowly, almost invisible against the dun mat of humus, and sniffed Hunter's bare foot. He snatched it and crushed out its life before it could even squeak, and nibbled at its twitching body as he watched the sun set.

Not a bad planet at all.

3.

When I turned eighteen, my mother took me down to New Orleans to celebrate my birthday with Aunt Helen. Eighteen was the legal drinking age in New Orleans, and I was ready. Aunt Helen lived there, and knew all the watering holes, and the three of us had walked up and down Bourbon Street and Decatur and St. Charles, comparing the quality of mint juleps in various places. I probably lost track after three or four.

Brennan's is the place where I learned about treating a hangover with booze, their traditional champagne breakfast. It was a strange medicinal compound of champagne and Pernod, with orange juice on the side, and it worked so well we kept drinking champagne for a while, even after the hangovers were buried.

Aunt Helen—"Hell," she liked to be called—had by then turned this cycle into a way of life. The hangover would start to gather about the time the coffee was perking, so she'd spike it with a gin Bloody Mary and get on with life. I sincerely hope she outlives us all.

That breakfast had started out airy and French, a soufflé made with berries, and then anchored with hot Andouille sausage and fried potatoes, washed down with imported beer. I don't think I had eaten better in my life at that time, and have only a few times since.

Of course this visit to the Big Easy was going to be less festive. Not easy.

After eighteen hours on the bus, sleeping fitfully after I finished the short Hunter chapter, I was ready for a little walk. The ticketmeister drew me a map on a three-by-five card and said it was a little more than a mile. It was not quite eleven, and I'd told Kit "about noon," so I set out into the gathering heat.

Quite a bit of foot traffic, but it wasn't unpleasant, tourists happy to be where they were, not yet sweltering and cross. I resisted the automatic reflex to take out the cell and check for calls, or call Kit to reassure her. They're probably listening; why make it easy for them?

Of course there was a chance we had lost them now. In my mind's eye I could visualize them crawling over Kit's car, looking for clues. There wasn't one molecule of evidence that we were going to New Orleans. They would find the directions to Baton Rouge, crumpled up and kicked under the seat, but otherwise I hoped our trail stopped there, in the long-term lot outside the St. Louis airport.

They would get the rifle. That gave me a little chill. Would they bench test it without first checking—lock and load and fire the second round into the blocked barrel? If it killed or injured some DHS or FBI agent, they would probably up the ante. If it was the people who'd supplied the rifle in the first place, who knows? They wouldn't have any reason to test-fire it. Maybe it would show up in our motel room in Key West, still fatally booby trapped.

The line for Brennan's was half a block long. After a minute or two,

long enough for me to fall into a reverie, Kit tapped me on the shoulder.
"Hey, sailor—new in town?"

We kissed and she steered me across the street to a place with tables
in the front garden. She'd already gotten us a table and a carafe of coffee.

The coffee was strong and bitter with chicory. Thick real cream and
honey to take the edge off. A waiter came over immediately and I ordered
a beer and a pile of sausage and bacon.

"Breakfast of *champignons*?"

"Living on candy and carbs, on the bus," I said. "Dreaming of that
sausage."

"And coming up with a master plan, I hope."

"I have some ideas. You?"

"One you won't like."

In other words, one I'd better accept. "What?"

"We should both change our appearance radically. Look like we
belong in the Quarter. Chop my hair short and dye it, go butch."

"I love your hair."

"It'll grow back. Likewise you: off with the beard and moustache,
and shave your head."

"Shave my *head*? I'd look fucking gay."

She nodded, expressionless. "Look around. Black jeans and tight
black T-shirt, little earring. You get hit on, just say no. I do it all the time."

I couldn't argue with the logic. If your appearance gives off a specific
sexual signal, most people won't see anything else. "And then we get
fake IDs?"

"You said this would be the place."

"Yeah. True." Maybe I could go home for just one minute and grab
the file of notes I had on the subject, for the novel. "Smoke shop, head
shop, is the place if you don't need anything heavy-duty. Out-of-state

driver's license." I looked at her critically and stroked my beard. "Think you could pass for twenty-one? Little girl?"

"In your dreams. Wet dreams." She could pass, actually—even for a teenager if she dressed the part.

A pile of pig protein and lots of muscular chicory-flavored coffee, and I was ready to face a bunch of spies, or at least a barber.

He didn't speak much English, but he got "Take it all off." The feeling of a straight razor sliding along your skull was a new kind of discomfort for me, which I hope never to repeat. He also did an expert job on my beard. In the mirror I looked like one of those children with progeria, a baby's face with age lines and basset eyes.

Kit's haircut cost three times as much, and looked like the result of an industrial accident. You shouldn't lean so close to the lathe, babe. But I hardly recognized her, which was the idea: bleached blond riff brushed out stiff with a purple accent.

She looked in the mirror and started to cry. But then she laughed brightly and wiped her eyes. She put on some lipstick that I didn't know she had, and a little mascara. Stuck out her tongue at the reflection.

We split a pair of earrings, black pearl studs that she had in the bottom of her purse. I hadn't worn one since I was an undergraduate, so it hurt and bled.

As a mutual disguise, though, it worked pretty well. We did look like a couple of thirty-ish tourists trying to look younger. On the Bourbon Street sidewalk, we blended in like cows in a herd.

A restaurant on St. Charles, Korn Dogs 'n' More, needed a dishwasher and a waitress. The manager looked like he had just stepped out of a Yale faculty meeting, but he didn't blink at our appearance or at Kit's story that we'd been robbed and had no IDs.

The dishwashing wasn't hard. Piled up after lunch and then was quiet until about five. Pretty busy till the place closed at ten. The pots and pans took another hour after that, Kit helping.

I probably would have hated it if I'd had to do it for a living, up to my elbows in greasy water. Doing it as protective coloration was kind of fun.

The Italian owner, Mario, cooked nonstop but had lots of stories, and was obviously happy to have a new audience. He'd also been in the desert, so we bonded over that.

Once I didn't respond when he called me "Jim," my temporary name, and he gave me a big wink.

He had a friend who rented rooms by the week a few blocks away, and gave Kit an hour off to get us a place. We finally crashed there a little after midnight.

The computer beeped at ten. Kit was already in the shower down the hall.

The room had a coffee machine. By the time I had it charged up and dripping, she came back, rubbing her hair with a towel. She shrugged out of her robe and handed it to me, then giggled when I put it on. "We'll have to get you something without lace and flowers."

I looked in the mirror and almost didn't go down the hall. Baby-blue posies clashed with my skinhead asshole look. I showered quick.

We got to work one minute early, and Mario seemed vaguely surprised to see us. But we were going to hang in there at least six days, until the first paycheck. Or until somebody caught up with us.

4.

We got our first week's pay and the phone call the same day, no coincidence, I suppose. Even paid by cash, there would be a record. My "James Kinney" ID probably went straight into a federal database of false IDs, and a face recognition program linked it with the person I used to be.

The phone rang at Korn Dogs and someone asked for me. Mario put it on hold and asked whether I was here.

"Someone want Jim Kinney?"

"Well . . . 'the person who calls himself James Kinney.' Want me to say you haven't come in yet?"

No, they might be watching. I shrugged and held out my hand. A woman's voice asked if I was Jack Daley.

"Or Jim Kinney, yes. Who is this?"

She was agent Sara Underwood, who had been "partnered with"

James Blackstone. She asked me whether I had any information about him.

I was tempted to say that if the federal government couldn't keep track of its own people, how are they going to track down the bad guys? "No, not since our interview last week. I called his office once, but he wasn't in."

"What business did you have with him?"

"He asked me to call in if I had a change of address. He wasn't there, though."

There was a long pause. "Agent Blackstone has died, under odd circumstances."

"Oh, my god. I'm sorry."

"Yes. We're calling everyone who had contact with him recently. You were not a person of interest in any of his ongoing investigations, but you did speak with him the afternoon of the seventeenth. About a sniper rifle?"

"Yeah, we called on Tuesday last week, I think. Someone left a weapon in my car, the sniper rifle that I thought I'd gotten rid of, with a suggestive note."

"Yes, we know that from his desk report. I'm afraid we have to confiscate the rifle now."

I tried to respond but my throat had closed up.

"Mr. Daley? We need that rifle. You don't have to ship it to us. We can pick it up now."

Sirens outside. A black-and-white screeched to a stop in the side street. I signaled Kit and she stepped into the ladies' room.

"I—I don't have it."

"Where is it, Mr. Daley?"

Two uniformed cops banged into the store. The black one had his hand on his gun, the Hispanic on a Taser. I raised my free hand. "The police are here."

"*Where is the gun?* Mr. Daley."

"In the trunk of a car in St. Louis. Airport parking lot! That's what I told—" The cops towered over me. I covered the phone. "I'll be right with you," I said. "Talking to the FBI."

"Put down the phone," the black one said. "Right now."

"I mean Homeland Security," I said.

"We've recovered that car," Sara Underwood's voice said, and then she said something else, but I couldn't hear it because the Hispanic officer had snatched the phone away.

"Are you going to cooperate?" he said.

"I'm *already* cooperating! Talk to the lady on that phone!"

He opened the phone and looked at it. "Says 'call blocked.'"

"Yeah, of course." I stuck out my wrists. "Let's go."

"We don't do it that way," the Hispanic one said. He grabbed my arm and hauled me out of the chair and had my hands cuffed behind my back in about one second.

"Take it easy, for Christ's sake!" One held me while the other patted me down roughly.

"Homicide," the black one said, in explanation, as he goosed me. "Up in Indiana or someplace." I almost said "Illinois," but decided to leave him uncorrected.

At least they didn't get both of us, I thought, and didn't look at the door to the ladies' room.

They stuffed me in the back of the patrol car and managed to belt me into the shoulder harness with both hands behind my back. Maybe my one phone call would be to a chiropractor.

It didn't last long. We went a couple of blocks with the siren going, the black officer driving slowly while the other said incomprehensible things into the radio. Then they pulled over and helped me out of the car, took off the cuffs and gave me back my cell phone.

"Be careful now," the black one said by way of apology, and they drove away.

If something like that happened in Iowa City, I'd go down to the station and get on their case. False arrest, harassment, intimidation. Not in the Big Easy, I think.

I walked back down St. Charles for a few blocks and then sat down at a sidewalk café to think.

Was I being watched? Not obviously. Wouldn't make any difference anyway, if it was just Homeland Security and the FBI and the New Orleans cops. But how far behind are the ones who gave me the rifle, twice?

A pretty black waitress came out, looking bone tired. End of the night shift. I ordered white coffee and a beignet, playing knowledgeable tourist. After I ordered it I chastised myself. Black coffee and a doughnut would have saved me three bucks.

I talked to an operator and then a secretary in the Springfield Homeland Security office, and got a call back from Sara Underwood. "What on earth is going on down there? You're in trouble with the New Orleans police?"

"You tell me, Ms. Underwood. My girlfriend and I are getting jacked around six ways from Sunday, and all we've done is try to cooperate with the authorities. I was just now handcuffed and thrown in the back of a police car, and then released, all without a word of explanation. You tell *me* what's going on!"

There was a long silence, with some clicks. "I don't know what kind of trouble you might be in, down south. You're in some trouble here in Springfield."

"What do you mean, *trouble*? I haven't done a damned thing illegal."

"That may be, Mr. Daley. But this is a homicide investigation now, and you are more than a 'person of interest.' You were interviewed by Agent Blackstone, with negative results. Agent Blackstone was found dead this morning."

It was a sunny clear morning, but I could feel walls closing in on me. "I didn't do it. I couldn't have done it. How could I? I've been in New Orleans for a week!"

"Well, you were in New Orleans a week ago and you're there now. You could have gone to Singapore and back in between."

"Yeah, I'm sure you guys wouldn't notice. But you said you got the car?"

"The car?"

"Before New Orleans's finest picked me up. You said you'd retrieved the car from the airport in St. Louis."

"We did, yes."

"Then? You were about to say something else."

There was a sound like papers being shuffled. "I was going to ask you . . . about firing the rifle. You did do some shooting with it."

"Just a few rounds. As I told Blackstone. Just to zero it in."

"Why?"

"To zero it in."

She sighed. "I mean why would you want to zero it in if you never planned to use it?" That blocked me for a moment. "Hello? Doesn't that seem odd to you?"

"The note . . . there was a note!"

"We found a note, crumpled up on the floor of the car." She paused. "It says, basically, you'll be paid $100,000 to kill someone, and there's a down payment in the rifle stock. Nothing about zeroing the weapon."

"No, I'm wrong. I'm sorry! It wasn't the note; it was a phone call right afterwards—a woman told me to take the rifle down to the Coralville dump and zero it in. Then police up the brass and targets."

"What about the police?"

God, was this happening? "*Police.* It's a verb. It means to clean stuff up. I was supposed to pick up the brass from shooting it. The spent cartridges."

"So was it a phone call or a note? Or was it both?"

"Both. It was both." I took a deep breath. "Someone put the rifle on my doormat back in Iowa City. Put it there while I was asleep, and rang the bell and drove away."

"And you didn't call the police then because?"

"We told all this to Agent Blackstone."

"And he's dead now. You didn't call the police?"

"There wasn't time! I opened the box and while I was looking at the rifle, the god-damned phone rang. A woman warned me not to call the cops, and then said to take the rifle out to the Coralville dump and zero it."

"She actually said 'Don't call the cops'?"

"I don't remember her exact words. But she threatened to kill Kit if I didn't cooperate."

"In so many words? 'We will kill Catherine Majors'?"

"No . . . I don't know. She said they'd done it before, and she had me Google some kid's name. Who had died of mylo something. Mylo-thrombosis? It was pretty convincing."

"And on the strength of that?"

"What do you mean? They threaten to kill my girlfriend and 'on the strength of that' I go zero their fucking rifle? Yes! You wouldn't?"

"What were you supposed to do after that? Did they say who you were going to shoot with the rifle?"

"I don't think they ever did . . . no, never. Just that he was some-one bad."

Paper rustled. "'You will agree that the World is a better place with-out him.' The word 'World' is capitalized."

"I noticed that. And a couple of other grammar things. So he's not too literate?"

"You never know, Mr. Kinney—Mr. Daley. 'He' might be a female, and more literate than you or me, faking it. Though you're right; on the surface it appears to have been written by a person with little education, probably male.

"Of course that generates the question of how and why some semi-literate person could and would set up and execute this complex stunt."

Her use of the word "stunt" was interesting. "Wait. Do you still think that I might have done this 'stunt' myself?"

"Nothing is off the table, Mr. Daley. My personal opinion is that you didn't do it. People who haven't seen the recording of your interview, who don't know anything about you, might think otherwise."

"But it's ridiculous! Why would I go to all that trouble just to get into more trouble?"

"You're an educated man, and a writer. You know that people do things for odd reasons, or no reason. That you or someone else would set this up is 'odd,' but odd things happen."

That was almost exactly what Blackstone had said. Maybe it's a mantra you have to learn for Homeland Security. "And I suppose my fingerprints are all over the note."

"In fact, no. That piece of paper has been folded and unfolded and crumpled up, but as far as we can tell no one has ever touched it without gloves. You do admit to reading it?"

Shit. I loved where this was going. "Of course. I told Blackstone—"

"Why would you put on gloves to read a note? Why would an innocent person avoid leaving fingerprints on anything?"

I had to admit that was a pretty good question. "I . . . I guess I was in a suspicious frame of mind. Cautious frame of mind. I started to take the rifle out of the box but then I thought, hell, I'm taking this straight to the cops; don't want to mess up any prints that might be on it."

Long pause. "But in the event . . . you actually didn't take it to the police."

"*No!* Like I said! That's when the woman called."

I heard her exhale in exasperation. "I'm trying to make a list here. First your doorbell rang, late at night."

"Morning. About four in the morning."

"What were you doing up at that hour?"

"I *wasn't* up! The *phone* woke me up."

"Calm down, Mr. Daley. I'm trying to decipher the notes from your conversation with Mr. Blackstone. You went to the door and there was no one there."

"I heard a car leaving, peeled out. Before I opened the door."

"There was no sign of them when you opened the door?"

"Nothing but the box. I heard tires squealing while I was getting dressed."

"What did you think it was? Four in the morning."

"I don't know. Kids, I guess."

"Why did you go to the door when the phone rang?"

"Not the *phone*! The doorbell."

"Okay. Kids rang the doorbell and left behind an expensive sniper rifle."

A really bad feeling was growing in my head. Could I open my mouth without screaming? It would feel so good to throw the phone into the traffic.

"Are you there, Mr. Daley?"

What would it sound like on her end, when a car ran over it? Would it be loud enough to be worth the cost?

"Mr. Daley?"

I took a deep breath. "Add this to your list. I've had enough abuse for the day. My shoulders and wrists hurt from being manhandled by jackbooted fucking storm troopers. On your list I want you to write down the time of day. Call me exactly twenty-four hours from now and I'll answer. If the phone rings before that I will throw it in the fucking Mississippi." I snapped it shut with a sound like a rifle shot.

An elderly couple sitting down at the next table smiled and applauded softly. "Whoever they are," the old lady said, "fuck them."

I gave her a V-sign. My grandfather's generation. God bless the sixties.

The phone rang again. I opened it. "Didn't you hear what I said?"

It was a familiar woman's voice, but not Sara Underwood's: it was the mystery woman who first talked to me in Iowa City, and threatened me with the story about the boy who died of myelofibrosis.

"Jack? We know where you are now. Are you ready to talk?"

I threw the phone into the street and got up to rush to Korn Dogs.

Bikes in a Box

1.

Something must have shown on my face when I returned to the restaurant. Mario was by the grill chopping onions and he came over with the big chef's knife in his hand. "Something wrong," he said.

"Hate to leave you in the lurch, man. We have to get out of here." Kit untied her apron wordlessly and started folding it.

"You have to?"

I nodded.

"Shit happens," he said, setting the knife down. He went around the counter and punched the cash register hard and scooped out two C-notes and a fifty from the till.

"We couldn't, Mario," Kit said.

He put the money on the counter and looked at me. "I never seen you guys." He turned to go back to his onions. "Good luck anyhow. *In bocca al lupo.*" He'd taught us that phrase, like "break a leg."

We had Plan A mapped out completely. Every morning before we left for work we packed everything we owned into two knapsacks, so we could go into the apartment and out in seconds.

There was a bike shop on the way. The two we'd picked out, a couple of sturdy touring Treks, had been sold—but two new ones had just come in; he'd unboxed them this morning and almost had them together. It seemed like a good omen, starting out fresh, so we bought them and two sets of rear baskets.

While the kid was bolting the baskets on, we went back to the apartment and picked up the knapsacks and left the key on the dresser. As an afterthought Kit left a note saying we'd been called north, and expected to be back before the first, but if we weren't, go ahead and rent the room. We left our Jazzy Pass RTA cards with the note.

We had two detailed route maps that took us from New Orleans to Miami on back roads, and then down A1A to Key West. We would travel apart, Kit leaving an hour before me, the routes slightly different wherever possible. They'd be looking for a couple our age traveling together.

Not trusting cell phones, we'd bought a pair of kids' walkie-talkies from the Phone Shop. I would call her every hour on the hour, and let it buzz once. If she didn't buzz back soon, it meant she was in trouble—or we'd been betrayed by cheap Phone Shop technology, not impossible.

We split our cash down the middle, $4,320 each. Decided to go ahead and use her credit card for the bikes, since the Feds knew where we were anyhow. All my cards were flat.

I'd downloaded lists of bicycle-friendly hotels for the states we'd be going through. We chose one just out of town, about twenty miles away, for the first night, and I sent Kit on ahead.

Locked my bike up outside the Black Cat, our favorite tavern, and had one last imported beer before taking off into the land of country general stores and Bud Light. We'd made up our routes from a library copy of the Southern Tier Trail "southern tier" tourist maps, which kept you away from highways and cities, and decent beer.

It's very close to what my hero in the novel was doing, in reverse, but the only reference to that in the whole world was buried in Duquest's files; maybe my agent's. Under anybody's radar.

Kit was carrying the fake Glock, the pellet gun with the orange nose spray-painted black, figuring that if one of us was going to need it on these deserted country roads, it would be her. My thinking had gone a little beyond that, though.

The one morning drunk at the bar got up and left. I took a G-note out of my pocket and smoothed it onto the bar. "Jimmy," I said to the bartender, "maybe you can help me with a little problem."

———————

Two hours later I was down in bayou country, headed east on Route 90, a bright red accessory bag on a quick-release clip in the center of my handlebars. It held my wallet, maps, some nuts, and a candy bar—and a snub-nosed Taurus .38 Special, the favorite little pistol of TV detective actors. Actual criminals probably favor something with more punch, but a new .357 Magnum would have cost nearly a thousand more.

I didn't want anything bigger anyhow. When I unsnap the bag and carry it into a convenience store, I don't want the clerk to gauge its weight and reach for his own gun.

I'd bought it from a black guy who had conspicuous tracks on his left forearm and hadn't bathed in a while. But his hands were steady and his eyes clear, so I assumed he was a cop, or worked for them. Which didn't bother me too much. If somebody tried to bust me I would have

Sara Underwood rain some Homeland Security shit on them. Though she might just ask them to lock me up and throw away the key.

There was enough truck traffic to keep me from being bored, and the road was pretty rough. The bikes were set up for endurance rather than speed, medium-fat tires with Kevlar inserts. Fewer miles per day but no flats, and we could go off-road if necessary.

There were no good scenarios that involved that, though. If someone was after us with a car, we were just caught. I wasn't going to hit the dirt and lay down a field of fire, not with five rounds of .38 Special ammo indifferently aimed. Twenty-five rounds if I had time to reload a few times, which didn't seem likely.

I guess the gun was more a psychological crutch than actual protection. As my M2010 had been in the desert, most of the time—if you live with a weapon 24/7 it becomes like another limb, and anytime it's out of sight you start to panic.

(So when is a crutch not a crutch? When you could walk better without it?)

I'd gone unarmed for most of eight years, but the feeling of symbiosis, of dependence, came back immediately. It made me feel more calm, in control, even though my rational brain knew that was nonsense. If any of our enemies produced a weapon, it would trump the hell out of a Dick Tracy snub-nose .38 not-so-Special revolver.

But it was better than nothing. Nothing would be total helplessness, being a target rather than a foe. And even though Sara Underwood probably already had a memo on her desk with the serial number and exact provenance of my .38, whoever was after us probably didn't know yet. That might buy us a second or two in a few of the less likely futures that we faced.

2.

We had figured that it would be safe enough if we came together each night. Two people on bicycles might be conspicuous at a mom-and-pop motel, but two car-less bikers at two separate motels would be even more conspicuous, and we felt safer together.

She called me on the walkie-talkie and said there was a vacancy at the place we'd tentatively chosen, the Southern Comfort motel, a half mile up the road. On the way there I stopped at a convenience store and bought a pint of that odd beverage, honey-flavored whiskey. At a 7-Eleven. God bless Louisiana's liquor laws!

We celebrated our first day as two-wheeled fugitives with a couple of big plastic cups of ice and the sweet liqueur, sitting on folding chairs on a screened porch overlooking some bayou. The mosquitoes were pretty fierce for our being technically indoors, but after we swatted a dozen or so they showed us some respect.

We'd brought the bikes inside the motel room rather than risk them being stolen or identified, and Kit had just nodded when I showed her the .38. She didn't bring it up until we were halfway through the "Judy Collins Juice," as my father called it. The sun was a dull crimson ball behind a confusion of spindly trees and power poles and lines.

"You know about guns and I don't," she said, "but I thought we decided back in Iowa . . ."

"Yeah, we did." I could've bought a regular pistol at the Kmart where I'd bought the pellet gun. But I didn't want to raise the ante, at the time. "I guess it was Blackstone getting killed. Like they're playing hardball now."

She nodded, staring at the dying sun. "Hardball. You sound like somebody on TV."

I laughed. "Guess I do."

"But guns are real to you, from being a soldier. That's something we'll never share."

What could I say? "Hope not."

The sun disappeared and a dozen birds swifted by overhead, talking about dinner. A good still moment.

"Would you show me how?"

"How what?"

"How to use the gun. If something happens to you that doesn't happen to me."

"'Course." I stood up and stretched. "Not that I'm an expert."

We went inside and I unzipped the red bike bag and took out the pistol, feeling a little foolish. The thin film of gun oil had collected some lint and grit. I took a tissue from the box on the desk and wiped it clean.

I thumbed the catch and the cylinder swung out. Looked down the barrel, using my thumbnail to reflect light up; it wasn't even dusty.

Shook the cylinder into my palm but only one round dropped;

I used the built-in ejector rod to push the others out. "Never had one like this," I said apologetically. "Couldn't fit an assault rifle into the bike bag."

I snapped it shut and passed it to her with the nose pointed to the ceiling. "Rule Number One, they say. There's no such thing as an unloaded gun."

"That must save a lot on ammunition." She took it. "Sorry; I'll be good."

"It does hurt a lot of soldiers, forgetting the round in the chamber. I don't think you will, though."

"No." She held it like a ticking time bomb. "Heavier than it looks."

"Always." I passed her the handful of cartridges. "Load it up?"

She fumbled and dropped two, which was a complete lesson in its way. "Easier in the movies," she said with a nervous laugh.

"I hear it happens to cops," I said. "They practice for years, but when they have to reload under fire they're all over the place."

"I won't be doing anything 'under fire.' Running, maybe." She pushed the cylinder into place with a soft click.

"Me, neither, I hope." I took it back from her and unloaded it again. "You don't really aim a gun like this. You can't hit the wall with it, anyhow, no matter how well you aim." I pointed it at the TV and click, good-bye weather girl. "You know what a sight picture is?"

"No, I never heard the term."

I handed it to her. "Point it at the door?"

She did, and I stood behind her and wrapped my hand over hers, and raised the pistol up to eye level. "The thing in the front is the blade sight. You line it up with the notch in the back and the bullet ought to go in that direction."

She rocked it up and down. "You can't focus on three things at once."

"That's right." I peered over her shoulder and thought about what my eyes were doing. "I guess you look at the target, then bring the front sight in line with it, and then the rear sight, and then squeeze the trigger." She did, and the hammer clicked down.

"I didn't 'squeeze' it. I just pulled it."

"Yeah, and the nose went up a little. But you're just trying to hit the wall. Do it again?"

This time she held it level and the nose stayed down when it snapped.

"I never used one in combat," I said. "The Glock, we had one day of disassembly and cleaning, and a half day on the range, mostly safety procedures. I was never really issued one." I did carry an automatic for a week, when I was TDY'ed to Shiraz, but I was advised to keep it inside the shrink-wrap so I wouldn't have to clean it. Not exactly hardcore.

"Well, you're a boy; you have it in your blood."

"You never played with cap guns as a kid?"

She laughed and it felt good on my chest. "Mom would have a heart attack."

"With dear old Dad a soldier?"

"Especially." She raised the back of my hand to her lips and kissed it. "He's so jealous of you."

"Getting shot. He can have it."

"You know what I mean." She set the gun down on top of the TV and rotated inside my arms. Her voice was muffled in my shoulder. "Is it true you soldiers are really good lovers?"

"I think you mean bicycle riders." She smelled so good. "Soldiers can get it in the hole they're aiming at, usually. Bike riders know to hug the curves, though."

"Idiot," she said, and pulled down my shorts.

3.

The road made us go northward for a couple of hours, which annoyed me in an obscure way. If we just wanted to go to Key West, we could've flown, or even hopped a train in New Orleans. False names, tickets bought with cash; in one day we'd be off the grid and almost off the map. But we'd also be, to complete the trio of clichés, at the end of the line. And not that hard to trace.

If they did follow us to Key West, we'd be cornered. Just as true with bicycles as a train or plane, but maybe after that much pedaling, we'd be in good enough shape to dive in and swim for Cuba.

I hadn't been to Key West since I was a little boy, but from what I heard it sounded like a good place to drop out of sight. Like New Orleans, it had lots of off-the-grid work for low pay, though in fact we did have enough cash to live on for a few months, a year if we were parsimonious. Best to find a little room and disappear into it. I could write well that way, I thought, and Kit was content to read and draw.

Give "the Enemy" time to lose interest in me. We started calling them that. Sometimes you could hear the capital E in both our voices.

Agent Underwood hadn't called. Just before noon, I called her number; someone said she was out of the office and would call tomorrow morning. That was okay by me. I can handle truck traffic, and I can handle spies, but I'd just as soon not do both simultaneously.

After a day of pretty serious riding we were dead tired. We took a couple of McDeathburgers to the Holiday Inn and almost fell asleep during the thrill of eating them. I slept ten hours, about four more than usual, and woke feeling like I'd come in second best in a bar fight. Some hard roads, and I'd been off the bike for a couple of weeks.

Holiday Inn coffee is nontoxic and the machine was quiet enough not to wake Kit. In the pool of light from the desk lamp I made a list of the facts we knew about the Enemy, and the assumptions we held. Sometimes the distinction between fact and conjecture was not clear.

1. They were not "the government" in any conventional sense. Sara Underwood would have acted differently if she worked with the Enemy. (Maybe some sinister cabal of meta-spies like in the movies. Not likely.)

2. They nevertheless seemed to have resources comparable to a government agency's. But Kit pointed out that this might not be true if, for whatever reason, I was their only project. If you really wanted to fuck with one person's mind this way, it wouldn't even be a full-time job.

3. This raised the interesting possibility that I might be somebody's hobby. An agent like Blackstone could be a one-man

"Let's drive Jack Daley insane" club, working a couple of hours a week. But why would he?

4. There might be an army connection. They had easy access to my records, and of course had plenty of M2010s lying around.

5. They were watching us—and not being obvious about it. We'd been on the lookout since Iowa City, often on deserted back roads, and hadn't seen anything.

6. It seemed likely they could track me from a distance. Maybe a tracer implanted when I had surgery in Germany.

7. They were serious enough to kill a federal agent. They used a rifle like mine, possibly. Setup or coincidence? An unrelated murder? Sure, there are snipers everywhere.

But it all pointed back to the big question: Why me? There were probably a hundred thousand people who could shoot a rifle as well as I can. A small fraction of them would probably shoot a stranger just for the thrill, or for the hell of it, let alone for a roll of G-notes. (Thriller writers sometimes assumed there were people on the government payroll who would do this sort of thing, but I always doubted they could keep it secret. A civil servant whose morals allowed him to murder on assignment could also be bought by a tell-all journalist.)

When Kit got up she read over the list. "Number 6, the implant. I guess we'll find out about that. If they show up now, they must be physically tracking you."

I thought for a second, and agreed. "In a city, even New Orleans, we'd be on security cameras enough for them to follow us by face recognition software. They caught those spies that way in Chicago." It had been fodder for a lot of *Big Brother Is Watching You* editorializing. The Ramirez couple had even had cosmetic surgery, but it didn't fool the software. They should've left the city instead.

Florida would be safe from that. Their courts had followed North Dakota's lead, and declared the ubiquitous camera network an unreasonable invasion of privacy.

"But New Orleans is still bothering me," I said. "Suppose that *is* why the cops picked me up—computer sorting of routine security images. That's not the real mystery—I mean, hell, we were on the run. Using false identities, working for cash. They might have picked me up on general principles."

She nodded. "And so?"

"So the real mystery is not why they picked me up, but why they let me go! The cops talked to someone back at the station, on the car radio, and immediately pulled over and uncuffed me and let me go. What did someone, headquarters, say to them?"

"Maybe that what they were doing was illegal. They can't just grab someone off the street."

"Yeah, but they *can*, if you're a criminal. They definitely were sent to pick me up, or us. I didn't think fast enough. I should've asked to see a warrant or something."

"They'd just invoke Homeland Security."

"But how could they? Homeland Security didn't know where we were! I hadn't talked to the DHS woman for two minutes before the god-damned cops showed up!" Though maybe two minutes would be enough, if we were on the right list.

She got up and split the remaining coffee between us. "Maybe it was somebody else in the DHS. They're not just one woman with a phone up in Illinois."

"Yeah, and it may not have been Homeland Security business at all. Maybe the guy who sold me the gun ratted on me."

"Yeah," she said, glowering theatrically. "Ya shoulda plugged the sumbitch."

"Next time, Muggsy." We both laughed.

4.

We dozed till noon and then picked up a cheap cell at a convenience store next to the motel, just to make two calls. Didn't want our families to worry enough to call the authorities—all we needed was state troopers from Iowa to Mississippi sharing their databases, looking for us as missing persons.

From researching my first novel I knew how to engage a proxy cell host, to make it look like we were calling from New Orleans. It wouldn't fool a government agency—or the Enemy, presumably—but it would cover our tracks on the domestic front.

Dad wasn't home, so I left a message saying Kit and I were leaving the New Orleans heat on a road trip up to New England. Kit's father answered and she improvised a little, saying that we'd probably visit an uncle up in Maine, verifying his address. Didn't know when we'd get there; she'd be in touch.

I checked my e-mail one last time and there was a note from my agent saying hey, no big rush, but Duquest wants to know how the monster story is coming along.

"Let's get into Mississippi," I said. "Find a place in the middle of nowhere and stay for at least a day. I'll write up another little chapter."

"And maybe print it out?" she said.

"Yeah, if we find a place." I was getting nervous, too, not having a paper copy. I did e-mail the manuscript to myself every couple of days, but the dime store computer's word-processing program was Neolithic and had a small mind of its own. I eased the thing shut and for about the thousandth time regretted not spending a few bucks more, for a machine that could talk to a thumb drive or something.

I'd mailed a paper copy home when we first got to New Orleans, but I was at least thirty pages past that now, and had made changes in the earlier chapters as well.

"Should you call the Underwood woman or somebody?"

I wasn't sure. "Maybe not. Let's see what happens if we don't make it easy for them. But maybe . . ."

"Maybe what?"

I opened the phone and contemplated it. "We've got nine thousand some dollars. Enough to go maybe nine months?"

"I think so," she said, "living simply, under the grid. With no emergencies."

"Still not enough. Let me call my agent, see if she can wire us another ten grand or so."

She was with another client, but called back in a couple of minutes. I told her I was in a real jam, a legal problem I was advised not to tell anybody about.

"Ten grand?" she said. "Jack, if I had ten thousand dollars to spare it would go to the rent on this god-damn place. I'm way overextended."

"It's really serious."

"Life or death?"

"I think it could get there."

"Want me to try your movie guy, Ronald Duquest? He's got millions, and I can pretend he owes me a favor." I said sure.

Hooray for Hollywood. Duquest told her he'd consider it an additional advance against the movie rights—pretty generous, considering that ten grand was all he'd actually paid anyhow. He took a penny away for some IRS thing, and deposited $9,999.99 in my PayPal account.

I couldn't exactly shake the computer until the cash came out, but it would stay there until we needed it. Once in Key West, I could use nested firewall proxies and retrieve at least 80 percent of it without leaving any trail.

Outside the motel room I gleefully stomped the cheap phone and bundled its mortal remains with our trash and tossed it in the parking lot dumpster. Pure paranoia. There was no way the Enemy could have put a tap on a random phone from a convenience store—but could our benevolent government? Every phone in every cheesy little store? Could the Enemy know everything the government did?

I could worry about it or I could get a new phone next week.

CHAPTER ELEVEN

Hunter slept for twenty hours and awoke around midnight, pale lunar light filtering through drapes. The warm trailer still had a stale smell of roasting meat. Sharp sweat tang.

He had a painful small erection, which he couldn't see over the mound of his belly. He pulled on it until it emptied, and lay thinking, calculating.

There was enough meat in the freezer for about ten days of his normal diet. Two weeks if he stretched it, but he knew if he got too hungry he might do careless things.

The woman's purse held enough money for months of food, five or six sides of beef. The idea of nonhuman meat turned his stomach now, but when he was hungry enough he would eat anything. Anything animal. The closest he could come to a vegetarian diet would be eating vegetarians.

Which he had probably done. Not Ms. Cooper. Out of curiosity he had squeezed out the contents of her large intestine, and could see that she had been a meat-eater. Too little fiber in her diet. It would have killed her one day, much more slowly.

What had he lived on before he came to Earth? His dentition was similar to a human's, though presumably a dentist could tell he was different. He could crack bones with his molars, and his jaws were strong enough to tear apart humans and other animals. Clothing was sometimes too durable; he could break a tooth on a zipper or bra clasp. Though it was peculiarly satisfying to tear into people through their clothing, and it made the remains look more like an animal attack.

But his little talks with them were probably more interesting when they were naked. They were more frightened, which made them taste better. He knew the Chinese would beat dogs before they butchered them, partly to tenderize the muscle, but also for the endocrine tang of fear. When he had taken humans by surprise, killed them without warning, their flesh had been relatively bland. Much better to play with them for a while, and let ductless glands work their magic. The taste of hope, and the loss of hope.

Thinking made him hungry. In the back of the refrigerator he had a pair of hands in a large jar of dill pickle juice. He fished one out and had it with bread and butter, gnawing around the small female bones. Then he threw the bones into the stockpot simmering on the stove.

That pot had enough evidence to hang him four times over, in this state. He would ask that they do it without the hood. He wanted to see their faces when he plunged through the trapdoor and hung there alive, smiling, at the end of the tether.

He grinned and picked bits of Ms. Cooper from between his teeth.

5.

Kit quietly closed the top of the computer. "Maybe let's not have breakfast."

"Oh, come on. It's not that bad."

"Okay. Just don't order a hand sandwich."

"Or finger food?"

"Seriously . . . don't tell me that scene's going to be in the movie."

"I guess not," I admitted. "Wrong genre. No chainsaws or goalie masks. But the book has to go a little further than the movie."

"So what does he eat in the movie?"

"Well . . . that particular scene isn't in it. Later on, he ladles a spoonful of broth and sips it."

She smiled. "That's a distinction. You're grosser than Ron Duquest."

I shrugged. "Different medium. Besides, you want to be over the top on the first draft. Easier to cut stuff than to add it."

She nodded microscopically, not looking at me. "Yeah, you explained that."

Storm signals. "It bothers you that I would even think of such horrible things."

She didn't say anything for a couple of seconds, lower lip between her teeth. "Really, it's all right. You've seen worse, I keep forgetting."

I tried not to think of yards of intestine unspooled across a dusty road, the owner festering in a ditch, arms wide in dumb supplication. Why was that so close to the surface?

She put her hand over mine. "If you want to talk about it, we could."

Actually, we couldn't. There was no vocabulary. Smell, heat, pain, always the edge of nausea. Just the smell of diesel exhaust made me clench my teeth. The somatic memory of it back behind the sinuses, shit burning in diesel, rot, the buzz of fat flies. Mud spatter, blood soaking desert sand. The guy had looked like a Matthew Brady daguerreotype, mouth open in dark bloated features. The second dead man I had seen, but the first had only been a dusty bundle.

"Honey? You want to lie down?"

Actually, I wanted a drink. But maybe I'd better not say that. "Naw. Get some chow."

She smiled. "Okay, soldier. Make a mile first?"

"Check the map." I unfolded it and found our motel. There was the Burger King across the way, but nothing else on the map for about twenty miles. "Let's see what they've got across the street."

"If it's hands, we go someplace else."

"Deal." We rolled up yesterday's clothes and repacked the bikes in about a minute. The air was cool and clean, and if it had been just me I would have gone on down the road. But if she doesn't have breakfast she turns into something dangerous, so we crossed to the Monarch of Mediocrity.

In truth, Burger King wasn't half as bad as McDonald's. I got three little hamburgers and fries while she had some egg thing. On impulse I asked for a salad. The high-school girl behind the counter acted like I had asked for a human hand. *Would you like guts with that?* She wrinkled her nose and said it was breakfast time. Hamburgers, sure. Salad, no.

There's something weirdly satisfying about hamburgers for breakfast. Some would disagree. Kit made a face when I squirted mustard and catsup on them. "Caveman," she said.

"Og like meat. Meat with blood and the yellow stuff."

"Your internal clock is off. Hamburgers and fries?"

"I suppose." Actually, she knew I didn't like regular breakfasts unless I fixed them myself. Eggs completely dead, no evidence of their actual origin . . . which isn't all that appetizing, if you think about it. Og not eat that. It come from bird's asshole. Cloaca. Same difference. An asshole by any other name, the poet said, would smell just as sweet.

The sun was still low behind us when we took off down the service road that paralleled 90. Not much traffic, no wind or weather. It would be a great vacation if we were on vacation. Riding alongside quiet bayous, wading birds oblivious to us, stalking breakfast.

But I couldn't not think.

How deep shit were we in, and with whom?

Besides the Enemy, we were in at least shallow shit with the forces for good in the universe, Agent Underwood and her ilk. Presumably they would understand why we had dropped out of sight.

Kit was reading my mind. "Should we let somebody know where we are?"

"Maybe. Who would be safe?"

"God knows. If they're tapping phones, they probably have our parents covered, and your agent. But you say they can't tap a random phone from the 7-Eleven?"

"No way. Not unless they had possession of it first, got at its software."

"So why did you destroy that one this morning?"

"Just caution." I was on shaky ground—I'd researched it for *High Kill*, but that was four or five years ago. "They couldn't tap the phone, but maybe they could track it. Given the information they could pick up from our parents' phones."

"Think so?"

"Well . . . at the very least, they could call us back and as soon as we answer, they know where we are." Or where the nearest booster antenna is? "Wish I'd taken some engineering courses."

"Me, too," she said. "Amazing how little help quantum electrodynamics is in real life."

We switched places; my turn to lead. I preferred following, since all I had to do then was keep an eye out for her and drop back when she came into view. I was a stronger cyclist, so if I was in front I tended to pull away steadily, especially if there were hills—power up and streak down. On the level like this, I had to keep an eye on the speedometer, keep it below thirteen or fourteen miles per hour.

If it were only about logic, it would be sensible for her to lead all the time. We found out in a couple of hours that that didn't work; she pushed herself, trying to stay in my comfort range, and was dead tired by noon. Whether that was competitive or accommodating, I wasn't sure.

It bothered me a little that she was upset by the direction the novel was taking. I wanted to stick to my guns, though. The first stuff I really loved reading was the horror fiction of the late twentieth, early twenty-first century—Stephen King and Peter Straub and those guys. Though it started with Poe, which must often be the case—books your parents let you read because they were in somebody's canon, even if they were more dire in their own way than horror movies or slasher comix.

When I was in grade school I read to the other kids on weekends and in the summer. There was a construction site at the end of my road; when the workers weren't there we'd crouch in the shadows with a candle and stolen matches, and I would intone Poe in the spookiest voice my short unformed vocal cords could manage. *For the love of God, Montressor!* In a squeaky voice.

I hadn't thought about that in years. How much different is what I do now? The stories aren't spooky, I suppose, except when they are.

If I'd known then that I was going to be a soldier, killing people and getting shot myself, I would have been thrilled. *And then you're going to spend the rest of your life in a small room pecking away at a keyboard. No, Montressor! For the love of God, no!*

One of the guys in our outfit—I don't remember his real name; his radio handle was Hotshot—he was going into the private sector after he separated, hiring out as a mercenary soldier. They were getting about triple our pay, doing stuff that looked less dangerous.

Still, we all agreed that he was fucking crazy. He laughed and agreed, too. But you could tell he really loved the work. His eyes actually gleamed; he smiled when other people looked grim. Loved guns and grenades—and guys, you had to suppose. In a thoroughly manly way.

Though that must be cyclic. One thing Grand-dude despised about the army in his day was the aggressive locker-room masculinity of it. Brutal hazing for anybody who was quiet or intellectual. I guess we had some of that; I took some ribbing for always carrying a book everywhere in Basic and AIT. But in actual combat all of the men were more quiet.

More serious and introspective. Repeated exposure to death and suffering plays hell with your sense of humor. Or tilts it in a gallows direction, anyhow. Like putting a lit cigarette in the ruined face of a napalm victim, between his bright teeth. We laughed so hard we almost shit. But I guess you had to be there. It's not so funny in the recollection.

Cyclic, cultural. When I taught the short workshop in Iowa, none of the kids had heard of the Grand Guignol. But then when I was their age, the image of an audience laughing at nipples being cut off with lawn shears was pretty extreme. They probably do it on soaps now.

Before I finish the book I should spend a couple of days watching daytime television. Kit is shocked by the things that go through Hunter's mind, and life. But she's no more mainstream than I am. Maybe they're eating babies on prime time now.

To thine own self be true. I'd read *Hamlet* on my own before we got to it in school, and I Magic Markered that line. Embarrassing to find out that Polonius is a fathead, and the profound observation was a laugh-line to the Elizabethan groundlings. *And it must follow, as night the day, thou canst not then be false to any man.* So if you're a fathead, and are true to yourself, you say fatuous things. *Quod erat demonstratum,* we may have learned the same day.

"A penny for your thoughts." Kit had pulled up alongside of me.

"Polonius," I said.

"I've got to pee-lonius. Next billboard?"

No shops or gas stations for miles. "Sure."

The next billboard was a weathered relic that some anti-abortion group had stopped paying for. A faded fetus claiming that it had a heartbeat at two weeks. Was that true?

The unpainted latticework that formed the base of the sign didn't really offer more than symbolic privacy. She took the small roll of toilet paper and went behind it. I turned my back to her and watched the road.

A big black SUV slowed as it approached. The passenger window rolled down and a man pointed out a camera with a fat lens. They passed close enough for me to hear the shutter go chop-chop-chop three times, like a newsie covering a game or a speech. "Pervert," I said.

He lowered the camera and smiled.

It wasn't a leer. It was a smile of quiet satisfaction. Did I recognize the face? Fat white guy with a dark tan and a shock of white hair. White moustache.

The license plate number was partly hidden behind a crust of mud. But it hadn't rained in weeks. They rolled to a stop about two hundred yards away.

"Shit," I said, and unzipped the handlebar bag.

"What's he doing?" Kit said.

"I don't know. Get down flat." I let the bike go, dropped to one knee, and tried to get a sight picture with the stubby revolver. I'd be lucky to hit the car, let alone something the size of a human. I pulled back on the hammer, unnecessarily, and it clicked like a quiet door latch, cocking.

The passenger door opened slightly. I held my breath and squeezed the trigger.

The flat *bang* was louder than I'd expected. If the bullet hit the car, it wasn't obvious. The door opened more and then slammed shut, and the tires squealed as the car peeled away. I kept the sight picture but didn't fire again.

"My god," she said. "My god."

I was busy keeping my asshole tight, and didn't say anything. This was too much like reality. I willed my trigger finger to relax. But I kept the sight picture until the car went over a rise and disappeared.

"Jesus," she said. "Did you have to do that?"

"I don't know. If I did have to, it might have saved our lives." I clicked the cylinder around so the firing pin rested on the empty shell. "If not, I guess we'll be talking to the cops pretty soon."

I could hear her pulling up her Lycra shorts. "That's not something I ever looked forward to before."

I picked up my bike and put the revolver back in the handlebar bag, but didn't zip it shut. I studied the map carrier. "Nine or ten miles to the next town. Or should we head back to New Orleans?"

She had picked up her bike and was adjusting her helmet. "Nearest phone. You ought to call Underwood."

"I guess." Where had I seen that face behind the lens? Could it have been Springfield? "Did you see the guy?"

"With the camera? Kind of."

"Look familiar to you?"

She paused. "Just from old movies. A bad guy."

"Yeah, the enemy spy in James Bond. But somebody real, maybe in New Orleans?"

"I don't know. I must've had ten thousand customers at Mario's. Maybe a thousand had white hair and tans."

My ears were still ringing from the gunshot. Hands shook and my chest was so tight I could hardly breathe. "I shouldn't've stomped the phone."

"As it turns out, no. But how do you think they found us? If it *was* them."

"Who else would it be?"

"Ja-ack . . . I had my bare ass out there in the sunshine. You see it every day, but to some other man it might be worth a picture."

"All right," I said lamely, "but someone who had a fancy big-lens

DSLR sitting there ready to go? 'Maybe I'll see a pretty ass to shoot'? I don't think so."

"Okay. But then why *didn't* they shoot? I mean with a gun. If they were the bad guys?"

"I don't think that's part of the plan. They've had all kinds of chances, if they wanted me dead." I clenched the handlebar to stop my hands from shaking. "Probably didn't even have a gun in the car, if they were smart."

She didn't say anything. I turned and saw that she was crying silently. Dropped the bike and went to hold her. Awkward, with her bike still leaning against her hip. She let it fall away and wrapped her arms around me. "I'm sorry," she said.

"Nothing to be sorry for." My mind spun out of control. If I'd only had a camera, instead of a gun. A phone with a camera, like normal people. Or both phone and gun; aim both at the same time? Click, bang, click, bang. How the fuck did they find us on a back road in Mississippi, and was anyplace on the planet safe? Hell, if Iowa isn't safe, where would be?

"You know what you told me about racing cars?" she murmured into my shoulder.

"Racing cars?"

"You said if you're in a race and the car in front of you gets into trouble, you aim for him. Because he's liable to go anyplace but straight ahead."

"That's right."

She rubbed her face against my shirt and I could feel the tears. "So we should just keep on. Go the direction they went."

"What if they double back?"

She looked up at me with bright eyes. "Then shoot the one with the camera."

6.

We went eighteen map miles down that little road, peanut farms alternating with acres of weeds and spindly trash trees. The motel that was supposed to be at the eighteen-mile mark was a weedy burned ruin with the words "Ffriendly Ffolkes" fading under broken neon tubes. British orthography or Americans trying to be classy? But it was only another four or five miles to a Comfort Inn.

Traveling by car, you can afford to have contempt for chain motels. But when every mile is forty-eight calories, they look pretty good.

There hadn't been much traffic, not even one car a minute. No black SUVs with bullet holes.

The next motel was still standing, but ramshackle. "Try this one?"

"Anyplace with a bed," she said. Her color wasn't good, cheeks pale and forehead flushed, and she was breathing a little too hard. "Let's get these bikes out of sight."

The black woman behind the desk was huge and suspicious-looking. "Where's y'all's car?"

"We're on bikes," Kit said, convincingly clad in bright Lycra and sweat.

"Sure you are." When I said we'd pay in cash, she nodded with grim satisfaction and handed me a corroded brass key on a plastic tag that might once have borne a number. "You go to Room 14."

The room had a single low-watt bulb in the ceiling and a TV set that hissed and had no picture. Lots of roach tabs in the bathroom and closet, but no actual bugs. It smelled stale, but there are worse smells.

The drapes were stuck in blackout position. We got a slight breeze going through, with the front door and bathroom window open. The other windows were glued-shut plastic.

The fat lady directed me up to Bradley Road, where there was a mom-and-pop store and a porch where some old characters sat to drink beer and stare at alien invaders on bicycles. I got us a four-pack of tall cold no-name beers and some cheese crackers and a strip of what claimed to be alligator jerky.

Whatever the jerky was made of, it had a soporific effect. Or maybe it was the beer. Or maybe Jane Austen; the five-and-dime notebook had a few freebie book files, and I read about three pages of *Pride and Prejudice*. Kit was snoring by then, and I joined her.

I woke up about three, restless, mind racing. The hot water from the tap made something like coffee. Back to Hunter's world.

CHAPTER TWELVE

He had thought they were closing in on him. Twice yesterday morning he had seen unmarked police cars cruise by with men listening through headphones. A good thing his captive was gagged.

But nothing for more than twenty-four hours now. If they had brought in dogs it would not take very long, with all the buried bones around. Dogs would like that. But they didn't have them, he supposed. Not a rich county.

If it did come to that, he could move into another level of discourse. He could try to negotiate with them, essentially with a knife to her throat. Inviting a simple head shot from a police sniper.

Or he could cut her up and scatter pieces of her through the woods, hoping to distract them from his avenue of escape by repugnant over-kill. Of course that might make it harder on him if they caught him—or maybe not. If you're brutal enough, they call you insane, and treat you as if you were handicapped. Though it is they who are handicapped, by timidity.

He approached the trailer in a large circle, checking seven suspended threads that crossed every route to the place. He retrieved his shotgun from the bushes and entered the trailer silently without turning on the light. He listened in the darkness to her irregular breathing. Drank in her smell. Then he pulled down the bandana that gagged her.

"Can we talk?" she said to the darkness.

He eased the safety off, and the small click was loud.

"If you're trying to scare me, you've succeeded." Her tone of voice had told him that. He aimed the shotgun at her voice and touched the light switch.

"So that's what you look like." He had grabbed her from her tent in the darkness and tied her up in the trailer without light. "You . . . you're even bigger than I thought."

"Uglier," he growled, the first word he had spoken in weeks.

"Are you the one they're looking for?"

He shrugged and stepped closer to her. Her breath was mint-sweet. His made her flinch away. "I'm sorry," he said. "I didn't cook the last thing I ate. It had been on the road for a while."

She coughed. "I'll do . . . whatever you want. Really." She took a breath and straightened up her well-toned body. "Anything."

"You wouldn't say that if you could see into my mind. Do you think there is nothing worse than death?"

She shook her head slowly.

He wiped his lips with the back of his hand. "What do you think you know about me? If I am the beast that has been on the news?" He smiled, showing too many teeth. "I am a beast, as they say. Not human."

"So they say." Her breath caught. "Of course we are all animals."

"Not in the sense that I am one. I really am *not human*. I don't even come from Earth."

After a pause she said, "So what planet are you from?"—as if that were an ordinary question.

"I don't know. It was a long time ago. I have memory issues." He studied his long blunt nails as if the answer might be there. "Thousands of years of memory issues." His eyes came up. "You think I'm crazy."

Her voice shook a little. "On the news they say you are." She tried to stare back at him but looked away.

"Now you're going to tell me that someone is looking for you. If I let you go, they will be easy on me."

"That could be true," she said quietly, looking at the floor.

"Not quite lying. I like that." He went to a window and peeked through the blinds. "Would you like to offer your body to me?"

"It's yours, of course. But you don't seem to want it."

"What if I wanted you from behind? Rough."

"That would . . . be all right. I've—"

"From the front?" He took a clasp knife from a deep pocket and shook it open with a snap. The blade was a dagger about eight inches long. "I mean the abdomen, as usual. Have you read about that?"

She shook her head in jerks, staring at the blade.

"Most newspapers haven't printed that. The fact is, not being a man, I have no particular interest in vaginas." He sat down on a barstool. "They look like a wound to me, even when they're not bleeding. I prefer to make my own wounds."

She started to say something, but just swallowed.

"I enjoy it that you're scared, as you may know. You will live a little longer for that."

"But not very long?"

"No." He tested the blade with his thumb. "Would you like for me to be kind, and end it quickly?"

"I want to live."

He smiled condescendingly. "I have a news flash for you: The universe doesn't care. Neither do I. But even if you were to survive this . . . little meeting, you would die very soon. A half century? That's nothing to me."

"How . . . how old are you?"

"I remember Pompeii. And a flood before that. I may be immortal."

"Or insane," she whispered.

He nodded. "Or insane. Maybe both." He picked up a sharpening stone, and drew the blade over it slowly. "Maybe I *was* sane, a couple of thousand years ago. And it wore off."

7.

There was a light on in the motel office, so I went in and printed out the chapter while a black kid about high-school age watched me. Making conversation, I explained about what a pain it was to try to do work on this dime store computer, not being able to just push a button and send it to my agent. He understood, and volunteered that they had a scanner, if I'd like to make an electronic copy and send it.

It felt kind of funny, switching between the twentieth and twenty-first centuries. I sent copies to myself and my agent, as well as Duquest.

Perversely, writing the nightmarish chapter helped me get to sleep. And when dawn showed through the drapes, Kit kissed me awake and slowly had her way with me, a quiet and dreamy kind of sex.

There was a message slipped under the door, evidently printed on the office computer:

RONALD DUQUEST

HOLLYWOOD

If you got this you know my number

This is fucking fantastic. Keep the girl alive, stretch it out, like the old Silence of the Lambs *. . . maybe a POV shift with some cops who can't figure out the craziness. You got a fucking movie here, man.*

It might be real money. I'll talk to some people.

rd

We took showers, laughing and chatting over the noise. Celebrate our good fortune and go back up to Bradley Road for breakfast.

But when I braced the door open and started maneuvering the bikes out, a kid, younger than the one who'd helped me, opened the office door and jogged over.

"Mister . . . guy said not to wake you up, but give this to you 'fore you leave." He handed me a heavy padded mailing envelope with no address. On the back of it, a crayon scrawl in green block letters: SOME-ONE THOT YOU SHD HAVE MORE FUN.

We went back inside and sat on the bed.

I tore open the envelope, causing a blizzard of gray shreds. There was a thick hardcover book inside—Dexter Filkins's old history of the Gulf War—but most of the text was missing. Someone had hollowed out a large enough volume for two thick packages of hundred-dollar bills, banded $25,000 each, and one big bullet heat-sealed into a plastic bag.

And the key to room 15, next door, and a car key.

We stepped around the bikes and opened the door to 15. On the bed, no surprise, a long rectangular box.

"He was in here," the boy said from behind us, "the one who give me the envelope. Musta left before the sun come up. Left his car, too."

"What kind of man was he?"

"Old guy."

"Old like me?"

"No . . . way old. Old white guy with a white 'stash."

I picked up one end of the box and let it fall, heavy. "What exactly did he say?"

"He say give you the thing."

"Nothing else?"

"Huh–uh. He don't say *nothin'*!"

"Come on. What did he say?"

"Nothin'!" The kid bolted. I got to the door just in time to see him run behind the motel.

"Did he threaten you?" Kit called out. "We could help." We could hear him crashing through the woods in back.

"Sure we could." I sat back down on the bed and tried to open the tough plastic bag. Finally punched a hole through it with the door key and widened the hole enough to get the bullet out.

"What is it?" It was heavier than a normal cartridge and had a small crystal lens on its tip.

"Smart round," I said. "Like a little guided missile. You fire it at the target and little fins snap out for steering. Self-propelled, slow." I pointed at the tip, painted light red. "It's an incendiary, for good measure. I'm supposed to shoot some poor dick with this and hope the ensuing fire will dispose of the evidence?"

"Or cause confusion," she said. "Would it be a big fire?"

"Don't know; I never used one except on the range. It doesn't look like it could be a big fire, unless you hit a gas tank or something." I turned it around in my hand, looking for clues. "Of course the red paint doesn't really mean anything; they could paint it baby blue if they wanted."

"Does it shoot like a regular bullet?"

"Yes and no." I opened the end of the cardboard box and slid out yet another M2010. This was a civilian one, the Remington Model 700, with a heavy blond wooden stock sporting expensive grain, and a big heavy finderscope. I eased the bolt back slightly; it wasn't loaded.

I pushed a tab on the side and a three-by-three-inch screen popped out beside the fat Leupold finderscope. It had a blurry picture with bright crosshairs and a faint bull's-eye. Hadn't seen one since the desert.

"Watch this." I slipped the cartridge into the receiver and pointed the rifle out the door; the picture on the screen snapped into focus, a bright picture inside a dark circle, like looking through a keyhole. The parking lot.

"So it shows where the bullet is going?"

"Exactly." I set it down and reached inside the carton. Taped into a square of Bubble Wrap, a little box with a joystick. "That's weird."

"How so?"

I set it down carefully. "I did spend a week training with things like this. But that was like ten years ago, twelve. They expect me to squeeze the trigger and then guide this thing into a target, with no practice? I couldn't do it even if I wanted to, not with any certainty."

She picked it up and studied it. "Maybe they don't know that? They seem to think you're one of the people you write about."

Odd but true. Maybe there were people with the combination of power and ignorance required for that kind of mistaken identity. The only thing I was sure of, though, was the ignorance on our side. "Let's think. We should just go to the cops. Homeland Security."

"Where they'd have your file open on the desk before you sit down."

"Granted. But the Enemy has way upped the ante now. Or again, rather. And I still haven't broken any law."

I eased the cartridge out and held it in my hand. "You can't buy this shit in a store, not anywhere. I don't think they let hunters take deer with incendiaries—Smokey the Bear and all. It's a plain terror weapon." The weight of it was both repellent and fascinating. In training we had fired off a box of these, one for each of us, aiming at old paint cans, each with a spoonful of gasoline inside. Boom, fireball. Better than winning a Kewpie doll.

"Pretty expensive?"

I nodded. "The sergeant made a point of that. The round was worth more to the United States Army than we were. So aim. Or you might have to be the target next week."

"They wouldn't do that." She was serious.

"Not really, no. You weren't disposable till you were overseas." I hefted the rifle. "This thing is *heavy*. I guess it's a match model, for accuracy. Deepens the mystery."

"How so?"

"It's wasted on me, really. I'm a pretty good shot, but I was far from the best in my platoon, even my squad. The army's full of people who could shoot one round from a sniper rifle like this and shave a hair off a fly's ass."

"None of whom wrote a novel about a sniper."

"More's the pity." I aimed it out the door. The scope really was beautiful, a hard bright image with no color fringe. I could spin the power up to 40X, but without support the image danced around like crazy; I couldn't even tell what I was looking at.

"Can I try it?"

"Sure." I spun the power all the way down and automatically made sure the safety was locked, not just "on." Product of a thousand spot inspections.

She put it to her shoulder and pointed into the parking lot, the muzzle waving around in a sloppy orbit. She craned her neck, peering into the scope. "Don't see anything."

"Your eye's too close. Back off to a natural distance."

"Like this?" She leaned back too far.

"No—" I reached toward her and the room suddenly darkened as a huge form blocked off the light.

"What you all—" the big black woman said, and then screamed, and backed away so fast she tripped into the parking lot and fell hard onto her back.

I ran out to help, and Kit was right behind me, still holding the rifle. The woman's eyes were open, showing mostly whites. I couldn't feel a pulse in her neck, but her wrist had a slight one. "She's alive."

"Call 9-1-1?"

"No! Jesus!" I looked wildly around; there didn't seem to be any eyewitnesses. "Leave the bikes. Get in the car and get the fuck out of here."

"But . . ." She looked as helpless as I felt.

"I know. Let's carry her in onto the bed and go!" She put the rifle down and took one arm. I took the other and we dragged the woman in through the door.

No question of lifting her dead weight onto the bed. I scooped up the book with all the hundreds. The loose high-tech round, the joystick. Picked up the rifle off the sidewalk.

"Maybe we should leave all that stuff behind?"

"No, maybe we'll ditch it someplace else. Let's just get outta here!"

We threw everything into the car and it started right up. I backed out carefully and turned it around.

In the distance, sirens.

"Fuck it!" I floored it and fishtailed out of the gravel lot onto the two-lane road.

"Don't!" she said.

"'Course." I took my foot off the gas and pulled over, reaching for my wallet. "'I wasn't running from the body, officer. Just the FBI and DHS.'"

Two Highway Patrol squad cars bore down on us, sirens screaming, blue lights flashing. They went right past the motel without slowing down. I clenched the wheel and watched them close in—and then pass us, engines roaring flat out.

We looked at each other. "So what was that all about?" she said. "We must not be the only criminals in Mississippi."

"At least they're not after this car." I put it in gear but sat for a moment. "We really ought to . . ."

"Yeah. She could be really hurt."

"We should check." Still I hesitated. "Hell. 'Avoid the appearance of wrongdoing.'" I did a slow U-turn and went back to the motel parking lot. The door to the room was still ajar.

She was still where we had left her, but her eyes were closed now. Still a pulse in her wrist. Her name tag said "Mary Taylor," and tasked her with Customer Relations. And everything else, I supposed.

"Mary?" I said. "Miz Taylor?"

I put my hand behind her head and raised it slightly. There was a little blood in her hair. Her lids fluttered.

"You fell and hit your head," I said, which was true.

"I was . . . you was . . ."

"You slipped on the gravel," Kit said.

She stared at Kit. "You had a gun."

"Hunting rifle," I said. "She was just checking the sights when . . . you came to the door."

"What you suppose to be huntin', this time of year?"

"Nothing yet. It was a present."

She rolled over onto an elbow and touched the back of her head gingerly. "Don't like guns."

"Me neither," Kit said emphatically.

The woman fixed me with a baleful stare. "This present. The man give it to you, why he didn't just knock on your door?"

"My uncle Johnny," I improvised, "he's kind of crazy. I mean, he's always doing stuff like this, elaborate pranks."

"With a gun? Sure." She sat up with surprising grace, and a groan. "Your Johnny, he give my boy a twenty-dollar bill to tell you look in that room. That's some uncle."

"Yeah. He's crazy."

"You wouldn't mind if I called the police." She said *po*-leese, mocking her own accent.

I might have paused too long. "Do what you want."

"Let me put it some different way. Would it be worth a hundred dollars to you fo' me not to call the police?"

"I suppose it would."

"Uh-huh. Then I suppose it might be worth a thousand."

"No way."

She rocked a little bit, thinking. "How 'bout for five hundred bucks I let you tear that page out of the logbook, and I never seen you, neither of you."

"I can't believe this," I said to Kit. "Bargaining with a woman we came back to—"

"You best believe it," the woman said. "I do appreciate you coming back, but get real. You got money and I ain't. You on the wrong side of the law, and I got a cell phone. You want that page for five hundred dollars?"

"We're not criminals," Kit said.

"I know you ain't that kind. If I thought you'd do me harm I'd be hiding."

"So you're just trying to make an honest buck," I said.

"Dishonest buck," she conceded. "You got a lot more than five hundred dollars, and I got a lot less."

"Okay," I said, "but you have to throw in the cell phone."

She nodded. "Six hundred, then." She unclipped the cell phone from her belt holder and handed it to me. Just a symbolic gesture, but I took it.

"Why don't you put the bikes in the car," Kit said, turning her back to count out bills from a banded stack. "I'll take care of the logbook."

"Okay." It wasn't quite that simple. I wheeled the bikes out to the hatchback, but they were too long to just stuff into the back. I had a panic moment—no tools—but Mary told me there was a tool kit under the counter in the office. I removed the front wheels and the bikes stacked into the back easily.

While I had a pair of pliers, I took the precaution of sabotaging this new rifle the same way—take the powder out of a bullet and fire just the primer, to lodge it halfway up the barrel. Useless to an assassin, but that was never really in my job description.

8.

I called Underwood on the lady's cell as soon as it was 9:00 in Washington but got a recording. I asked her to call this number back and also send an e-mail. Phone trouble.

We decided to stay off the expressway, and just crawl down the two-lane. Might as well make it easy for the Mississippi cops, if Mary Taylor decided not to stay quiet for $600. We had bigger problems.

How had the Enemy caught us? From the billboard encounter we knew that they weren't following cell phone information; I'd stomped the cell long before that. Maybe, far-fetched as it seems, the mystery did go back to the surgery in the army hospital in Germany—a tracer bug imbedded in muscle mass. What would it use for power? Can a tiny battery or fuel cell work after sitting for ten years? Maybe there was some biological thing, generating electricity from my own body chemistry.

As soon as we could stop for a few hours in a big enough town, I should arrange to have my hand X-rayed. I could complain about phantom pain from the missing finger, and who would refuse to give me a picture? If only to shut me up. A tracer could be tiny, but big enough to see.

I didn't say anything out loud about that. Of course this car had to have been bugged by whoever left it for us. We could assume they knew exactly where we were at any time, and could overhear us talking. Kit hummed a folk song from a couple of years ago: "Sittin' in my home alone / Waitin' for the god-damn phone. . . ."

She took the paper tablet and marker out of her bag and wrote HAVE TO DUMP CAR—GREYHOUND IN GULFPORT? in big block letters.

I nodded and scrawled CASH TICKETS TO TWO DIFFERENT PLACES? Keeping my eyes on the road.

It made me nervous, the idea of being separated. But we had agreed that it was a necessary step. There would come a future, I supposed, when every little Podunk bus station and train terminal would have spy-cams with face recognition software. For now, though, you might still travel through the country without Big Brother making sure you stay out of trouble. If you're careful to stay off the grid.

They would have our description, a man and a woman biking together, out in the middle of the country but without any touring gear. We'd be less conspicuous as individuals just taking bus rides to wherever.

(I don't think I was unduly paranoid about this—and my controlling metaphor wasn't Big Brother, actually, but Big Mother, the nanny state. If you really want to keep control of your children, you have to keep them on a leash. The image of the cyber-state as a harried young mother with children going every which way, straining at tethers, seemed pretty accurate.)

We turned on the radio and listened to dreadful Southern nova ska for the benefit of our supposed eavesdroppers. After about ten minutes, though, Kit made a face and slapped the search bar until it delivered some funky bayou jazz on NPR.

We did take an hour and a half to indulge my paranoia. We saw a sign and pulled into a small "urgent care facility" in the middle of nowhere, and I complained to the doctor about sharp pains in my hand, by the stump. He had a young man take an X-ray, and brought the film to me with a perplexed look, and put it up on the wall.

"Never seen anything quite like this," he said, "but then I don't get a lot of combat amputees." Where the bone for the little finger was cut off, there was an opaque perfect cube, maybe a third of an inch on a side. "The medics didn't say anything to you about it?"

"It was a confusing time."

"At a guess, I'd say it was something to promote healing. Never seen the like. Maybe you were a guinea pig, and they didn't follow up." He took off his glasses and rubbed his eyes. "Not allowed to do that, but they do. God . . . damned . . . army. You a disabled veteran?"

"Eighty percent," I said.

"You get home, get the VA on their case. Get a patient advocate and stand your ground. They can call me if you want." He handed me his business card and a prescription. "This is Tylenol with a little codeine. Don't drive on it."

He stood up and shook my hand. "Thank you for your service, son. Wish I could do more."

"You've done plenty." Kit and I both said good-bye, staring at the little white cube on the film.

We settled the bill in the waiting room and then stood for a minute in the small parking lot before getting in the car. "I don't feel good about leaving you now," she said.

"Not that much has changed," I said. "We figured it was something." I looked at my hand. "Know any amateur surgeons?"

By the time we got to Gulfport it was dark. The next bus going north didn't leave till seven in the morning. That didn't bother either of us; stop at a nice motel and have a decent dinner and a sleep together before we separated.

Not a good decision, it turned out.

The dinner was great, a deep-South crab and shrimp boil with small new potatoes and baby onions cooked in the broth. We tarried over it and had a bottle of wine and a plate of fresh gingersnaps, the house specialty.

Our lives might have been a lot simpler if we'd just picked up some burgers. Driven on.

We got back from the restaurant about eleven and there were no parking spaces in front of our motel room at Traveler's Rest. I let Kit off to run to the bathroom while I went around back to the auxiliary lot.

We were separated for less than three minutes.

When I opened the door, there was only a line of light coming from under the bathroom door. "Kit?" I called.

She made some noise from the bathroom and I stepped into the darkness. A sharp pain exploded in the back of my head, and I was conscious just long enough to think *Stroke?*

————————

It had been a stroke, all right; the stroke from a club or a blackjack. At three in the morning, 3:17 by the bedside clock, I sort of woke up, ears ringing, pain radiating in spasms from the base of my skull. A big tender swelling there. No blood. I swallowed back vomit and staggered to the bathroom and drank some water, and managed to keep it down. Splashed cold water on my face and rubbed it with the harsh towel.

There was an insistent buzzing in my ears that I eventually realized was coming from a strange cell phone, centered on the neatly made double bed. I got a tissue from the end table and picked up the phone like a master criminal, or an amateur one.

I pushed the button but didn't think "hello" would express how I felt. "Fuck you."

"Now, now," a familiar female voice said, "what if this was your mother calling?"

"I suppose I would ask her what the fuck was going on. But I guess I'll have to ask you. Who the fuck are you?"

"We are the people who have your girlfriend. That's all you need to know."

"So you've upped the stakes to federal crime."

"Technically, no; I think it was already a federal crime when somebody killed a DHS agent. But yes, the stakes will be higher . . . for you."

"How so?"

"It goes like this: we'll give your girlfriend back. If you cooperate, we'll give her back all at once. If not, we'll send you a finger first, and then negotiate the next part."

I couldn't speak. It was like my vocal apparatus was glued shut.

"You can reach me at any time by touching the REPLY button. Do not make a recording of the call. If you don't reply in one hour, or if you call the authorities, we will definitely give you the finger. Registered mail." She hung up.

I stared dumbly at the phone while it sank in.

They had me pretty well figured out. It might not work with an actual war hero; he would probably make the calculation and, more or less with regret, do what he had to do.

But to me? Killing some stranger, no matter who he might be, was not unthinkable; that had been my business as usual for more than a year, not that long ago. But allowing the woman I love to die—slowly, tortured by amputation? Through my inaction?

The ghost of my missing finger talked quietly all the time, in a language no one else could hear. Now it screamed. *You can't let them do this. Do this to her.*

It wasn't just the pain. The chest pain was worse, when it was bad. But nothing was missing in there.

The muscle below the stump flexed and flexed. The ring finger clawed in sympathy.

As it had done when I woke up in the hospital bed in Germany. The tight swath of bandages that covered the chest was nothing compared to the arm suspended just above eye level, twitching, broadcasting loss more than pain. *This will never grow back. Never be better.*

I pushed the button. The phone rang once, and the person who picked it up didn't say anything.

"So what do you want me to do?" I asked the silence.

A man's voice: "Do you feel fit to drive?"

I didn't, actually. Maybe I could walk to the door. "How far?"

"Some distance. You should sleep first."

"Sure."

"There are sleeping pills and aspirin in your shaving kit."

"I don't carry sleeping pills."

"You do now. Take two and I will call you in the morning." He hung up, a comedian.

My "shaving kit" was a courtesy zip-bag from Harrah's. It now had an aspirin bottle with eight aspirin and four purple pills.

No way in hell. Even if I knew they looked like sleeping pills, which I didn't, I wasn't going to take them on the word of a probably homicidal mystery man. I walked across the street and got an ice-cold quart of beer from a local place called Swamp Hawg Brewery.

It was not as bad as it might have been. I drank the whole quart in about ten minutes, while nibbling on stale cookies for my stomach's sake. I started to undress, but only got my shirt off. Decided I had to rest a bit before tackling my shoes.

Woke up slowly with shoes still on, eyelids stuck together, clothes twisted and heavy with sweat. The clock said 9:14. Dappled sunlight coming through the window by the bathroom. Funny feeling in my stomach, butterflies rather than nausea, and probably a bad case of Swamp Hawg breath.

Maybe nerves, too.

I set up the coffee machine and slumped to the shower. It had a head more talented than my own; I set it to a complex vibrating mode and let the thrumming hot water try to wake me up. When it turned cold I stepped out carefully, remembering a stupid accident in junior high. Slipped in a strange bathroom and laid open my chin.

No Time for Stitches, a good title for my autobiography.

I got the cardboard box out of the trunk and dumped the rifle out onto the bed. A lot heavier than the one I used in the desert.

I'd only used the sniper-mod M2010 once as a plain rifle, rather than a sniper weapon, and the results were more instructive than impressive. The bolt action that gives it such accuracy is a handicap when you're not punching somebody a new orifice long-distance.

There were seven or eight of us deploying in a roomy MaxiStryker, crawling up a steep hill with maybe a dozen other vehicles on our way from nowhere to elsewhere, and we ground to a halt when the vehicle either ran over a mine or was hit by an IED. We were all deafened, but otherwise unhurt. Smoke everywhere. There was some small-arms fire whispering from above us, and we all piled out on the downhill side to shoot back.

It was an unholy racket, even to the deaf; at least two Strykers blasting away with fifties and the littler machine guns and grenade launchers chattering and booming. I could see by tracers what they were aiming at, a dun-colored lump that was probably a pile of sandbags, and I managed to get two rounds in that general direction while the Strykers pelted it with about a thousand. Finally something hit something and it went up in a big orange-and-grey blossom. Some guys pumped fists and cheered, I guess the way Goliath did until his last engagement.

I remembered taking comfort in the rifle's weight and balance, back then, and now allowed myself a familiar fantasy: those guys pull up in their SUV and start taking pictures of Kit's bare ass—but instead of the piddling Dick Tracy toy, I pull out my trusty M2010. Right eye or left? Perhaps a new one, in between?

It occurred to me that this might be the same rifle I'd "modified" by plugging the barrel with a low-powered bullet. I slid the bolt back and looked down the barrel; it was unobstructed.

I could take it to the cops. Tell them my story. Some lunatic assholes gave me this rifle and want me to go to Washington and assassinate someone, and they kidnapped my girlfriend to make sure I do it. Here's a note that proves it.

Sure, son. Why don't you just put down the gun and sit over there while we check it out . . . you don't mind handcuffs, do you?

For some time I sat there and looked at the weapon. Then I carefully filled its box magazine with five fresh rounds, then pulled the bolt back and slipped a sixth one into the chamber.

Four rounds for the car and driver, and then two for the grinning schmuck with the camera. Chest and head. Take a picture of *this*, motherfucker.

9.

I was just about done with waiting, quarter to eleven, when the little phone buzzed. I pushed the button and didn't say anything.

"Do you have a pencil?" the woman said.

"No. Second." I found a ballpoint in my bag, and a folded-over piece of paper. "Okay."

"You have to be in Washington, DC, in four days. You have a room reserved under the name 'Grant Harrison' from the third of July until the fifth, in the JW Marriott Hotel, on Pennsylvania Avenue Northwest." She paused. "Do you have that?"

"I have it." I repeated it back to her.

"Your confirmation for the room, and a wallet with Grant Harrison identification, are in the glove compartment of your car. You will have to drive there, of course, so your luggage won't be searched."

I didn't bother to write that down. "I'm not doing anything for you until I know that Kit is safe."

There was a long pause. "Nothing?"

"Of course not. If you've killed her I have no reason to follow your orders."

"Oh. She is not dead." There was some line noise and a beep. "I've sent you a photograph of her. The picture includes the first page of this morning's *New York Times*.

"She still has all her fingers. But take note of the man standing next to her. If you call the authorities . . . we will give her to him.

"She will be killed. Repeat that to me."

"She will be killed."

"Keep that in mind. She will be killed, slowly, badly, and you will be to blame." The phone went dead, and then buzzed.

I clicked it for "Recents" and found a call with the current time, supposedly from "411." I opened it and found a photograph.

It was Kit, seated, gagged, wearing only frilly blue underwear. Which I had never seen.

A white rope thicker than clothesline was wound around her. Shoulders, chest, waist, legs. Her wrists were tied together in her lap, with what looked like telephone cord. Low coffee table in front of her, with a metal ashtray in the shape of a bird, filled to overflowing with cigarette butts. A corner of a window behind her showed a pine forest.

A tall thin man wearing a black mask hooded over his head stood next to her. In one hand he held a newspaper and in the other, a long-bladed fileting knife.

That was theater, of course. She was at the mercy of anyone, dramatic weapon or no. If not this theatrical knife-wielder, then the fat guy with the camera, or his black driver. The woman with the honey voice, the person who killed Blackstone, the man who'd just talked on the phone. And maybe some to whom I had not yet been introduced.

The background of the photo didn't reveal much. There were probably a million rooms just like it in motels and vacation cabins: fake log paneling, furniture that was worn blond Ikea or the like, many years old. I couldn't read the date on the *Times*, but the headline was current, "West Virginia Coal Miners' Strike Near Resolution."

I couldn't read Kit's expression, either. Wide-eyed, I supposed with fright, looking away from the camera, down at the table. The bandana pulled tight between her teeth, that must hurt. Her mouth would be dry. The dead-tobacco smell from the cigarette butts, rank and penetrating.

The man's eyes were visible, somewhat shaded by the hood. Windows of the soul, supposedly, though it's hard to read eyes with no other features. Safe to assume they were cruel. Cruel pulp-fiction eyes under a hangman's hood.

Would the long slender blade reach his heart if I thrust up under the sternum? That's what the master sergeant claimed in Basic Training. Maybe I would play it safe and just cut his throat. Shoot him a few times first.

Kit didn't have any blue underwear. White or nothing, usually nothing. She had been stripped and redressed.

An interesting word, "redress." Could anything really pay us back for all this?

The phone by the bed rang, and I snatched it up. It was just the office, asking if I planned to stay another day. I said no, and assured her I'd be out by eleven.

"Where you headed?" she chirped. I told her Washington, DC.

"Gonna be a madhouse, Fourth of July coming up."

I tried to laugh. "Guess I can handle it."

She might wind up on page three of the *Times* herself. *He seemed like such a nice boy. I saw that long box but didn't think nothing of it.*

That room in the photo could be a block away, or it could be almost anywhere with pine trees. Underneath the note I had copied from them, I did some calculation: They hit me over the head and took Kit around 11:00 last night, 2300. Almost twelve hours later, they sent me the photo.

If they were driving, they might have gone six or seven hundred miles. But they didn't have to drive if they had access to civil aviation. I called the desk, and the woman said there was a landing strip two miles down the road. Yes, she had heard several planes take off tonight.

In that time, a plane could get them anywhere in the hemisphere. Someplace with a *New York Times*, but no other constraints.

I went out and opened the glove compartment and took out a cheap plastic wallet. Illinois driver's license, library card, and Exxon and Visa credit cards for "Grant Harrison," the names of two presidents. One gave us Black Friday and the other was a nonstop talker who died of pneumonia after a month in office. From eating cherries in cold milk, which I never believed. I wouldn't have voted for either one of them.

Not much packing up to do. I put our bathroom gear back in her pink suitcase and the rifle back into its box. Went to the office and paid with a C-note, which caused the clerk to purse her lips. *I knew there was something fishy when he didn't use a credit card.*

I asked whether I could use her desk computer for a minute, though, and she decided I was probably not that dangerous. She wanted to go off to the little girls' room anyhow, she said; would I watch things?

Sure. The main thing I wanted to watch was the picture of Kit, bound and gagged. It took me a minute to transfer it to her machine. She didn't have Photoshop or anything, but I was able to enlarge portions of the picture.

What I mainly wanted to study was a small wall calendar that was nailed to the paneling at the edge of the picture, next to the window.

It was a freebie calendar from an Ace Hardware; I recognized the logo but couldn't read any of the lettering. Maybe the words under the logo were the name of the town.

I pushed the enlargement in and out. The first line looked like two words: four letter-blobs, an apostrophe, and another blob. Probably an "s." Then six blobs. The first one narrower; might be an "i."

The second line was five blobs, slightly larger. The name of a state? I called up a list of states, and there were only three with five letters: Texas, Maine, and Idaho.

A CIA genius or *Jeopardy!* winner might rattle it off instantly: a place name that was "somebody's" "something," in one of those three states. I Googled around and found a gazetteer that would search for place names with missing letters.

Texas and Idaho came up blank, but I scored on Maine: Swan's Island. It was a little pinpoint in the ocean, south of Mount Desert Island. Population 350.

I wrote all of that, and the latitude and longitude, on the back of a postcard extolling the virtues of Traveler's Rest.

It wasn't much, but it was all I had. What were the chances that somebody who *didn't* live on that little island would nail up a throwaway calendar from there?

I could hear a despised math professor from my freshman year sneering that the probability was non-zero. Which meant *not bloody likely, but the only chance you have.*

But wait. There was a retro phone with a rotary dial on the table. I selected it and enlarged it. Someone had carefully printed a number with clear block letters on the white circle in the center of the dial.

I scribbled that down and Googled "phone number" + "land line" + "find address."

It gave me a service called FindFone. I was never so glad to have my Amex card number memorized. I typed it in and FindFone charged me ninety-seven cents to divulge 127 Ring Road, Swan's Island, Maine.

The clerk came back and I thanked her and rushed back to the room.

Threw everything in the car and reviewed my options. I could go to an airport and take a chance; try to fly there on my illegal credit card. Airports are a little less forgiving than rustic taxicabs on that, though.

I drove for a couple of hours and then stopped to get a sandwich at a Pilot truck stop. Walked through the big convenience store, looking for inspiration, and possibly found it.

The car was parked behind a Dumpster, not visible from the shop. I got in and almost enjoyed the microwaved cheeseburger and an ice-cold Coors. Not my brand of choice, but there was nothing less American on offer.

I had bought three other items, cash, paying at a register that was not visible from outside: a sling for my left arm, masking tape, and a roll of aluminum foil. I wanted to reconstruct a vaguely remembered Science Fair project from junior high school.

One of the kids had a demonstration of the "Faraday Cage," basically a box that blocked electromagnetic radiation. He'd built boxes of chicken wire, fine-mesh metal screen, and plain metal. The demonstration involved putting a cell phone into each cage and calling it from different distances.

I couldn't remember what he had proved with it, but it gave me an obvious idea. Would a container made of aluminum foil block a radio signal?

Maybe you wouldn't need a whole room with aluminum wallpaper. If I wrapped my hand in aluminum foil, would it block the transmitter buried in the flesh? If I wrapped the arm up past the elbow, would that keep radio waves from leaking out?

Wished I knew more science. The "open" end of the cylinder of foil would be full of muscle and bone. How well would radio waves travel in and out through that?

Car radios work, inside a "box" that's mostly metal. But I vaguely remember something a teacher said in school about how they got around that. I was probably studying the back of Rosy Bender's neck, and trying to imagine the rest of her skin, and somehow didn't quite get what he was saying about radio waves.

Looked around and didn't see any witnesses, and the car's windows were tinted anyhow. I tore off a long sheet of foil and wrapped it around my left hand and arm, molding it up past the elbow. Having a right angle in the tunnel of foil might help; there wouldn't be a straight line from the bug to the outside world.

Good thing I'd gotten a wide roll. It overlapped with plenty of room to spare. I wound masking tape around the whole thing generously, then managed to hide most of it inside the sling.

I would still be able to fire the rifle or the revolver, but probably couldn't reload either of them without tearing the foil off the left hand.

Well, if it came down to shooting, I wouldn't be worried about radio waves.

I'd worked out a vague plan. Might as well get going.

A county road paralleled the interstate for two dozen miles, so I'd follow that. I put the cell on the passenger seat, in case I had to do dangerous stuff, like driving while talking on the phone, or shooting at people. Started the car and moved out.

The road was almost deserted. After a few miles, the cell buzzed, and I picked it up. "What?"

I resisted the urge to laugh into the awkward pause. "Your . . . car is moving," the woman said.

"It's your car, I think, and it's headed for Washington," I said. "Isn't that what you wanted?"

"Why aren't you on the highway?"

"I have three days. It's an unfamiliar car, so I'd rather not speed. Why is that a problem?"

"Take your next right. Get back on the highway."

"Okay." He didn't say, *We seem to have lost your hand.*

Maybe time to confuse things more. Steering with my elbows, I unwrapped the foil from my hand. Then as I drove along, I covered it up for a few seconds at a time. Then I left it uncovered. Let them think that the battery inside my hand was failing.

My half-formed plan was to set them up so they wouldn't panic if the signal from my hand flickered on and off. Over the next three days, I wouldn't cover it up for more than a minute. But if I ever did want to drop off their radar screen, I could do it, and the first thing they'd think was battery failure.

Of course they could track me anyhow, as long as I stayed in this car. That was okay for the time being. Since I didn't know where Kit was, my only hope was that their directions would lead me to where she was being held.

I did take the next right, and obediently got back on I-85. The screen button said I was 980 miles from Washington. What could I do in 980 miles?

Sleep a couple of times. I picked up the phone and thumbed it. "This car doesn't have Supercruise. How long do you think I can drive before I fall asleep at the wheel?"

"We will tell you when to stop." The woman again.

"What if I have to pee?"

"Go ahead," she said, a trace of amusement in her voice. "It's not your car."

I drove along eight or ten miles, until the next exit sign. Picked up the phone: "Seriously, I need some coffee if I'm going to stay on the road. There's a place in two miles."

"All right," she said. "Use the facilities. Treat yourself to a candy bar."

I would, actually; get the blood sugar fired up. I pulled into the rest stop and parked. I watched for a few minutes, and no black SUV followed me in.

Well, if they could assassinate a president, or someone important, they could probably afford a second car.

On impulse, I opened the back door and took the rifle out of its box. I propped it up diagonally across the passenger's seat, then left the car unlocked and went to get my coffee.

I took my time in the bathroom, then got a coffee and a pastry. I stood and enjoyed the block of crumb cake with apricot filling, watching the car from the rest-stop foyer, in air-conditioned comfort. Just as I finished the crumb cake, a fish took my bait.

A stern-looking state trooper watched me saunter out with my half-finished coffee.

"Is this your car, sir?"

"Yes, it is."

"You left it unlocked with a weapon in the front seat."

"Really?" I took out the keychain and pushed the button twice. The car honked. "Good grief. Careless of me."

"Well, be more careful, sir." He walked away, without asking for my license and registration. What kind of a police state is this? How do you know I'm not headed to Washington to shoot the god-damned president?

I hoped he at least had written down the license plate number or taken a picture. Maybe he had one of those microcameras in his hat.

But I put the ignition key in and turned it, and nothing happened. Took it out and tried it again. Then a big dark shape pulled up behind me and stopped.

A state police tow truck.

The cop came back with a friend, a very stern-looking woman with a Smokey-the-Bear hat and her left hand on the butt of the automatic pistol that rode too high on her hip. The other hand hovered over a spray can on the right side.

Her voice was a staccato chirp: "Sir, we have to ask you to come out of the car and keep your hands visible please."

"Sure." I opened the door slowly and eased my tired bones out. "What else can I help you with?"

"Are there any other weapons in the car?" he asked.

"No—yes! I mean, not in the car. In a suitcase in the trunk, there's a gun."

"Would you please open the suitcase and show us? We won't confiscate it without reason."

Even with reason, I wondered whether they were on shaky legal ground. Could they make you open a suitcase without a warrant? The rent-a-cops at airport security did it routinely, so maybe they were covered.

I opened up the suitcase and stepped away before she could order me to. "Take a look."

The snub-nosed revolver was in sight on top of the clothes. She searched through them anyhow, and didn't find anything else interesting.

"Have I broken a law here?" My half-formed plan was to get the police suspicious enough to follow me. Hopefully without throwing me in the slammer.

The male officer took off his sunglasses, revealing soft features in a big round face. "There is a law against creating an 'attractive nuisance,' sir. A nice rifle begging to be stolen qualifies, I think."

"So I could be arrested for somebody else's theoretical lack of moral fiber."

"You're not being arrested, sir," the woman said. "Though I will issue a warning to you." She reached for a notebook very slowly, I guess so as not to spook me in case I had yet another gun squirreled away. She asked the other officer what the code was for "attractive nuisance," and he didn't know either, so they settled on 999. They gave me the warning and abjured me to have a good day, and please put the weapons where they weren't in plain sight.

The warning wasn't a citation. It was somebody's brilliant PR idea—a smiley face with "Friendly Warning" printed across the top. No name or license number involved, how friendly. I probably wasn't in any state police computer for it.

The tow-truck door slammed and then there was a solenoid click down by my starter switch. So they could turn off this car's engine by remote control, which I'd known was true in a couple of states. Another reason to stick to bicycles.

I did put the rifle in the trunk but also, perhaps unwisely, took the .38 from the suitcase and slipped it into the front door pocket, tucking a map over it for camouflage. Not that I was going to quick-draw it from the driver's seat, with my left arm incapacitated.

It was right next to the plastic wallet with Grant Harrison's identification. Maybe I should have used it. *Remember this name, officers. It will be in the papers soon.*

My fingers tingled and so did my toes, a not-completely-unpleasant feeling I remembered from combat. Like feeling a change in the weather: a shitstorm may be gathering, but at least it won't take me by surprise.

I studied the parking lot, feeling a little sheepish, and didn't spot any tanks or snipers. I touched the EST. TIME button on the map, and numbers appeared under route lines. I was five hours from Huntsville. Figure on stopping there for dinner and a rest.

As I pulled out of the parking area, I told the phone to recharge itself from the car's system while I drove. It had one message, which had come in while I was being interrogated by the Smokies.

We will call you with instructions this evening at eight o'clock your time. You have to be checked into a motel or hotel by then. You might want to get some rest.

That was thoughtful of them. It would put me on the other side of Huntsville, but 8:00 was late to be looking for a room. I'd start looking well south of the city.

The phone buzzed, and I picked it up wearily. So soon. "Yeah?"

"Hey, babe. What's up?"

The voice was only vaguely familiar. "I don't know. What *is* up? Who are you?"

"Break my heart, babe—this is *Ron*! Ron Duquest, the only guy between you and a million bucks."

"Jesus! How on Earth did you get this number? I just *got* this phone."

"What do you mean?" he said. "You e-mailed me the number this morning from . . . Missi-fucking-sippi? What the hell are you doin' down south?"

What should I or could I tell him? Of course we were being overheard, at least my side of the conversation. I chose my words carefully. "Unlikely as it sounds," I said, "I'm doing a little thing for the army. Secret."

"The *army*? I thought you hated them."

"What can I say, Ron? Their money spends."

"That's great, babe. But what about *me*? And my money? The army takes precedence over my monster?"

Jesus. "Didn't I just send you a chapter?"

"Jack, yeah, you sent me a chapter, like a week ago."

"Couple of days," I said.

"The monster's got the bikin' guy," he said. "He's about to fuckin' *eat* him, and the cops are closing in while he sharpens the fuckin' knife, and you have to do a job for the fuckin' *army*? One of us is crazy, man, and I'm sure as hell it's not fuckin' *me*!"

I had to smile in spite of everything. "It's me, Ron. I am totally fuckin' bug-fuck." I checked my watch. "Look, I'm about to knock off driving for the night. I'll stop at a place with Wi-Fi and do you a couple of pages."

"You got to, man! I gotta know, does he eat the guy—no, don't tell me! I wanna *agonize*!"

"Okay, Ron. I'll do as much as I can."

"Do *more*! I wanna know what happens to this fuckin' freak!"

"Do what I can," I repeated. "Talk to you tomorrow." I clicked it off and tossed it on the seat. A big sigh surprised me, and then I had to laugh.

If you only knew, Ronald. There are more things in heaven and earth than are dreamt of in your philosophy. Using the term loosely.

CHAPTER THIRTEEN

Hunter removed the tape from his victim's mouth slowly but gently. This one was also athletic, but not as skinny as the girl last month, good.

Hunter had duct-taped his wrists and ankles. He pushed the bandana that had been covering his eyes up onto his forehead. "If you make any noise, I will blind and gag you again. But I will hurt you first."

"Okay," he said hoarsely. "I understand."

"I do want you to understand," Hunter said. "I want you to know that what's happening to you is special."

"Thank you." His eyes tracked all around the trailer. A library of science fiction and popular science paperbacks in floor-to-ceiling bookcases. Large old medical books, anatomy and physiology. A too-large billiard table took up half the floor space.

Hunter crouched and lifted the table's false top of green felt, not straining. Underneath, a metal surface with blood gutters. Its white enamel had been scrubbed, but stains persisted.

"This will not be an autopsy, despite appearances." He opened a drawer and took out a plastic case of glittering scalpels and a pair of surgical saws. "Autopsies are for dead people. This will be more like a very thorough physical examination."

"At the end of which I'll be dead?" His voice quavered.

"We shall see." He took large shears out of the drawer and advanced on his prisoner.

"What are you doing?"

"Preparation." He started with the left arm of Steve's T-shirt, scissoring it open to the neck. Then he did the other side, slowly, shearing it all the way to the waist. The ruined garment fell to the floor. Then he snipped open his biking shorts, leaving him clad only in a jock strap and incongruous running shoes.

He looked up defiantly. "Does that do it for you? A helpless victim gives you a hard-on?"

With a thumb Hunter pulled down the front of his own shorts, exposing nothing. "Not really."

He stared. "You're not . . . aren't you . . ."

"There's something there. Not what you might expect, and small."

"What . . . are you?"

"Not human. You will have to die for knowing that. But you would die anyhow."

Steve's body was pale as wax under black hair. "What . . . what will you do?"

"Eat you, ultimately," he said in a playful tone. "You are prey, after all, and I caught you, fair and square."

"No."

"It's not a movie, though, so you won't have to watch as I consume the minor pieces. I will kill you more or less quickly, and feed on you for several days. As you would a cow or a pig."

"No," he said, lying inanely. "I'm a vegetarian."

"Another one. Do you think carrots feel no pain? You tear their skin off and chop them up into—"

Someone pounded on the door. "Open up in there!"

Hunter picked up the shotgun in the corner, smiling calmly. "A friend of yours?"

The rapping resumed and he stepped toward the door. As Steve shouted, *"He has a gun!"* he pointed the shotgun at about chest level and fired one deafening blast, and then two more, blowing the flimsy trailer door to pieces.

The gunstock had an elastic band that held ten or a dozen shells. He reloaded three and then kicked out what was left of the door, and stepped through blasting.

Steve could hear rifle shots and then a burst from a submachine gun. He saw Hunter jump from the top step.

For a couple of minutes there were more shots, and the sound of men shouting. Then it was quiet, and a short man wearing SWAT armor lumbered through the door with an assault rifle. "You all right, sir?"

"I've been better." His voice was somehow flat and calm. "Thank you for coming." He looked out the door. "You killed it?"

"Oh, yeah. I hit him twice myself, and he walked straight into a shotgun blast right after."

"So it's dead?"

"Gotta be."

From farther away, a short spat of automatic-weapon fire. Then a shotgun barked twice, and a third time.

"Hope so."

EPILOGUE

The coroner of Ilsworth County, Georgia, has done hundreds of autopsies, but never one of such a huge person, and he's not looking forward to it. Mountains of messy fat to slice through before you get to the organs. But he prepares the body and makes his first incision. Then he staggers back, dropping the scalpel.

Inside, there's no fat, and not a single organ he can identify. Some of them are shiny metal.

Its eyes snap open.

10.

Never thought I'd be homesick for a Holiday Inn. This rustic-looking place was Mom's Home Away from Home, which brought to mind Nelson Algren's three rules of life: "Never play cards with a man called Doc. Never eat at a place called Mom's. Never sleep with a woman whose troubles are worse than your own."

Never *sleep* at a place called Mom's. And, I guess, never play cards with a man whose troubles are worse than your own, and for god's sake, never eat with a woman called Doc. Unless you're going to be sick, I suppose.

I couldn't sleep anywhere, anyhow. Worrying about Kit.

At least you could write at a place called Mom's, if you're writing a cheesy monster novel. I finished lucky chapter thirteen. Hunter joins the ranks of the Undead.

I'd started out writing with the .38 sitting on the desk in front of me, but it was too distracting. I'd just look at it and worry. I started to put it under the pillow, but didn't want to smell the gun oil all night, and try to sleep with the lump. Finally, I put it on the floor, slightly hidden behind the bedspread. I could still snatch it in a second.

Eight o'clock came and went with no call. I supposed they actually gained more by not calling; keep me in suspense. And for all they knew, I might be sitting in a police station or FBI office somewhere, waiting for the phone to buzz so the authorities could trace the call and rain cowboys all over their ass.

I hoped that the night's distracted writing would satisfy Duquest. Would it be gory enough? I was more into disgust than horror.

I tried to ignore the feelings left over from trying to sleep while worrying about murderers and listening to bugs scuttle in the night. I did finally get a few hours' sleep, but woke up feeling crawly. Crawled upon.

Quick shower and hit the road. When I turned on the shower and a thin stream of brown water came out, I was almost able to laugh. Instead I called the office, and a yawning old man came down with a key to another room, with a shower that worked. Beige water, tepid.

He acted miffed. Who would want a shower with clean water?

Turned out the place didn't have Wi-Fi, though the sign said it did—the same sign that promised clean, comfortable rooms. I'd get back on 85 and use the first rest stop. Maybe it would even have a shower, dream on.

The main reason for stopping at a little place was to be able to check the parking lot at a glance. No big black SUV with a bullet hole.

If it had been there, though, what would I have done? Call the cops? Take out the rifle and wait for a target of opportunity?

That's what we called it in the desert. Though that sounded inappropriately cheerful. It was rather the opposite of "opportunity" for the guy on the other end. No more opportunities.

I remembered a poem, "Dealing in Futures," written by a soldier friend, about all the futures he had destroyed. Maybe somebody he killed would have found a cure for cancer, a car that runs without gasoline, an end to war. I read that before I was drafted, but even then, my reaction was "but maybe the soldier you decided *not* to kill has the bullet with your name on it."

That was always on the top of my mind in the desert. I didn't hate the enemy; in fact, I sort of admired them. But they can't know that, and any one you spare might be the instrument of your own doom. "Kill 'em all," said a slogan on my grandfather's helmet cover in *his* war; "and let God sort 'em out." He didn't believe in God any more than I do, but he did believe in the power of statistics. The Law of Large Numbers was a phrase I remembered him using. If there's a large number of soldiers out there absorbing bullets, maybe you'll be the one who gets missed. Or something.

This enemy now, perhaps I should hate. They're probably after me just for profit, hired by someone who has political motivations. Of course they're not killing me, to be precise; just putting me in a position where somebody else can. As Uncle Sam did as my graduation present, all those ten years ago. Perfectly legal.

Maybe I should just walk out to the highway and stick my thumb out. Take me anywhere, as long as it's out of this bizarre life. But for Kit.

Went back to my own room and turned on the television, but the only channel that worked was Random Colors & Static. Turned it off and jerked open the end table drawer. It had an old King James Bible. I opened it and flipped through to Matthew, which had pretty good poetry. But I came to a verse that stopped me in my tracks—

"And if thy right hand offend thee, cut it off, and cast *it* from thee: for it is profitable for thee that one of thy members should perish, and not *that* thy whole body should be cast into hell." Good grief. I was glad it didn't say *left* hand.

There was a polite knock on the door. I went to open it, and as I pulled on the knob, thought of the .38 sitting on the floor ten feet away.

An older man in a coat and tie and an attractive woman, maybe thirty, wearing a tailored white outfit. A nurse's uniform?

"What's going on?" I said.

"Out," the man said. "You're going out." He stepped aside, and as I leaned to close the door, the woman kicked it open and shot me in the chest.

I staggered back and looked at my chest. There was a dart there with bright red feathers.

"Damn it," the man said. "I said not the chest!"

I took one very shallow breath and collapsed.

11.

It was not unpleasant as long as I didn't wake up. People moved me here and there, I knew, and I seemed to always wind up in the same places. A quiet hospital bed in a dark room. A huge warehouse where invisible people walked around me. Sometimes a railroad car that I think came from some movie. It rocked along uneven rails and I knew that there were Indians riding alongside, but I would be okay as long as I didn't open the curtains. For the longest time I was up in some future, lying forever in a bed, I think waiting for immortality.

I could almost remember an ambulance ride, but that kept turning into a familiar helicopter, some bastard medic pounding my chest, *Stay with me Stay with me* when all I wanted was to leave. Leave behind the mutilated hand, the blood in my eyes, the punched-out chest. And now a dart, too.

Then it became a nurse whose huge face shrank back to normal size. My hand came up and touched a plastic thing over my mouth.

"Let's try breathing without this," she said, and there were some clicks as she unhooked something behind my head. The plastic went away, and with it the cold breeze that had been whispering into my nose. "They gave you a shot to wake you up. Do you know your name?"

"Jack Daley not John," I said automatically. "Specialist First Class, US3482179813. You are not allowed to ask me for more than this."

"Doctor Lu?" she said. "He's responding now."

A slender Asian guy, probably Vietnamese, wearing surgical greens and a stethoscope. He checked my pulse and listened to my heart. "You are so in the wrong war," I said diplomatically. "My grandfather would kill your ass."

"I was born in Cleveland," he said. "I'm just as American as your grandfather, maybe more." He unbuttoned my hospital shirt and looked at the skin there. He touched it gently with his fingertip. "Does that hurt?"

"No. Not at all."

"Funny. How do you feel?"

"Okay. Woozy, I guess."

A deep voice behind him said, "He's talking?"

"Yes, lieutenant. But I think he should—"

"I'm a lieutenant *colonel*, doctor. It's like the difference between lightning and a lightning bug."

Wow, I rated a bird colonel. What kind of shit was I in now? They went out into the hall and conferred, and then walked away talking softly, I think arguing.

I had the room to myself. Three other beds, empty. What did that mean?

I napped and woke up what seemed like seconds later, refreshed. "Nurse?" I said quietly.

She looked up from her charts, smiling. "You're awake, sir? Let me go get the—"

"No! No, wait. Before I talk to any officers . . . could you tell me where I am and what I'm doing here?"

She put a cool hand on my forehead. "You've been in this bed several days. Your chart says you're under observation pursuant to a drug reaction. What drug did you take?"

"Didn't *take*. It was a dart."

She touched the gauze in the center of my chest. "It was your heart?"

"No, not 'heart.' A dart. Look. Where am I?"

"It's a military hospital, Keesler Air Force Base. You got a dart in your heart?" She smiled. "Like Cupid?"

"No, not *Cupid*!" Better not say a beautiful mystery woman shot me with a mysterious dart gun for mysterious reasons. "I guess it was kind of an accident?"

"That was clumsy," she said, her pleasant expression unreadable. "You shot yourself in the chest with a riot control gun?"

"Is that what it was?"

"Well, they don't say you did it yourself." She reached down and rattled the handcuff that attached my ankle to the bed frame. "They seem to think you were resisting arrest."

"Holy shit. That's not it, not at all." I sat up in bed, shaking off dizziness, and looked at the handcuff, ankle restraint, whatever. It looked pretty serious. "Nobody arrested me."

She looked out down the hall. "Yeah, the guys who dumped you here weren't MPs, despite their uniforms. I work with MPs all the time. What did you really do?"

"Truth is, I'm not really sure. But I didn't break any law."

"For what it's worth, I believe you. Those guys are creeps. They don't work here."

"So let me out of here."

"Oh, yeah, and get them on *my* ass." She shook her head. "Even if I could"—she rattled the handcuffs—"I don't have the key. Oh yeah, and I don't want to spend the rest of my life in federal prison."

"They're not real officers. And I'm not a criminal. I think my life's in danger."

She canted her head and smiled again. "Spy stuff, eh?"

"Kind of. More like criminal stuff. On their part."

She stepped to the door and looked out again. "Them? I think they're too dumb to be criminals."

"Why's that?"

"Don't know shit. They didn't treat me like a nurse, just another dumb black bitch—and those scrubs they're wearing, they don't think I know whose monograms they are? Like I've worked here so long they oughta name a disease after me." She turned to rummage through a drawer. "Not even clean. They stole them scrubs from a laundry basket."

"You've got to help me."

"No, I don't *got* to. I don't have to do nothing not in my orders."

She looked out the door again, and shook her head, then picked up a big towel. "Don't you go noplace." She hustled out and was back in about two minutes.

"Got my boyfriend's pickup." She unwrapped the towel, exposing a big greasy pair of bolt cutters.

Rather than cut the chain, she snipped through the cuff itself, and then cut it off at my ankle, too. "You take that and get rid of it somewhere. Outside."

She pulled open a drawer and lifted out my clothes and shoes, wrapped in tissue paper. "Move fast. I'm not here." She put the bolt cutters into a low cabinet, stepped into the hall, looked up and down, and walked away unhurriedly.

There was a heat-sealed plastic sack with my bag in it. No cash in the wallet, though; just a receipt for $4,109. A brown envelope had the stuff from my pockets, about thirty bucks in small bills and change, and keys to the car that was parked back at Mom's Home Away from Home, and the room key. Not too useful. Credit cards that I might be able to use in off-the-grid places. A dime store cell phone.

I dressed quickly and stuffed the blue hospital pajamas into a HAZ-ARDOUS BIOWASTE trash can and stepped out briskly, trying to look as if I knew what I was doing.

No way I was going to get that $4,109 out of the hospital safe. But I wasn't going anywhere without money.

The fifty grand inside the book, that was just gone. If the guy with the white moustache showed up, I'd just have to tell him that the *other* bad guys, Boris and Natasha, had beat him to it. Take it up with your god-damned supervisor.

I had to assume that they searched through the motel room after they darted me. But if they didn't know about the money . . . I'd closed the hollowed-out book and left it on the floor by the bed. Maybe some maid got a tip big enough to retire on.

I sure was worth a lot of money for a guy who barely had cab fare. Even in mundane reality. I had plenty of credit cards in my wallet; that was a couple of grand that I could tap at usurious rates, if I were standing in a bank in Iowa City. But between me and MidWestOne were plenty of search engines where my name would ring a bell. Or start up a siren.

I sat down in the hospital lobby for a minute, trying to come up with a plan. Went through everything in my wallet.

At the bottom of the stack of credit cards was a Visa I'd never used. It was from a dumb promotion thing where I'd get $10 of free merchandise at a Hy-Vee in Coralville—but that store was just a hole in the ground now; they'd closed it last year.

I'd never used the card because it had the wrong middle initial: "John B." All my other cards were for "C. Jack." When it came, I hung onto it with a vague idea of doing an experiment; see what happened if I tried it in a cash machine when I was broke.

Might as well be hung for a sheep as a goat, though I wasn't really sure what that meant. Might as well be hung for a John as a Jack.

I used the pen at the sign-in desk and scrawled "John B. Daley" on the card's signature block. Then I went outside and got in the next cab. "Bus station, please." The driver was a girl who looked about twelve.

"You want the one at the Amtrak station?"

"Yeah, sure." The cab had a beat-up card reading machine. I handed her the new one. She slid it through without bells or sirens.

"You got ID?" I showed her my driver's license and she scrutinized the picture and then studied my face. "You look better with the beard," she said, and handed it back. I guess Visa-Jack would pass for Visa-John if there were no computers involved, or sufficiently old ones.

She dropped me at the bus station annex. I watched her pick up a fare and drive away, then made a snap decision and crossed over to the train station.

I used the same Visa in a ticket machine, ready to run if it started beeping, but it obediently booked me to Washington. From there I could book to New York, and then up to Maine. The last Maine bit on the bus.

How to get from Bangor to Swan's Island without any money was a problem I'd have to deal with when I got there.

It wouldn't be smart to push my luck charging a restaurant meal. With cash, I got a handful of power bars and a hot dog. Still a few hours before the train. I picked up a discarded *Times-Picayune* and sat on a bench outside, reading with one eye and watching with the other.

I didn't suppose a police car would pull up with lights flashing. If a cop car did come up, I could slip off in a cab to nowhere and start over.

The breeze died and I realized I smelled too strong to sit next to anyone who didn't have a real bad cold. What performers call "flop sweat," I supposed. A difficult role, pretending to be an innocent writer from Iowa City who had no connection with murderous assholes or people with good plain haircuts from three-initialed agencies.

The men's room had a cologne dispenser that took a dollar coin. So I could at least disguise myself as a weary traveler who knew how bad he smelled.

The crossword puzzle in the paper was too easy. I did about half of it and quit out of nervous boredom. Then I picked it back up and filled in all the blanks with random words. That was a little more challenging. I got to cross AXOLOTL with LYNX, a biology experiment that would probably never actually happen.

It was three and a half hours till the train. I got up to look at the map on the wall and with a shock realized I was only twenty miles from the motel where I'd been kidnapped.

I hurried outside and went to the first cab in line. He looked like a cliché New York cabbie, fat and grizzled and unfriendly, an unlit cigarette dangling from his lip. In actual New York, I realized, he'd be from the Indian subcontinent or Northern Africa. Maybe that's why he moved to Mississippi. I tapped on the window.

"Yeah?"

"Could you take me to a motel in Quigman and back in two hours? Mom's Home Away from Home, off 85?"

"Twenty-some miles? Sure. Cost ya."

"How much, about?"

He tapped the dash map a couple of times and entered some number into his meter box. "Fifty-mile round trip . . . call it $250 plus waiting time?"

I handed him the card. "Give you three hundred if you can get me there and back in an hour, and you never saw me?"

He took the card and the back door sprang open. "Never saw who? I been off duty since ten seconds ago. Gonna drive the long way home."

I was sure the meter box would keep a record, but hell. The back of the cab smelled of stale cigarette smoke, which made me think of Kit, trapped somewhere with her face down by that overflowing ashtray.

My eyes stung and I closed them during the drive, just to rest them, but was sound asleep when he pulled up at Mom's Home Away from Home. "Here you go, buddy."

"Thanks. Back in a minute." I got out and stretched. Against all odds, the hatchback was still in front of number 15.

I went into the office and the querulous old man looked up. "Well, finally," he said. "Where the hell have you been?"

"In the hospital in Biloxi. Not sure how I wound up there."

"Oh. You okay now?"

"Still sore from where someone hit me over the head. Look, I left a suitcase and stuff in that room."

He stared at me with a mixture of confusion and suspicion. "Maid cleaned up. Guess you can take a look. You got your key?"

I took it out of the plastic bag and jiggled it. He decided to follow me to the room, putting a BACK IN FIVE sign on his door. The cabbie joined us, I guess to protect his investment.

The door to room 15 was locked, which gave me a moment of optimism. But the pink suitcase wasn't anywhere to be seen, nor the dime store computer. The Dexter Filkins book was on the floor, open, its hollowed-out pages empty.

"What happened to that book?" the old man asked.

"I don't know. Someone got mad at it."

I knelt down to pick up the book and yes, the .38 was still down there, not visible behind the bedspread. I swept it out and into my pocket as I stood. The old man hadn't been looking at me, and the cabbie developed a sudden interest in the ceiling.

Checked the bathroom and retrieved the shaving kit I'd gotten from the casino.

Nothing in the car but some road maps and a box of stale cookies. Aluminum foil and masking tape. A coffee cup with dried-up mold in it.

"You gonna take the car? This ain't no parkin' lot."

"Somebody'll be by for it tomorrow." State police or Homeland Security, but maybe not tomorrow. I wasn't going to take it and drive to Maine with a beacon: *Come shoot me again; maybe a bullet this time.*

On the cab ride back to Biloxi, the cabdriver and I listened to music on a country station. We didn't talk until we got to the train station and he opened the door. The cab machine took my card with no protest, and I tipped him up to three hundred.

"It's none of my business," he said, "but you better watch your ass. Listen to a fellow vet. Guns are never nothin' but trouble. Haven't we had enough trouble?"

"Yeah," I said. "We shouldn't go looking for it." He nodded and drove off shaking his head.

When trouble comes looking for you, though, best to be ready. A little revolver with five shells is five shots better than a pocket full of nothing. On cue, a train whistled in the distance. The train to Maine, soon enough.

I'll come to thee by moonlight, the poet said, *though hell should bar the way.*

12.

I probably could have upgraded my ticket to a sleeper compartment, but didn't want to push the one credit card too high. I did nurse a couple of glasses of wine, watching TV movies in the bar car.

The revolver seemed heavy and obvious in my Amtrak bag, and perhaps the idea of a gun clashed with its cheerful logo, but it would be more conspicuous in my pocket. I decided to use my layover in Washington to buy a shoulder holster. And a double-breasted dark jacket, with padded shoulders, to go with it. Mirror shades and a rent-a-girl to hang on my arm. Or maybe I should stick with the Amtrak bag.

Actually, an inconspicuous light jacket and a shoulder holster would be a good idea. I checked the web on the bar-car computer, and was amazed to find out (admittedly in an ad for shoulder holsters) how risky it was to simply carry a pistol in your pocket—at any second, the trigger could snag the pocket lining and blow your dick off! Buy a shoulder holster for the sake of your theoretical progeny! I'd gone all my life without worrying about that.

Actually, I'd be more concerned about a policeman saying, "Is that a pistol in your pocket, or are you just . . . wait! That *is* a pistol in your pocket! Hands up!"

The Amtrak bag seemed effective and inconspicuous, and the price was right. But I wondered whether I might be going into a situation where I would want a concealed weapon and both hands free. That might be worth the hundred bucks or so. Though I wouldn't put it on unless I was walking into an actual "situation."

I did get a solid six hours of sleep on the train, even getting up a couple of times to take the foil off for random intervals, to confuse things. As we approached Washington, I left it off for the last hour or so. The people who were renting the room in the Marriott would no doubt be listening.

I'd want it covered up all the time when I headed north, but also, naturally, I'd want it to be "not working" for hours at a time before I left.

Of course I had no idea where the listeners were located. Maybe they were in Maine, in the same room as Kit, which they implied. I must be ready to surprise them there, at least approaching with the hand quiet, wrapped up.

But first there was Washington to worry about. In all likelihood, they would expect to meet, or at least contact, me when I arrived in Washington. Perhaps I should do that, reassuring them just before I headed north, with my foil-silenced hand. If I checked into the hotel on schedule and *then* turned around, wrapped up the hand, and went straight to the train station, I could be halfway to Maine before they missed me.

By now, I hoped, they should be used to the intermittent signal from the hand.

When I got off the train in Union Station, I looked around, checking the time, as if I were expecting someone to meet me. Kept looking as I walked from the track through the huge station, but nobody contacted or, apparently, followed me.

I got to the taxicab rank and then doubled back to the ticket machine. Quickly bought a ticket up to Maine via Penn Station. There were lots of trains from Washington to Boston, but not so many from Boston to Maine. Two leaving in the morning, two in the afternoon, and a red-eye just before midnight.

I did toy with the idea of chancing a plane north. Of course the pistol was the obstacle. I could just ditch it and improvise when I got to Maine, a state with a lot of hunters. How hard could it be to buy a pistol in Portland?

Actually, I had no idea. But a gun in the hand is worth two in the bush, or something, conjuring the pubic ultimate in concealed weapons.

And I would actually only save about two hours, flying. There weren't that many flights to Maine from New York. I guess people in Maine took the train or stayed home.

The only legal gun store in the District of Columbia, according to the computer, was one operating inside the main police station—how handy for them. I'm sure there was a fascinating story behind that. But I just needed a holster, and Googling, found a list of sporting goods stores that sold them, one right in Union Station.

I got a hot dog and a Coke from a vendor and asked her where the sporting goods store was. She pointed down a long corridor of shopfronts. I sat and finished my lunch contemplating the question, "How do you look innocent while asking to see concealed-weapon accessories?" Then I went off to try it.

I walked through a huge assortment of balls and bats and gloves and hats, until I got to the very rear of the store, where behind a forest of rifle barrels pointing skyward and a veritable clothing store of desert- and jungle-colored garments, there was a glass case with dozens of bright new airguns. A few aisles down, I found stacks of various holsters.

The shoulder holsters looked a little too gangster-ish. But I guess gangsters preferred them for a reason.

"Can I help you decide?" asked a little round man with a nametag.

"Looking for a holster for a snub-nosed Taurus."

"Would that be a 605? An 85?" He looked left and right. "You don't have it with you?"

"No. No, it's for a friend." Wouldn't be smart to pull it out, I presumed.

"Good. Do you know if it's a .38 Special or a .357 Magnum?"

"Either, I think. I was told." By a highly trustworthy arms merchant in a smoky New Orleans dive.

"Will you be wearing it under your clothing or outside?"

"Under." He nodded and didn't ask to see my permit.

He picked up two cardboard cartons. "Under the arm or on the belt?"

"Belt, I suppose."

He handed me one. "This is best, I think, for men who aren't, well, very fat. Some policemen are."

"I've noticed." I took it from him. The belt clip seemed to be on the wrong side.

"It's not for cross-draw," he said. "Strong side."

I clipped it on my belt on the right hip. "You don't recommend cross-draw?"

"Your choice." He shrugged, I think meaning *not for the likes of you*. "You might want to wear it with a roomy jacket. Sports coat." I bought it and went to look for something inconspicuous to put over it.

There was a clothing store called Next2New less than a mile's walk away. Plenty of time before the train, so I strolled there, through a part of Washington the guidebooks probably didn't mention. I got a shabby tweed jacket for less than a hamburger on the train, and a well-worn beige shirt with the monogram MPX on the breast pocket. Michael P. Xavier, if anyone asks.

I changed clothes in a grubby men's-room stall at Union Station, throwing away the old shirt. My heart jumped when I did that: before the next time you change clothes, you'll face down the Enemy. Don't sweat, now.

Clipped the holster onto my belt and slid the Taurus into place. In the mirror I looked innocent enough. Would it fool a trained policeman? An untrained one? I put the gun back in the Amtrak bag.

On the way to the waiting room I passed the sporting goods store and hesitated. I'd reloaded the pistol after the billboard confrontation, but no longer had that box of cartridges. So should I face the bad guys with only five rounds, or go in and buy a new box?

I didn't know enough. Could you buy a carton of bullets as casually as a carton of milk here? Or would your face automatically appear on a Homeland Security computer screen with the notation "armed and presumed dangerous"? *Escaped from a military hospital where he was being held under armed guard.*

Here's your change, sir. You might want to run for the door.

Well, the depressing truth was that one box of cartridges more or less was not going to profoundly affect my fate. If five rounds didn't do the job, then thirty wouldn't either. Factor in the time it would take me to shuck out the used shells and reload, cowering behind that Ikea coffee table. Five would have to do.

If it came down to a firefight, my trusty snub-nose against however many serious weapons they had, I was going to come in second anyway. That didn't worry me as much as it should have, though; give a man a weapon and he starts to think with his balls.

Maybe when I get to Maine I can pick up a flamethrower or a machine gun. Or maybe when I pull the snub-nose out of its policeman holster, they'll all throw up their hands and surrender.

There were three computers in an alcove off the Union Station waiting room. Pretty shabby ones, keys yellowed with age and the grunge from thousands of random grimy fingers. I made a mental note to autoclave my hands when I was done, and used the Visa card as a key to the wonderful world of global communication.

Google Earth took ten seconds to show me an aerial view of a cottage with the address on Ring Road. At greatest magnification, the roof of the A-frame was a stark grey rectangle at the end of a brown dirt driveway off the "ring road" that circled the small island's perimeter. I bought a print of that view and also a map of the island; folded them up and put them in the bag with the other incriminating stuff—carefully saved the foil and rolled it up inside the sling that hid it.

This part had to be done quickly: I took a cab to the JW Marriott Hotel and waited in line for two minutes. No one sidled up to me. I showed the clerk the reservation receipt from the glove compartment of the car, and he gave me the key to 1138. I declined help with my bag.

No one else in the elevator. I went up one floor and got out, re-wrapped my hand with the foil, then walked back down to the lobby and went outside to the taxi rank and said "Union Station."

If they were able to follow me, well, we'd have our confrontation in a very public place. Not in room 1138.

Back at the station I found a place to sit with my back to a wall, and tried not to look too furtive while I killed a half hour with the *Washington Post* and watery coffee. When it was ten minutes to boarding time, I went toward the train. On the way, I stopped at the bookstore and looked for something that might keep me occupied for some hours. Thrillers were a little too close to real life, so I picked up a copy of *Stranger in a Strange Land*, which I'd read when I was too young. Maybe it would give me some tips for dealing with aliens. Assuming the bad guys were not citizens of the United States.

My seat was half occupied by a black gentleman who was sound asleep in the window seat, so I went on to the bar car, or "lounge," where I would have wound up anyhow.

I got a beer and sat down at a table not too close or too far away from the security guard, a serious-looking woman in a grey uniform with a Glock in a fast-draw holster clamped to her thigh. Had she been trained to detect nervous amateur spies carrying little holsters clipped to their belts? Evidently not.

I studied the *Post* editorials long enough to be able to discuss global ocean trash issues or the current revolution in Somalia with her, but she didn't come over.

The train was underground for some time, and then spent a few minutes speeding over the suburbs in elevated mode, and then slowed down to connect with the twentieth-century rails that served Amtrak through most of the northeastern corridor. Slowed down regularly for nineteenth-century curves.

After the Baltimore stop, I checked back in the coach and the black guy was gone; both those seats were empty. Clipped my ticket to the back of the seat in front of me and cranked back the seat; the train wouldn't reach Boston for another seven hours.

A conductor woke me up when the train was approaching Boston, about ten at night. I got off and South Station was a huge quiet cavern full of places to eat, all closed.

A sleepwalking rent-a-cop directed me to a twenty-four-hour place a couple of blocks away, the South Side Diner, which was full of interesting people. I probably was not the only one carrying a gun, but nevertheless felt somewhat out of place, neither intoxicated nor obviously unwashed. Though I wanted a shower so much I might have *used* the gun to force my way into one.

I'm sure there were fine restaurants still open in some other part of town, but I only had an hour. I nibbled on a fried-egg sandwich, which seemed safe in all respects other than cardiac, and went back to the station to wait for the late train north.

I felt like a time traveler marooned in the twentieth century, or the nineteenth.

The small crowd waiting for the train was mostly old black or Hispanic people. The few who were white or prosperous-looking were absorbed in their readers or papers. How many of them had sought out this slow venue because they were also carrying guns? How many were *not*? We were a fairly desperate-looking crowd, myself definitely included.

The gun was chafing my side, so I went into a men's-room stall and returned it to the Amtrak bag. I doubted there would be a quick-draw situation on the Portland train.

A good thing, too. I was exhausted from travel, and once I got to Portland it would still be at least four hours to Bangor on the bus.

When I got to Bangor, what then? Daniel Craig and Sean Connery would always appear all fresh in their tuxedos, with plenty of weaponry and ammo tucked away somehow. I couldn't visualize either with dark shadows under his eyes and his gun in an Amtrak bag.

At least I wouldn't look dangerous. And I could put it back in the holster before I confidently kicked down the door.

13.

It was not quite six in the morning when the squeal of the bus brakes woke me up at the bus station in Bangor. There wasn't an actual station; it was just a Greyhound sign outside a coffee shop. It said 24 HOUR SERVICE, but didn't look open; to be on the safe side I went to the back of the bus and used the noisome toilet there.

Good thing. The diner was locked, but when a church bell started tolling at six, a cab pulled up. He had a card on his dash that said BAR HARBOR AIRPORT $25. The window went down as another man and I approached.

It didn't look like an actual cab. It didn't have a meter that I could see.

"How much to Bass Harbor?" I said. That was where the ferry left for Swan's Island. The other man said he had to be at the Bar Harbor airport *right now* and would pay fifty bucks.

The cabdriver, who looked like a sleepy high-school boy with a fake beard, said to the other guy, "Get in." He checked a laminated card and said if I went along, he could drive me from the airport to the Bass Harbor ferry for $100.

I decided not to tell him that I'd have to pay with a dodgy credit card. We could work that out later. He read the other man's credit card with an iPod attachment.

The ride alternated between quaint New England hamlets and beautiful dense pine forest, with some neatly planted potato fields and a few random acres of inexplicable desolation. Like a war had happened, but only went for a block or two.

I tried to ignore how my left hand felt. It was throbbing, baking under the foil cover—closer to braising, I suppose, than actual baking. Cooking with moisture. But I was too close to Kit and her captors to take it off and broadcast my presence.

The last record they would have of my little beeper would be when I had checked into the Washington Marriott. Of course, by now they might assume I was on the run and could be anywhere.

We got to the airport, a low brick building with a pretty tall hotel, in about twenty minutes. I got out and stretched while the other passenger collected his bags and ran for the plane.

"Mind if I sit up front?" I asked. "I'm about to die back there." The backseat was broken and came forward at a little more than a right angle. That gave me an excuse.

"Come on up," he said, and took my card as I got in.

The iPod read it and beeped. He frowned and tried it again, and it beeped again. "Mister . . ."

"Be calm," I said, the .38 pointed at his midsection. "This is serious business. Government business."

"I won't . . . look . . . don't . . ."

"I won't pull the trigger unless you make me do it. I'll give you a thousand dollars to take me to Bass Harbor, and across to Swan's Island. A thousand dollars in cash, but I can't pay you until tomorrow."

"What . . . government business?"

"Homeland Security," I improvised.

"Do you have . . . let me see an ID?"

"Not undercover."

He looked at me, and then out the windshield, and then back and forth again. "This is crazy."

"Just drive," I said. "I'll tell you the whole story. But you have to promise not to tell anyone."

"Okay," he said slowly, and pulled away from the airport loading zone.

By the time we were back in the potato fields I had told him all about what I'd done to the Polish embassy and about the international espionage ring that had sent a hit man after me when they couldn't get to me "through channels" in Washington and Krakow. I said I'd give him the whole story once it all came down, in maybe a week. The poop was going to hit the pulverizer, I told him, using authentic spy euphemisms.

It was forty-six miles from the airport to the ferry boat. I wrote him an IOU for a thousand dollars and signed it, and used a felt-tip marker to put a thumbprint next to the signature. I gave him my Iowa phone number and e-mail address.

I actually did plan to pay him. And even tell him the real story, eventually. But when he pleaded, "Do y'have to keep pointin' that gun at me?" I said that in fact I did. Just accept it as a condition of employment.

We were pretty much in the middle of nowhere when we saw a sign that said five miles to the ferry. Just beyond the sign was a dirt road to the right; I told him to turn down it.

It was a forest fire road, arrow-straight most of the way. No sign of habitation; a state or federal forest reserve, perhaps. We went a couple of miles and then the road just stopped. Ran out of funds or hit a county line or something. "Back up and turn around," I said.

He wasn't an experienced driver. It took him six or seven sloppy tries. "Okay, stop. Give me the keys. And your cell phone."

He looked at me on the verge of tears, mouth trembling. I gave him my water bottle. "Don't drink this all at once. It will take you a while to get back to the road. I'll leave the car at the ferry station with the keys and the cell under the floor mat."

"What?"

"Even if you don't get a ride, you should reach the ferry before dark. That thousand bucks is yours, plus another thousand, if you don't say anything to anybody. Did you ever make two thousand dollars in a day before?"

"I don't, but I don't get it."

"Spy stuff, man. Don't try to make any sense of it." I motioned with the gun and he got out. I slid over, and he handed me the cell phone. Gave him a little wave as I drove off and, in the rearview mirror, he waved back weakly.

How many state and federal laws had I just broken? Steal a car at gunpoint, kidnap the poor schlub who owned it, and abandon him in the woods after threatening murder? Maybe I could write it up as a TV show and use the royalties to hire the best lawyer on the planet.

The clock was ticking, but I had no faintest idea of how long I had. How likely was it that the kid would take me at my word and become my accomplice? More likely that some forest ranger or farmer would find him out there on that dirt road and he'd spill everything.

Which might not be bad if the timing was just right. Have a boatload or chopper full of cops coming to back me up at the cabin. But not so soon that they would arrest me instead.

I got to the main road and pulled over to the shoulder to think. I looked at the boy's cell phone. Damn, the battery light was blinking yellow. Kids nowadays.

Why not just call the cops?

Well, they might arrest the wrong person. Me. *Yes, I took the kid's cell phone at gunpoint and stole his cab, but you have to understand—*

Even if they did go along with it, a large force converging on that cabin might endanger Kit.

Or no. If the Enemy hurt her, they would have nothing to bargain with.

Which presupposed the Enemy would think rationally under stress.

What about me? Could *I* think straight? Was I?

My plan: go to Swan's Island and sneak up on these desperados with five rounds in a .38 Special peashooter. Brandish the gun and snatch Kit and take her back to safety?

If that's the question, the answer is "You and what army?"

I didn't have an army, but I did have certain resources, chief among them the ironic one of being a fugitive. And thus perhaps a lure. But again, who would I be luring?

What I really needed was a pissed-off Sara Underwood, mad enough to rain some serious shit on me, focusing on a tiny island off the coast of Maine. Unfortunately, the phone with her number in its memory was in shards in a dumpster in Louisiana. That had been a smart move.

I didn't even know what state her office was in.

But I did have one name and one place. I started driving and, throwing caution to the winds, picked up the phone and punched 4-1-1. I asked some guy with an Indian accent to put me through to an operator in Springfield, Missouri.

"That will not be necessary, sir. I have all those numbers right here."

"I don't need a number. I need a human being on the line."

"I am a human being, sir." He did not sound like a friendly one.

"I need one in Springfield, Missouri."

"That will not be possible, sir. If you give me a name in Springfield, Missouri, I will connect you to his phone."

"Okay. James Blackstone. Homeland Security. Springfield, Missouri."

"Thank you, sir. One moment." After about a hundred moments he came back. "Sir, the operator says that party is deceased."

A sign said one mile to the ferry.

"Call them back and ask them if they want to know how he died."

"Sir, I am not allowed to elicit or transmit information to or from a third party. And it is not yet eight o'clock in the morning in the state of Missouri."

"I'm calling from the state of Maine. Listen to me. It's a murder. James Blackstone was killed."

"Yes, sir." The phone went dead. Perhaps life is cheap in New Delhi.

No, it was probably the battery. The light on the top of the phone had stopped blinking yellow; it turned red and dimmed.

I went over a hill and there was the sea, or at least the bay. I parked the boy's car by the ferry office and put the key under the mat. Kept the cell phone. Maybe if I didn't use it, the battery would come back for one bleat.

The ferry was approaching. I bought a twenty-dollar ticket and watched the heavy craft ease into its berth, escorted by a cloud of seagulls.

Did they think it was a fishing boat? Maybe there was nothing else for a bird to do.

The weather was about to change, and not for the better. A band of golden light to the east was fading as charcoal clouds boiled in from the west. I went back into the ticket office and bought a two-dollar plastic slicker from a box by the cash register.

The first drops began to fall as I walked down the ramp to the *Captain Henry Lee*, which smelled of new paint and old fish.

There was an enclosed waiting room that added the smell of diesel exhaust and a whiff from the head. I stood outside after a couple of minutes and enjoyed the rain after I struggled into the slicker.

That would make a fast draw even more problematical. *Would you mind putting that gun away while I untangle mine?*

This would be one time in my life, however much of it was left, when I could justify smoking a cigarette. Looking for a machine gave me something to do for a few minutes. But the boat was disgustingly healthy in that regard. I was sure that I could bum one off some old Mainer standing in the rain puffing away, but he must have had an oncology appointment.

Would the Enemy be waiting for me? Could be. They had shown me the picture of Kit, but would they suspect that I could deduce from that where they were?

It was placid and pretty, the light rain sprinkling down on the green islands that bulked out of the mist. Then a sudden stab of lightning and thunder blast, just to keep me from getting too relaxed.

The ferry backed and filled into its place at the dock, and I followed the one car out onto the road that sloped up into the woods. No passengers waiting, which I supposed was good.

I checked the map. Go to the left and walk about a mile and a half down Ring Road. The cabin was at the end of the fourth dirt driveway.

The rain made a constant rattle on the plastic as I walked along. Feeling conspicuous as a bug on a plate.

But none of the cabins were visible from the road. And the bad guys wouldn't be looking for me yet, I hoped.

They might be. Presumably they knew I'd made it to Washington, but wasn't in the hotel room. Maybe they'd figured out that I could turn the signal generator in my hand on and off. They probably had seen the sling by now, and might deduce that it was hiding something.

They knew I was armed, assuming the guy with the camera in the cowfield had been one of them. That might not be an advantage; not if it made them nervous.

With the revolver in its holster, there was nothing I really needed in the Amtrak bag. Two candy bars that I transferred to jacket pockets. The Heinlein book and a litter of receipts. All tax-deductible if I wrote it into a book.

A lot of good books had been written in prison; I could become the Camus of my generation. If I could learn to like cheap red wine and boys.

I decided Heinlein could wait, and stuffed the bag with his book into an RFD box, which surely broke another federal law. Perhaps they would put me in a cell with other hardened postal offenders.

The house before the turn-off looked deserted, storm shutters over the windows and no cars. So I walked down the dirt road as if I belonged, and passed behind the house to the rocky beach. The rain started coming down in buckets, for which I should have been grateful. Surely they couldn't expect anyone to come sneaking up through this weather.

Unless they actually were experienced criminals, with criminal minds. I've had two bikes stolen in my life, both of them in weather like this. Criminals assuming that nice people would not go out into the driving rain.

I struggled to keep my footing on the slippery rocks. Slick seaweed brought me down twice, hard enough the second time to cut my knee.

The leg stiffened up. I studied the terrain and picked my way carefully but clumsily from rock to rock. Clattering.

I had almost made it to the grass when a yellow light gleamed. The cabin's back door.

A man came out with a rifle or shotgun. I stumbled the last few yards with my hands up.

He waited for me, the weapon pointed in my general direction. It was a large double-barreled shotgun. So if I untangled myself and drew on him, he would only have two tries to blow me in half. And then reload.

He yelled over his shoulder, "It's the guy!" A woman came running out, pulling on a raincoat. She and the man approached me together.

"Watch out," she said. "He's got to have a gun." So much for surprise.

"It is him, ain't it?"

"Oh, yeah," she said. To me: "Out for a walk?"

I shrugged, an odd gesture with your hands up. She frisked me and took the pistol. "Nice holster," she said, and wagged the pistol in the direction of the cottage.

I recognized her voice from the phone. The man had been the driver of the car in the cowfield, I thought.

They walked me up a gravel path to the back door, and then through a rustic kitchen. "Company coming," she called out.

It was the living room in the photograph. Kit was bound in the same chair, but was wearing different clothes, jeans and a man's work shirt.

She didn't seem harmed, but had a bandana tight over her mouth. I tried to smile and she tried to smile back.

Seated next to her on a couch, similarly bound, was Ron Duquest, wearing a white silk suit, all California. It had probably looked pretty sharp a couple of days ago. He was pale and shaken.

Standing by the fireplace, the man who'd had the camera in the car. Whom I had last seen over the sights of the snub-nosed revolver. He had a broad grin and a Glock in an army-issue shoulder holster. He looked drunk.

"The writer," he said. "Marksman." I couldn't think of anything to say that might improve the situation, so just nodded.

I catalogued the weapons. Shotgun and pistol, mine, behind me, and who knew what else. Another handgun in front of me and, leaning up against the fireplace, a pump shotgun. On the coffee table, the sniper rifle with the fancy grain, with the futuristic Leupold flip-out scope.

Perhaps with a bullet still jamming the barrel.

They had more weapons than people. Pretty grim. The woman nudged me in the small of the back with my own snub-nose.

"There are too many variables in this equation," she said. "You know what I say."

"Kill 'em and dump the bodies," said the man next to her, and looked at his shotgun. "That may be good for you, but I personally have never killed anybody. I don't want to hang for your scheme."

"There's no death penalty in Maine, chickenshit," said the man by the fireplace. "Remember?" He picked up the sniper rifle.

"Careful," the woman said.

"You be careful," he said. "This asshole never shot at you." He cocked the bolt up and down and took aim. "Just nick the ear."

My only chance. "Big man," I said. "You don't have the balls to pull the trigger."

"No!" she said, and then a wave of concussion smacked me.

The man's face became a splash of crimson as the jammed receiver exploded just below his eye.

I half turned and kicked out at the woman. If the snub-nose went off, I didn't hear it. My kick caught her between the legs and she folded—and then *my* bad leg gave out and dropped me on top of her. The pistol skittered away and I snatched it up. The double-barreled shotgun went off like a sledgehammer, searing the side of my face, as I fired the snub-nose into its owner over and over.

I levered myself up, pulling on the arm of the couch, and aimed wildly left and right, not sure whether the revolver had any shots left. The air was grey with gun smoke and there was a lot of blood.

Some of it was mine. It dripped off my chin when I looked down.

The woman was very dead. The double blast that had singed me had excavated her chest.

The man who'd done it was bent double on the floor, twitching, clutching his abdomen, the emptied shotgun under him. I put the muzzle of the revolver behind his ear and happened to look up.

Kit was shaking her head frantically, weeping, no.

A strange calmness came over me.

She would never understand.

The dead people, this dying one, and me. All of us were Hunter. And all of us were prey.

I set the pistol down and watched him die.

Epilogue

I had gone into the kitchen to find a knife to cut Kit's ropes when I heard a helicopter laboring through the storm outside. I had her hands free and was working on the tight-knotted bandana gag when someone kicked open the front door and four men charged in, wearing black body armor with "FBI" in white letters, front and back.

I put my hands up. "What took you?" I think I said.

In fact, it was amazing that they had gotten there so fast, or at all. Reconstructing, I found out it started with fast action on the part of that annoying operator in New Delhi. He was on the line long enough to hear me say I was in Maine and "It's a murder. James Blackstone was killed." That operator queried a stateside operator, playing back the recording, and within a minute or two an FBI analyst was listening to it. Agent Blackstone's name was still hot enough to trigger a response.

A helicopter with a SWAT squad took off from Boston while FBI computers chased my credit card trail down to the Swan's Island ferry.

The black helicopter was already over Cape May, speeding north by northeast, when the FBI verified the location of the cabin and sent them a satellite photo and a map.

I have to wonder, as fast as they responded, what might have happened if they'd showed up a few minutes earlier. What would the bad guys have done if they'd heard a helicopter coming? It might have prevented a bloodbath. Or precipitated a different one.

The whole bizarre story came out in Ron Duquest's trial. I had just missed my big chance at fame and fortune.

Duquest had concocted a scheme for a kind of cross between an action feature and reality TV. He hired a couple of lowlifes in Los Angeles and had them drive out to the Midwest, then Louisiana, then Mississippi, to put Kit and me through what he conceived as a fantastic paranoiac chase scene: Who is after us? Why does the sniper weapon from my past keep cropping up? Who's on first? It would be a post-postmodern version of classic old television serials like *The Fugitive* and *Lost*, with the delicious variation that the star didn't know he was on camera.

He testified that he knew me well enough to trust that I wouldn't commit any serious crime, and the men he hired were under orders to just harass us; not break any laws themselves. But that all went out the window when I actually shot at them.

They had guns, too, it turned out, and an attitude problem that escalated into a runaway kidnapping scheme. Duquest lost control of them and was afraid to call in the police.

I've told the rest of the story here. Except for the happy ending.

The slight scar on my cheek from the shotgun just makes me look "interesting," Kit says, and together with the missing finger they mark the beginning and end of my decade of violence.

This decade will be parenting, we just found out last week. Starting lives rather than ending them.

We're even getting married, continuing a family tradition that started with old Grand-dude, back in the sixties: pregnancy, then marriage.

When the other hippies asked why they bothered, he said that one thing the world didn't need was yet another bastard.

Oh, and the cube in my finger? Nothing to do with anything. The army won't even tell me what it was. That probably means it never worked. Typical. All that aluminum foil wasted—and I'd been so proud of myself. Our tax dollars at work.